Praise for S

"*Secret Dead Men* is the most inventive, uplifting, hilarious, moving novel since *The Catcher in the Rye.*"

Ken Bruen, author of *Galway Girl*

"A profoundly psychotic hilarious whodunit fantasy ... It's as if [Swierczynski] simultaneously channeled Philip K. Dick, Eugene Ionesco, Richard Matheson, Raymond Chandler, and Charles Willeford."

Ed Gorman, author of the Sam McCain mysteries

"Filled with fascinating creations and memorable scenes. [*Secret Dead Men*] takes the traditional forms and puts a unique spin on them, reflecting the mind of an author with both new ideas and an idiosyncratic personality."

Philadelphia Inquirer

"Fresh and idiosyncratic ... Offbeat, quirky and confident, revealing Swierczynski as a talented newcomer."

Chicago Sun-Times

"One of the most surreal, amusing crime thrillers in recent memory. A masterpiece of weirdness and humor."

January Magazine

Praise for Duane Swierczynski

"Duane Swierczynski is a much-needed breath of fresh air in the book world ... This guy is a great storyteller. I never know what he is going to come up with or where he is going to take me. I just know I won't be complaining about a thing once I get there."

Michael Connelly, *New York Times* bestselling author

SECRET DEAD MEN

DUANE SWIERCZYNSKI

TITAN BOOKS

Secret Dead Men
Print edition ISBN: 9781835410486
E-book edition ISBN: 9781835410578

Published by Titan Books
A division of Titan Publishing Group Ltd
144 Southwark Street, London SE1 0UP
www.titanbooks.com

First edition: September 2024
10 9 8 7 6 5 4 3 2 1

A CIP catalogue record for this title is available from the British Library.

Printed and bound by CPI Group (UK) Ltd, Croydon, CR0 4YY.

For Meredith, who wasn't afraid of the bloody axe.

WOODY CREEK, ILLINOIS

Labor Day 1975

1

ONE AND A HALF DEAD BODIES

Alison Larsen's body went undiscovered for about six hours. Local children found her first. The paper never reported this, but a couple of the kids organized an impromptu club with a mandate to "experiment" on her corpse. *What will happen if we put rocks in her mouth? Can her eyes still see? If we cut her, will she still bleed?*

Twisted bastards. Did they think to call an ambulance? Scream for a neighbor? No. The first thing they did was grab a rock the size of a softball and shove it into Mrs. Larsen's mouth. According to the report, her teeth were chipped where the rock made contact. Alison was a petite woman. They had to push hard to shove that hunk of granite into her face.

There was no official effort to prosecute the children. Big mistake, in my book. This kind of behavior, left unchecked, often results in severely disturbed adults.

Then again, what do I know? At the time, I was a dead man impersonating an FBI agent.

* * *

Ten hours after the discovery, top brass—in other words, me and a bunch of agents from the Chicago office who I'd just met—sped through the weedy flatland somebody once decided to call "Woody Creek" and arrived at the Witness Protection house. The "safe" house. What a joke. *If we cut her, will she still bleed?*

After we pulled up, somebody handed me a doughnut and a Styrofoam cup. I thanked him and peeled off the lid. The coffee was lukewarm and milky. I prefer my coffee hot and black. But it'd been a long day—flying from Vegas to Chicago, and then this drive. I was grateful for any kind of stimulant. We all started up the front driveway.

The local clean-up crew had arrived a few hours before us, so I didn't see any of the corpse mutilation firsthand—I only read the report. The crew had checked Alison Larsen's body for vitals (as if there were any to be found), made the requisite notations, zipped her up in a plastic bag, and loaded her into the van.

Mrs. Larsen's body may have no longer been here, but her blood certainly was. It was splattered on the tan shag carpet at least three feet in every direction. "Shit," somebody said. I stepped over the soiled area and walked into the living room. There was a cluttered desk with its chair tipped over, one leg broken. A fat book was split open on the floor. I walked into the kitchen. Glass cupboard doors were shattered; broken pieces littered the hardwood floor. I noticed a smear of dried blood along one wall. The radio was playing "The Air That I Breathe," a Hollies tune from a couple of years ago.

"Who turned this on?" I asked.

"Nobody," replied an agent. "It was on when we got here. We left it."

"You think it might cough up some evidence?" I joked.

"Possibly," the agent said, all poker-faced.

A dark-haired man with a thick neck and clothes that were supposed to be stylish approached me. "Agent Kennedy?"

"Yes," I replied. I flashed the temporary photo ID I'd received upon arriving at the Chicago office. I'd told them I couldn't believe I'd forgotten it, but I'd been in such a hurry to make the plane I must have . . . blah, blah, blah. They'd bought it.

"I'm Agent Nevins. Welcome to Illinois."

Dean Nevins, SAC—Special Agent in Charge. I'd heard a bit about him from the boys on the two-hour drive down from Chicago. One-word descriptions flowed freely: territorial, obtuse, egotistical. Only hears what he wants to and beats the piss out of anyone who says different. When you're on a Dean Nevins case, they told me, you're in Dean Nevins' world. Keep your head down and your questions to yourself. He loved murders, too. Couldn't get enough of them.

"You have the name of a great man," Nevins told me.

"Yes, I know."

I told Nevins I wished I was here under better circumstances, it was a beautiful state, and all that. I wanted him to point me to Brad Larsen's body right away, but I thought to do so might

11

seem weird. Instead, I asked him to walk me through what had happened.

Nevins gave me a funny look, as if I'd ask him what brand of underwear he wore.

"Well, this all went down yesterday," he said. "Early Sunday afternoon. We assume the gunman took her by surprise, at the door." He led me deeper into the living room. "The guy knocked, and Mrs. Larsen went over to answer it."

I shook my head to indicate my disgust.

"Next thing you know," Nevins said, punctuating his words with a thumb-and-index-finger pistol, "blammo. Hubby stands up, and somewhere in here"—he paused to point to the middle of the room, in front of the desk—"hubby makes a break for it. It's typical. These WP guys are almost always Grade-A, USDA-approved pussies."

I nodded as if I agreed. "The body was out back?"

"No." Nevins continued into the next room—a small kitchen, done over in way too many earth tones. He pointed at a puke-green wall. "The perp nailed hubby here and smacked his head into a glass cabinet." I saw the blood. "They must have scuffled and backed into this table." Or what was left of it. "Then hubby runs for it again and skips out to the back door. The perp follows."

We walked past a bedroom to a flimsy aluminum door through which I could see outside. The porch overlooked a thin stretch of Woody Creek. Agent Nevins led me out onto the back porch deck, but a nervous-looking member of local law enforcement interrupted the agent's compassionate, insightful description of the Larsens' double murder.

The man's face lit up. "Was it the Mafia?" he cried. "One of dem Manson cults? C'mon, you gotta tell me!"

"I'm sorry, Sheriff . . ." Nevins started, then paused to look down at his notebook. ". . . Alford. This thing is ours now. Nothing to worry you."

"Hey! I found the body! I knew she weren't creek folk, I called you guys . . ."

"We appreciate your cooperation," Nevins said, "but it's better you leave it to us now. We'll take care of her. I promise you."

The sheriff shuffled off to another part of the house. I looked at the water for a few moments, waiting for Nevins to continue his story. But then a junior agent—Fieldman, I think his name was—approached with a clipboard. "You were right," he told Nevins. "Blood type matches Larsen. Wit Protec number two-three-three-oh. How did we let this happen?"

"Wait a minute," I said. "You haven't found Larsen's body yet?"

"His blood's all over the deck," said Fieldman. "We think he's in the drink, but nobody's spotted him yet. We found another blood type, too—probably our suspect."

"Aw, fuck a duck," Nevins said. "Okay. Call in the cleaners, take our samples, then strip the house. Leave nothing but a shell. And have some guys out to check the creek already. I know they don't like getting their Thom McAn specials all wet, but it's part of the job."

Fieldman nodded.

"And another thing," Nevins said. "We're not going to file a report today."

"What? Agent Nevins, you can't be serious . . ."

I asked myself a similar question: what the hell was going on?

Nevins enunciated each word: "We. Don't. File. Which part of that did you fail to comprehend?"

Fieldman didn't breathe for a moment. This clearly boggled his mind, and/or sense of how the world should work. Then he cautiously ventured: "Don't you want to—"

"You want to be the one to tell the world this program can't be trusted?" Nevins said. "That some of our esteemed colleagues sell addresses to hired guns? That the fabric of our judicial system is routinely ripped open like the panties of a whore?"

Fieldman looked around to see if anyone else was hearing this. When he saw we were alone, he turned to me. I kept my face blank. This was not something I wanted to be in the middle of—at least, not right now. Finally, Fieldman turned back to his boss. "No, sir," he said.

"Fine, then. Raze the house. And take care of the sheriff. His name is . . ." Nevins glanced at his notebook. "Daniel Alford."

"Daniel Alford," Fieldman repeated.

I looked over the creek again. It looked like the water in a backed-up bar toilet.

As Fieldman was walking away, Nevins called out to him, "Shoot the bastard if you have to."

Now *that* was gratuitous. But so what? Everything was gratuitous this morning.

I turned to follow Nevins back into the house, and my foot bumped against something. A book. *John Donne*, the spine read. *Standard Edition*. I picked it up, flipped through a few pages. Daubs of dried blood speckled the orderly lines of verse.

Damn. Nobody should read poetry right before they die.

* * *

Twenty minutes later, when nobody else was looking, I walked back outside and climbed over the porch railing. Hanging on the framework below, I swung hand over hand until my legs dangled over the choppy, muddy ground. I let go and miraculously landed on both feet.

I took the time to breathe, then listened to make sure nobody had stepped out onto the deck. I started along the shit-mud bank as quietly as possible. It wasn't much of a creek—not much to feed it except freak storms and floods. When I got further out, I craned my head up to look back at the house. The deck was still empty. I turned around and headed downstream.

Why bury this thing? According to the FBI's own files, Brad Larsen was the "key to exposing organized crime in the greater Las Vegas area." Unless . . . well, unless, of course, The Association's influence had pushed its way upstairs, all the way to Special Agents in Charge. But it didn't make sense; not from what I'd heard about Nevins. He was too much of a Boy Scout to be in somebody's pocket.

Finally, after a quarter mile of wading, I found Larsen's body, tucked behind a small pale bush and half-submerged in an eddy. The poor bastard looked like he'd been dead for no more than half a day.

Perfect.

2

A CONFESSION

My name is not actually Special Agent Kevin Kennedy. My name is Del Farmer and I'm a soul collector.

Not that this is a bad thing. I don't collect souls to torture them, or to steal their essence of life or something depraved like that. I'm no vampire. I use the souls for informational purposes only, to perform acts of mercy and justice. Or at least, acts my moral compass tells me are merciful and just. The souls I collect are damned anyway. Like Brad Larsen's.

His body lay twisted in the muddy water. Clearly, he'd been trying to fight his way down the creek. Going to call for help? Probably. Trying to pull it together so he could march back up and kick the shit out of whoever had killed his wife? Maybe.

There wasn't much to help him along in either direction. At least he was safe from the neighborhood kids back here.

I scooped him under his arms and dragged his body to semi-dry ground. I touched his neck. It felt like a slab of ribeye right out of the refrigerator. "It's going to be all right, buddy," I told the corpse.

The meat couldn't hear me, but I knew Larsen could. His soul was still nearby.

* * *

Collecting a soul is a fairly simple procedure. If the soul is still somewhere near its body, that is. If you wait too long, the link between body and soul is severed and it's tough to locate the soul. It is possible, depending on the circumstances and a bit of afterlife detective work—which I would have been forced to do, had Larsen expired more than a day ago. (After twenty-four hours or so, souls start to figure out they should get going into the next plane of existence.) And sometimes, if you go poking around in the afterlife too much, it can suck you right in. German philosopher Friedrich Nietzsche was perfectly on-target about that "looking into the abyss, the abyss looking into you" thing.

But I would have gladly done it. Brad Larsen was extremely important to me. I had tracked him down this far and wasn't about to give up now. I knew he was a hot-dog witness, important enough to The Association to warrant a hit, important enough to the government to keep him protected. Larsen knew *something*.

But what? And why hadn't he coughed it up yet? That's what troubled me. Usually, spilling your guts was the requirement for receiving a new name and house in the middle of suburban nowhere, courtesy of the US government. If he had, I would have heard about it. After all, I am a Special Agent with the Las Vegas branch of the Federal Bureau of Investigation.

Okay, not exactly. I collected the soul of the real Kevin Kennedy—and glommed his credentials—seven months ago, and I've been playing the part ever since. Before that, I kept an office as a private investigator in Henderson; before that, I was a county clerk in Reno. The jobs had to change. After a while, even the best cover story will fall apart. You *will* be found out. It *will* be time to move on, to adopt a new identity. The point remains: I would have heard.

The first step was to lure Larsen's soul back into his body. I knew he was still around, hanging on to this earthly plane by his astral fingernails. The vibe was strong; stronger still when I moved close to his corpse. The link hadn't been severed yet.

* * *

I won't go into the specific details of luring a soul; let's just say it's no more difficult than a birdcall or a sleight of hand card trick. Besides, if I told you, you might be tempted to try it. God forbid you do this in an old house or graveyard. You never know *what's* gonna answer your call.

I made my move, and after a moment or two Larsen's eyes opened. I'm not sure what he was looking at—there wasn't much. His shirt was ripped and covered in dark maroon blood. Or maybe it was mud. It was unclear where the creek stopped and the man began. "Mr. Larsen?" I said.

His eyes turned in my general direction.

"Hi there," I said.

Brad stared at me.

Now came the next step: soul collection. I had to work fast—a soul can't animate a corpse for long. It's a trick, really. The meat thinks it's back on the job, and it takes a while to realize, *Hey, waitasecond . . . I don't think I'm alive anymore . . .*

I knelt down next to Brad and scooped some water onto his face. I needed a better look at him. "Listen to me," I continued. "You've been murdered. I'm here to investigate. Your full cooperation will help bring your killer to justice."

His eyes rolled down at his body; his eyelids fluttered. Typical reaction. The victims are always curious, even after being pulled back from the dark wonderland of discorporation. A few check to see what they are wearing. Some even try to fix their hair. Brad tried to say something, but his throat was apparently blocked. I scooped another handful of water and poured it into his open mouth. He choked, then coughed up a dollop of mud and insects. I scooped more water onto his face, wiping the mud away. He was a handsome guy.

"We're in this together," I told him. "All you have to do is look at me."

"Sh-Sh-She . . ." he sputtered.

"Who?" I asked, but instantly regretted it. Clearly, he was talking about his dead wife, Alison. Shit. I had to switch gears. No sense having him freak out now.

I said, "I need to ask your permission for this." Not true, but I always made it a point to make this soul-collection thing sound like a matter of free will. "Will you join me to avenge your murder?"

"Sh-Sh-She's . . . c-c-cut . . ." Brad said, shaking.

Good enough. I snapped my fingers, which caught his attention, and then I collected his soul.

* * *

How, exactly? An excellent question. And I'll admit that I don't know.

Maybe this analogy will be useful. You probably drive a car, right? And you know how to use the gas pedal, and the brakes, shift into reverse and neutral, and operate the air-conditioning and the radio and windshield wipers and window crank?

Of course you do. But I'll bet dollars to doughnuts you wouldn't be able to explain the mechanical functions behind those operations. You probably don't even know how an internal combustion engine works. Which is fine. Neither do I. Nor do I understand the technical details of my soul-collection abilities. But rest assured, I know how to drive a soul, just as well as you know how to drive your Datsun.

I've been driving souls for five years, and I've gotten good at it.

In an instant, Brad Larsen became part of me. We were now Farmer-Larsen. I allowed Brad momentary control of my body so he could get whatever he needed to get out of his system. Kick at the mud, punch the air, curse God, whatever. Better to have his psychic anger dispelled on the banks of Woody Creek than inside my head.

Surprisingly, Brad didn't do a thing. I couldn't even guess what he might have been thinking. The connection was too new. All he did was use my eyes to stare down at his own dead body.

Me? Back when I was first soul-collected—after the initial exhilarating rush of being absorbed had passed—I cried. I was faced with a voyage into dark, terrifying turf. My collector, Robert, spent hours calming me down, explaining things to me.

But Brad only looked at his corpse as if he were looking at an interesting piece of modern art. I felt my head cock. He didn't ask a single question or voice a single complaint. Which was fine with me, as I didn't have time to explain it all to him.

"Relax, Brad," I told him, unnecessarily. "You're gone, but not forgotten." Then I regained control of my body.

* * *

Usually, next came the tricky part: stealing the victim's face. Thank God I didn't have to take Brad's right then and there.

A soul has its own momentum; it can propel itself anywhere, given the push or shown the right image. After all, a soul is built for travel. You can trick it back into its body, you can collect it and stick it in your own mind, no problem. A face, on the other hand, was dumb meat, stretched and burned and replenished and readjusted over a period of many, many years. Which meant, to steal Brad's face, I had to stretch and burn and replenish and readjust my own face.

I knew it would be worth the effort, however. Whatever priceless information Brad Larsen had locked away in his mind would become a more powerful weapon if I *became* Brad Larsen. On the day I confront The Association, I want to wear a face they fear. The fact they had sent somebody 1,200 miles to smash Larsen's face meant I'd found one.

But there was no time to do a full reconstruction here in the creek—plus, my FBI friends would be sure to hear my hellish screams—so I whipped out my trusty Kodak Instamatic and used an entire roll of 110 film on Larsen's corpse, for later reference. I also tried to memorize the features (just in case): the stiff, bony forehead and the high cheekbones and short, upturned nose. He had a strong jawline, but not so strong as to detract from his boyish good looks. This was definitely going to be an improvement over Special Agent Kevin Kennedy. No offense to the dead.

3

BRAIN HOTEL

I placed Brad Larsen's soul in one of the rooms inside my head, then thought up a mild brain sedative. He took it without complaint. In fact, he didn't even seem to be aware I gave it to him. These "rooms" are simply mental constructs, built to house the souls I collect. Consider it a Holiday Inn of the brain. How would *you* like to be plucked from death, only to find yourself floating around some ethereal space inside somebody else's skull? For souls to retain a sane, working version of their earthly memories—and not be corrupted by the strange limbo of my brain—they had to retain a semblance of earthly surroundings. So, I had a hotel in there.

From the soul's point of view, it's a sweet deal. Each soul

receives a two-bedroom apartment, and is allowed to furnish it as desired. After all, it's their own mental power doing the creating; I merely supply the guise of walls, floors, water, gas, and electric. They are free to pursue any kind of art or hobby they wish, or consort with the soul of a prostitute named Genevieve I'd absorbed a few years back. If they want a professional oak pool table, it's theirs. A wet bar, a color television set—not to mention whatever programming they desire—presto, bingo, there it is. Not a bad afterlife at all.

I do my business on the first couple of floors of the Brain Hotel. There's the lobby, reserved for social functions and meetings. I have my office to retreat to when the need arises. I've resisted the urge to absorb the soul of a secretary . . . though it *is* tempting. There is a series of interrogation rooms—ranging from a clean, comfortable lounge to a shithole dungeon with a scratchy, houndstooth couch—depending on the suspect. It helps with the acclimation process.

I had five souls in residence in my Brain Hotel. Brad Larsen made it six. I suppose I made seven, since I also lived in the hotel—that is, whenever I wasn't busy controlling my real, physical body.

I don't keep the souls locked up in the Brain Hotel all the time. Once in a while, as a reward, I'll allow one of them to take control of my physical body, so long as it doesn't interfere with my investigations. Most times, the soul will merely want to experience the taste of real food again.

Unfortunately, I'm the one who pays the gastrointestinal tab. Once, I allowed a tub-of-lard ex-bookie named Harlan to take control of my body. He promptly stuffed it with three Gino Giants, two cans of Campbell's baked beans (with bacon strips), six large Grade-A scrambled eggs, half a loaf of Stroehmann's bread, two cans of B&M chili con carne, and an entire New York-style cheesecake. I had been resting in my Brain Hotel office and hadn't noticed until it was too late. I spent nearly three hours in the men's room of the nearest motel, rotating my rear end and head into the business end of a white porcelain toilet.

As punishment, I made that fat bastard move into the dungeon with the houndstooth couch.

It is necessary to stress that the entire Brain Hotel—from the interrogation rooms to the restaurant to the Olympic-sized swimming pool to the Irish-themed pub—exists for a single purpose: to destroy The Association. It had been my mission for quite some time, and it even predates my current occupation of this body and management of the Brain Hotel.

* * *

The details aren't too important, but regarding my previous life: I was an investigative reporter in Las Vegas during the late 1960s. It was a great time to be a reporter; people still took you for an authority figure. My most prized possessions were my Underwood portable typewriter and General Electric tape recorder with detachable interview microphone. Pens and paper you could find anywhere, but a reporter without his typewriter and recorder was truly lost.

I had been checking into a case of election fraud, which I was sure was linked to earlier incidences of bribery, extortion, drug dealing, and DJ payola. A single name kept popping up—a mysterious "JP Bafoures"—as well as the same methods. Even to a wet-behind-the-ears kid like me, it sounded like a crime syndicate. I nicknamed it "The Association," and I was sure one of these days I'd find the link that tied it all together. It would be my way out of the desert and into a real newspaper.

But before I had a chance to break the election story in the *Henderson Bulletin*, I had a run-in with members of what I could only assume was The Association, sent by this "JP Bafoures." Even though I'd been writing about their activities for more than two years, it was my first physical encounter with any bona fide member of the organization. And my last.

They had picked me up as I was leaving a bar. Three of them. "Farmer?"

"Yeah?"

A quick punch to the gut; they grabbed my car keys. A few more shots to my kidneys and head. I was shoved into my own backseat. One of them started driving. Another went to his own car and followed us.

"Wh-Where we headed, guys?" I was trying to sound nonchalant, but it's awfully hard to sound nonchalant when you're sniffing blood up your nose.

The one to my left said, "For a drink."

Which, for some reason, terrified the shit out of me. My imagination started running away with me. Were they going to drown me? Force booze on me and send me driving off a cliff? Cut my wrists and make me drink my own blood?

Not quite.

When we reached a seemingly random destination in the desert, they threw me out of the car and served me my cocktail in a rusty gasoline canister. "Bottoms up, college boy," someone said, forcing the plastic siphon to my lips.

A shot of fuel rushed past my mouth and down my throat. I vomited it back up two seconds later. While I was on my knees, retching, they poured gasoline over my head and back. I reached out to steady myself; one of them snapped two of my fingers back, breaking them. I bawled like a baby and was force-fed more gas. Again, I fell to my knees, puking. I received another shower and a few kicks to my ribs. I hadn't had that much fun drinking since my freshman year of college.

Soon, I was back in my car, behind the wheel. I couldn't see anything—my eyes were burning too much to register images—but I knew what they were going to do. I imagined them fumbling for the matches and pouring a thin trail of gasoline far enough away to be safe. I remembered hoping my dentist kept good records. I didn't want to be forgotten, my work to go unnoticed forever.

Mercifully, before I could feel myself burn alive, I vomited one final time—blood, I think—and my head hit the steering wheel and I died. Possibly from the beating, maybe from gasoline poisoning, but most likely from sheer terror.

* * *

Not long after, my soul was collected.

One moment, I was trapped in a useless, burned pile of flesh. The next, I was looking back down at it, full of pity. Was that me? That broken, pathetic skeleton-man at the wheel of a baked Chevy Nova? It's quite amazing what a change of perspective can do for you. You feel it in tiny ways. When you look at a photograph of yourself, for instance. Distance gives you power. Or at least it allows you to place yourself in the past, where you didn't know any better.

I heard a voice in my head, and that's when I realized I was in someone else's body. *Relax, Del Farmer*, the voice said. *You're gone, but not forgotten.*

An odd thing to say, don't you think? But to this day, I can't think of anything more appropriate. So that's what I say whenever I collect a new soul.

Later, after I'd had a chance to settle down, my collector introduced himself. His name was Robert. He too was interested in the criminal organization I called The Association, and had collected my soul (after trying in vain to save my life, of course) to see if I would be willing to help him.

Are you kidding? Me, a kid raised on *Shock SuspenStories* and *The Vault of Horror* comics, turn down a chance to avenge myself beyond the grave? Please. I was happy to tell him all I knew, even to the point of retyping some of my stories on a Brain Underwood he'd provided. In time, I came to be much more than a source; I became a vital part of Robert's investigation. For three years, Robert showed me the ropes—how to collect a soul, how to build additional rooms in the Brain Hotel, and much more.

Eventually, before he left the hotel for the nicer neighborhood of the Great Beyond, Robert allowed me to assume control. He didn't explain why or give me any kind of warning. All I found was a note taped to the door of my Brain room:

Del:
Took a bunch of the souls on to a better place. It was time. But not for all of us. Keep up the good work, will ya?
Yours,
Robert

I understood that Robert was leaving me with a mission: to continue soul collecting until I had enough information to stop

JP Bafoures and his Association, once and for all. And after two years of dogged investigation, I thought I had finally collected the right soul for the job: Brad Larsen.

Robert would have been proud.

4

FIELDMAN'S TRIP

With Brad Larsen's soul safely checked in to the Brain Hotel, I started back toward the deck. I figured I would thank the Feds for their Midwestern hospitality, catch a free ride back to Chicago, use the bureau files to enhance my own Association case file, enjoy a tender slab of porterhouse steak somewhere near Lakeview Drive, then catch a plane back to Vegas and drink a couple of those miniature bottles of free booze they give you.

A few steps away from the house, I heard voices above me:

"Where is he?" (I recognized it: Nevins.)

"Nobody's seen him. He must have jumped into the creek." (Unidentified male.)

Oh boy. I slunk back beneath the deck and wedged myself between two wooden supports.

"I don't believe this," Nevins said. He paced a few steps, directly above my head. I could make out his stocky shape between floor slats. "You telling me this guy just sailed through your office? Without any of the usual . . ."

"He had clearance."

"*Had* being the operative word, asshole."

Damn. They knew. A voice in my head taunted me: *I told you they'd find out, jerk!* The voice belonged to the real Special Agent Kevin Kennedy.

"Be quiet," I muttered.

Take it from me—Feds don't enjoy being dicked around. They're gonna skin you and hang your skeleton out to drip-dry.

"Quiet," I repeated, then heard the footsteps above me stop. A whisper I could barely make out: "He's nearby." Then, the snapping sound of pistols being removed from their standard-issue leather holsters. Cautious steps to all sides of the dock.

This was beautiful. I tried to put together some options. I soon realized I didn't have any. My only chance was to sneak around the twenty-man FBI team, steal a car, then motor my ass out of here.

I stepped through the mud, using the dock supports to brace myself, trying to not make a sound. Once I reached the edge, I looked up, and saw a single leg swing over the side of the dock. Someone was coming down to have a look. My eyes scanned the ground for anything weapon-like—a stick, a rock, a chewing gum wrapper, anything. But no luck. I balled up a fist, wondering if I could hit fast and hard enough to knock the agent out before he could cry out—and without the sound of the blow reaching above. Not likely.

I shrunk back against a support, then slid myself around it. The agent hung from the rail for a moment, then dropped to the muddy ground, just as I had. He removed his pistol from its holster.

I sucked in my gut and tried to make like a pole.

The agent spun around, checking his surroundings. He missed me on first pass. Then he started walking away, down the creek, toward the recently reanimated body of Brad Larsen.

Okay, this was it. Fight or flight. In about thirty seconds this guy was going to see the body, yell for his buddies, and I would be swarmed. I wouldn't be missed a second time. So I took a chance and started a slow jog upcreek, hoping nobody was looking. Each step felt like a week. I sensed eyes behind me, watching me dance up the mud like an idiot. Any second now I was going to hear Nevins bark, "Freeze!" and I'd turn around to see the sun glinting off nineteen shiny pistols, each one pointed my way.

I dove behind the first shrub I encountered. Looked back; nobody had spotted me. I had to run further ahead, ducking trees until I found a way to the main road. I tried to remember it from the ride down. There weren't too many houses around, which meant not too many cars. I thought about tuning out for a second and checking the files in my office—you see, back in my Brain office, everything I see is instantaneously recorded in the form of typewritten logs, for later study. Consider it a highly organized version of the human subconscious.

But there was no time for that now. What would Robert have done?

Then it came to me.

I closed my eyes and pictured a phone. I dialed a nonsense number and thought about who I wanted to reach: Harlan, the gluttonous bookie. Deeper, somewhere beyond my ordinary range of hearing, I heard a phone ring.

Then a voice answered the phone in my head.

"Yeah?"

"Harlan," I whispered. "It's me. You've gotta do me a favor. But hold on first."

"What?"

I opened my eyes, then peeked over the top of the shrub. Nobody looking. I shut my eyes again.

"Okay. You still there?"

"Whaddya want?"

"I'm going to give you a chance to earn your room back, fat boy," I said. "Listen carefully. In a few seconds, the door to your interrogation cell will pop open. I want you to walk to my office and open the file in my cabinet marked with today's date. Go to the stack of papers for the past hour. Within the text, you should find a detailed account of the area surrounding the safe house in Woody Creek."

"So?"

I couldn't believe it. The pudgy bastard was still busting my balls.

Then, I heard a sharp cry: "Nevins! Get down here!"

Uh-oh.

"Harlan, you tub of shit, go in there and study the area. Help me the hell out of here. Find a car and lead me to it."

I heard him laugh. A deep, phlegmy chuckle. "I'm going to need more incentive than that, chief."

"No, you're not. Because if I don't escape, I'm going to be caught by the FBI. And most likely, I'm going to have to make a run for it, because it's my only chance to save the investigation. Even more likely, some sharpshooter is going to put a bullet in my head before I escape. Which means you and five other souls are going to be wandering a muddy creek in Butt-Hump, Illinois until the end of time."

"On my way, boss," Harlan said. He might have been a greedy bastard but he knew when to listen to common sense.

I opened my eyes to see a swarm of Feds hopping over the rail. Until Harlan found what I needed, I had to improvise. I climbed the steep, rocky hill along the side of the house, then crouched down next to the front porch. Took a peek over the rail; nobody there.

I listened for voices, and heard some fevered yelling, but couldn't make out anything. There were about ten yards between my current position and a tree. I decided to go for it. I stood up, looked behind me—just to make sure no agent had doubled back and found my footprints in the muddy bank—and started to run.

"Freeze!" a voice yelled.

I indeed froze. Slowly, I turned my head to see Junior Agent Fieldman, clipboard-carrying Boy Scout, holding a gun larger than his hands and pointing it at my chest.

"Don't move, Kennedy. Down on the ground. Hands behind your head."

This was not good. Fieldman was green and twitchy on the trigger. I didn't want to have the investigation end right here in Woody Fucking Creek. "Excuse me!" I shouted. "Did you just order a superior to drop to the ground?"

"You heard me. Down." Fieldman scanned my body,

looking for a hidden weapon. Of course, I had none. Unless you counted my eyes.

"Look at me, Fieldman," I said.

He did.

And that's when I grabbed his soul.

In my years of soul collecting, I'd only worked with the recently dead, or the near-dead. It was *weird* snatching a live one. Kind of the difference between shucking crab meat from a dead shell and ripping live, functioning tissue from a pissed-off crustacean. Fieldman fought it every inch of the way. He may not have known what was happening to him, but I'm sure he knew it wasn't a good thing. Fieldman's body collapsed to the ground in pieces, like a puppet with cut strings: first the gun, then his knees, torso, arms, shoulders, and, finally, his head.

I'd always wondered what would happen to a live body if its soul were to be removed suddenly. I wanted to observe how long his vitals would maintain themselves, but there was no time. Fieldman's colleagues had surely heard him cry out and would be back in no time. I had to work fast.

I closed my eyes, lay down on the ground, and surrendered control of my physical body.

To do this, I relaxed a certain part of my brain. It's hard to describe to someone who's never known about it being flexed; trust me, every human being does. Until someone makes you aware of it, you have no idea you're holding it tight, even when you sleep. If people were aware of it, suicide would be a hell of a lot easier than razor blades and unlit ovens.

Then, as usual, the blackness started to pulse with waves of deep light—like when you close your eyes and press your palms into your eyeballs.

An instant later, the lights came up. Walls, ceiling, and not-so-tasteful Oriental carpet formed around me. I was standing in the lobby of the Brain Hotel, right in front of the entrance. This was the symbolic gateway between the hotel and the real world; whenever I wanted to go back, I simply walked out the front doors. If any other soul tried it without permission, they'd run into a brick wall. Literally. (My touch. I couldn't resist.)

Fieldman's soul was standing in the lobby, too, holding an imaginary pistol. His soul had arrived a second or two earlier.

"Relax, Agent Fieldman," I said.

"Wh-Wh-Where am I?" he stuttered.

The poor guy. One minute he's having his soul removed from his body; the next, he's standing inside the lobby of a cut-rate Holiday Inn.

"You're having a bad LSD trip. Some jokester in the unit laced your coffee; you're going to wake up in an extremely bad mood. In fact, you're going to want to pummel the first agent who crosses your path." I had no idea if a hypnotic suggestion given to a discorporated soul would work, but what the hell.

"I am?" Fieldman asked.

"Yep. And you're not going to remember any of this, either." I coldcocked his soul with my spectral fist—you can do that, you know—then walked through the front doors and back into the real world.

I stood up and dusted myself off. Then I closed my eyes again, and visualized Agent Fieldman. Once I had him, and started to feel the weight of his conscious mind, I popped open my eyes and flung Fieldman's soul back into his physical body. A moment later he popped back to life, choking and writhing. In my professional opinion, he'd live.

I started to run down the road. My head pounded something fierce. I wasn't used to collecting and flinging souls around like that. About twenty yards later, I heard Harlan's voice in my head. "Uh, boss? What am I looking for again?"

Boy, was I going to hurt that fat bastard when this was all over.

* * *

Two miles and four pounds of sweat later I found a black Dodge, recent model. My dress shirt was drenched. I removed my jacket, wrapped it around my elbow, smashed the passenger window, unlocked the door, brushed broken glass off the seat with my jacket, and slid across. I couldn't stop sweating. My head felt like a garden hose with a hundred leaks. I wiped my forehead with my coat sleeve. Wonderful. Another $35 investment down the tubes.

It was time to call for backup. I closed my eyes and visualized a microphone with a big black button on its base. I mentally depressed the button—which triggered a set of speakers in the Brain Hotel—and started thinking out loud. *Doug Isom. Paging Doug Isom.* Doug was this hippie who used to steal stereos to buy marijuana. I'd absorbed him for moments like this.

"Hey, Del!"

"Hi, Doug," I said. "No time to chat. I'm going to surrender control to you in three seconds. I need you to start this car."

"Right on, man."

Since Doug could grow all the Brain pot he could ever use in the comfort of his own room, stealing was now strictly for fun. In many ways, Reality was a bigger high for Doug—especially parceled out in tiny snatches, here and there.

I nestled back into the seat, closed my eyes and slipped away, and found myself inside the Brain Hotel lobby. Doug was there, smiling lopsidedly at me.

"Go ahead," I said. "Body's all yours."

Doug walked through the front doors and into total blackness. His image vanished as his consciousness was transported to Reality. And let me tell you, Reality must have been a serious rush for this baked potato. But he didn't let it affect his professional abilities. He cracked the column, pulled out a wire, and sparked the ignition.

"Your car, sir," Doug said upon his return. He was laughing to himself. He was always laughing about things that, quite frankly, were not even remotely funny.

"Thanks, Doug," I said as I passed him and walked back through the front doors.

I hammered the gas pedal like the back of a long-lost friend.

* * *

I wanted to drive west, to return to familiar turf, but my instincts told me to head east, away from the maelstrom. Indiana came and went, and I'd barely registered the state. Not much to it: a lot of highways and random office buildings interrupted by farmland. The only thing that kept me sane on the trip was the car's AM radio. Thank God it worked. I'd missed listening to my albums back home—sometimes I think pop music holds the tattered and worn fabric I like to call my "life" together. Songs pin down times and places like nothing else. I can remember what song was playing the day I drove home from college graduation ("True Love Ways"), the first time I had sex ("Sweet Pea"), and the day I was hired as a reporter at the *Bulletin* ("What is Life").

Right now, the station I'd found was playing Lynn Anderson's hit, "Rose Garden." Big hit in 1970—the year I was collected.

Yeah, pop songs were comforting all right, but sometimes they could be a huge pain in the ass.

5

PEPPERONI AND CHEESE

After several hours of solid driving, I found a trucker's motel in a part of Ohio called Buckeye Lake. The names kept getting better and better. Whose job was it to name towns in Ohio, anyway? I mean, who looked at a dirty puddle and thought, "lake," then attached that grandiose description to a name that belonged to a one-eyed pirate? This is but one of the many mysteries that had gone unsolved during my lifetime.

Actually, the place wasn't so bad. The bed was pliable, the bathroom was scum-free, and the towels weren't too stiff. The room even had a TV—the fancy push-button kind, with giant rabbit ears. Not that I planned to watch anything except the local news. I dropped my shopping bag on top of a battered bureau that doubled as a desk and unpacked. A six-pack of Fresca, a package of store-brand crackers, a pound of Cracker Barrel sharp cheese, a slab of imported pepperoni, and a copy of a local newspaper. I walked over to the sink and found a cheap plastic tray with a plastic ice bucket and two plastic glasses wrapped in clear plastic. The guy in *The Graduate* was right about plastic, I guess.

I took the tray and brought it back to the desk, then used my Swiss Army knife to chop the pepperoni and cheese. I opened one of my Frescas and took a sip to prime the system. Then I tore into the pepperoni and cheese. It was the best meal I'd had since the FBI coffee the day before—and I was going to need my energy if I was going to do a full-face reconstruction. I only wished I had a Budweiser instead of a Fresca.

I pushed the bureau closer to the bed, so I could have a proper seat. I then checked the local paper, but couldn't find a mention of the Woody Creek incident. Stuff on the Ford assassination attempt was all over the place—something about a Manson family freako chick named Squeaky. (Seems like Sheriff Alford was on to something about those Manson folks, after all.) I didn't think I'd see something about Brad Larsen, or about the Woody Creek incident. Nevins had made it clear this venture was quashed, effective immediately.

But during the last ten hours of solid driving, my mind started playing tricks on me, and I'd hallucinated headlines like ROGUE FBI AGENT ON THE RUN. In reality, there was nothing. Whatever manhunt I'd caused, it was being conducted in secret. Which made sense, from a public relations point of view.

The best part: soon, I was going to be safe. The Feds were looking for Special Agent Kevin Kennedy—gaunt-looking male in his late thirties, with a sharp jaw and receding hairline. Height: 5'11". Weight: 175 pounds, soaking wet. Light blonde hair, green eyes. While the height and weight still applied, no other similarities remained.

Soon, I would have ice-blue eyes, rich, reddish-brown hair, and the kind of baby face that didn't need to shave often. I was going to lose at least ten years in the transaction, too. The only way it would backfire would be if some enterprising Feds put Brad Larsen's face out on the wire, but why would they? For all they knew, Brad Larsen was sitting in the middle of Woody Creek with his baby face blown to smithereens.

Right, Brad?

Brad wasn't answering. During the drive, I would pull over from time to time, close my eyes, port myself into the Brain Hotel, and peek into the interrogation room where Brad lay sleeping. Not a peep. He looked like a college kid sleeping off a hangover. I wanted to check on him again but wasn't looking forward to more disappointment. Besides, he'd come around soon enough. All souls did.

* * *

I stuffed a few slices of meat and cheese into my mouth. I wasn't hungry, but I had to keep my strength up, just in case I had to skip out and drive another ten hours. I was trying to pry a thick hunk of cheese from the roof of my mouth when I saw the sirens flash through the slats of my window blinds. My body snapped to attention and I dove across the bed, reached into my jacket for my pistol, then rolled along the carpet until I was hidden beneath the window.

They couldn't have found me this fast—could they?

I snatched a peek from behind the curtain, then slid back down. A sheriff's car, lights whirling. Not many others—a few curious truckers. This wasn't a Fed deal, unless they'd sent advance word, and the local boys were here to scoop me up. If they were, it would be better to find out now. (And besides— locals, I could handle.) I stood up, brushed the wrinkles out of my trousers, then walked over to the bureau. I ate a few crackers to cover the smell of Fresca, then tucked my piece under the mattress.

Once outside, it became clear I was not the focus of attention. A couple of blues were entering a room a half-dozen doors away from mine. Other motel occupants had come out of their rooms, too; I was merely one of the crowd. Finally, somebody cut the flashing lights. I heard some woman mutter, "Thank the sweet Lord." The cop who'd spared our collective retinas started walking in our direction.

"Nothing here, people," he said, holding up his hands. He was young. "A li'l family squabble. Go on back to your rooms and watch some TV."

"Bull*shit*," mumbled a thick guy next to me. His eyes found mine. "I heard they got blood all over a shower down there."

"You're kidding," I said.

"Wish I were."

Meanwhile, the kid cop was still trying to put everyone to bed. "Come on now . . . please return to your rooms." He tapped his nightstick in his right hand, pretending it was something he'd used before. The crowd did start heading back to their beds, but not because Captain Nightstick was putting the fear of God into them.

The thick guy and I started walking together. "What happened?" I asked.

"Who knows?" he said. "Some couple checked in yesterday. Now, nobody can find them, and there's a whole lot of blood all over the bathroom. This is all I need—some friggin' nutbag slashing my throat in the middle of the night."

"They think it's a serial killer?"

Thick Guy gave me a stupefied look. I'd strayed out of his vocabulary. I amended: "Some kind of nut?"

"Yep."

At this point, we'd both reached a door—his. "Well, happy dreams."

I wished him the same and wandered back to my own room.

I wondered if it was me, or if the world was becoming increasingly, strangely, violent. I ate more pepperoni, drank some Fresca, then pulled my pistol out from under the mattress, tucked it beneath my pillow and tried to sleep. Soul collecting took a lot out of a guy. Ordinarily, just to keep the Brain Hotel functioning, I needed about ten to twelve hours sleep per day. Any less and the residents started complaining about maintenance problems. Considering the events of the past few days, I was going to need to sleep for three days straight.

* * *

After two days of lounging in the motel, I decided I'd stalled long enough. I'd had plenty of food and rest. Brad Larsen's soul still wasn't in shape for any kind of interview, and nothing else was worth investigating until then. So now it was time to get down to the dirty work. It was time to rearrange my face.

Boy, did I hate this part of the job.

This is important, I reminded myself. They feared his face.

I packed a small paper bag with a few necessary items, left my motel room and drove outside of the Greater Buckeye Lake area. It took about one minute. Eventually I came to a grassy area that seemed relatively abandoned, so I scooted my car into a spot that couldn't be seen from the road. I opened my paper bag and spread my supplies on the dashboard. I flipped down the visor and taped up some of the photos I'd taken of Brad Larsen's corpse. I set my first aid kit on the passenger seat and fastened my seat belt.

I wished this were as easy as absorbing a soul. Why did the gods who invented these strange abilities make this one so difficult? Why bother calling it a "gift" if it was so hideously painful? The last time I did this, I almost went into shock and died.

Okay. No more procrastinating.

They feared his face.

I got to work.

I closed my eyes and visualized a control panel. Robert had taught me it really doesn't matter what I look at—the panel was a symbol. It had a miniature screen, with two buttons on each side. The screen was divided into four perfect squares; each button corresponded to a square.

I opened my eyes and looked at the photo of Brad Larsen. Then I closed my eyes and imagined it appearing on the miniature screen. Opened my eyes, studied the photo, closed my eyes, visualized it on the screen. I repeated this process for a good twenty minutes. To an observer, it probably looked like I was playing a marathon game of "Peek-a-Boo" with an imaginary friend.

Finally, after endless opening and shutting of my eyes, I had a sharp picture of Brad Larsen on my mental control panel. The image had burned itself into my mind and divided into four quadrants.

Yep, there it was. Ready to go.

Yessir.

Oh, shit.

It was time to push the first button. The lower left button, which corresponded to the lower left face of Brad Larsen.

Did I mention I *really* hate this part of the job?

Mentally, I pushed the lower left button, and an astounding, hideous pain seized the lower right portion of my face.

Ever have a blind pimple burrowed beneath your skin? Okay. Now amplify that by about a thousand, then imagine squeezing a fat thumb on the sucker. *Hideous* pain, let me tell you. Dr.-Jekyll-turning-into-Mr.-Hyde kind of pain. The kind that makes you want to swear never, *ever* to touch your face again.

On screen, the lower left quadrant vibrated slightly, like a television image struggling for proper reception. I hardly saw it, though, because sheer agony was blinding me.

The worst part: this was but one of the forty pushes required to mimic one quadrant of Brad's face. And there were three other quadrants to go.

Robert had explained it to me this way: each mental push of the button sends a complex message to my brain to electrically jolt the nerves in the corresponding area of the face. The jolt forces the flesh and bone to react. After enough pushes, that part of the face is more or less reshaped.

"Great," I'd said. "How about the button that supplies the novocaine?"

Robert smiled. "If only the afterlife were that simple, my friend."

Still, I've gotta think there's a way to apply some mental painkiller to this process. If I can drink a Brain Scotch, then why can't I concoct some superdrug to numb my physical body? If I could, I'd be invincible, and would be able to swap faces at will. I'd be the unstoppable detective. The ultimate mystery man. I'd uncover and crush The Association in a matter of days—nay, hours—then move on to wipe out all evil from the face of the earth.

I pushed the button again and whined like a whipped dog.

A few minutes later, I pushed it again. And again. And again.

Soon I settled into a horrific rhythm, pressing the other buttons of the other quadrants of my face in a slow sequence. It always progressed this way. It reminded me of the times my father punished me when I was a child. Dad was a card-carrying member of the Spare the Rod, Spoil the Child Social Club. The Rod in his case was a thick brown leather belt he wore. Wore, that is, until I came home with a bad grade, or stayed out past curfew, or committed some other terrible childhood crime. Then the belt would be released from its loops, folded in half, and smacked across my ass cheeks. The first was always the worst. After a while, I would start to float above the pain. Still feeling it, to be sure, but also outside of it. In a roundabout way, Dad and his belt did prepare me for my future. Just like he always said.

About a half-hour later I reached the final punches of the button. My face was alive and on fire. At some fundamental level, my own cells and nerves asked: what the fuck are you doing?

A few more pushes and it was over. I passed out.

In my dreams, a pointy-detailed demon with oversized mitts kept punching me in the face. It looked like Charles Manson.

47

It was night when I finally woke up. I had been slumped forward, hanging on my strained seat belt. I wiped away some eye-funk and immediately winced. Ow. Still fresh. Gotta be careful with the new mug.

I took a look at my new face in the rearview mirror, then compared it with the picture of Larsen taped to the visor. Not bad. I looked exactly like Larsen, if Larsen had gained a couple of pounds. My hair was still dark, and too short, but nothing Miss Clairol and a few hours couldn't fix.

Of course, the biggest difference would be my height and build—basically, everything from the neck down. The body was the one constant, no matter how many souls I collected, or how many times I switched faces. It wasn't even my original body (it'd burned in the car fire) or Robert's. Maybe it belonged to the guy who had collected Robert's soul. Robert only mentioned him twice by name—"Ralph"—and never talked about where he'd ended up. I figured original ownership couldn't have gone too far back; the body was still in decent physical condition. Sure, a few sagging lines here and there, and I wasn't pitching a tent every morning, but that was to be expected. Maybe it was forty years old? Forty-five, tops? I wished this thing had come with insurance papers and a title.

What this all boiled down to, of course, was that this job wasn't going to go on forever. At some point, like a car, this body was going to hit a certain mileage and fizzle out. I hoped I wasn't in the driver's seat when it happened.

6

THE FACE THEY FEARED

The next morning, I woke up and brushed my teeth—carefully—combed my hair, and tried to substitute my coffee with a piss-warm Fresca. It didn't work.

It was time for a talk with Brad. No excuses now. Yeah, he'd been through a brutal murder. Sure, he'd watched his wife die. But enough was enough. It was time for him to start blabbing.

Besides, it was something to distract me from the raw, throbbing pain in my newly crafted face.

I lay down on the bed, closed my eyes, and transported myself to the new Brain Hotel room where I'd been keeping Brad. I didn't bother to knock.

There wasn't much to it. Just your college dorm room basics: single bed, wooden desk, metal chair, sink, mirror, wastebasket, couch, mounted shelf. (In fact, I had modeled most new rooms after my own college dorm room, from Nevada State, circa 1963.) Brad was sitting on the couch, fully awake, reading a newspaper. Or at least the pieces I'd absorbed last night. I wonder how it looked—random sentences and images, interrupted by white space?

"Good morning," I said.

Brad looked at me for a moment, then nodded and looked back down at the paper.

"We have some business to discuss."

"Yes, we do," he replied, his voice quaking.

"Do you have any questions?"

"Only one," Brad said.

"Go ahead."

"What year is this?"

I hadn't expected that. Usually, a newly collected soul will spit out something like, "Are you Jesus?" or "Where's my momma?" or "Where are the gates and the clouds?"

I frowned at him. "Why do you ask?"

Brad folded the newspaper and tucked it between the cushions. "Well, the last thing I remember, it was Sunday, August 31st, 1975, and I was being stabbed to death on my back porch. But today I wake up, and I appear to be fully healed. A rational mind would assume quite a few years—not to mention, extensive plastic surgery—were to have passed for this to happen."

"I saw you reading the paper," I said. "Check the date."

"Yeah, I know. It says September 5th, 1975. But if it's September 5th, then how can my body be completely healed?"

I smiled. "Because that isn't your body."

Brad's eyes narrowed. "Oh no?"

"Nope."

"Okay. I'll bite. Whose is it?"

"Nobody's. When you look down at yourself, you're seeing your own mental projection."

"Oh," Brad said.

There was an uncomfortable silence.

"Aren't you going to ask *where* you are?" I said, finally.

"Well, there's no need, is there?" he said. "It's clear that I'm dead and have gone to Hell. To be honest, I had considered the option. But it all felt so real to the touch—my face, the feel of air in my lungs . . ."

"The brain is a powerful tool," I said. "Even back when you were alive, everything you think you 'felt' came to you through your brain."

"Ah-hah!" Brad exclaimed. "I still have a brain, thus I am still alive."

"No," I said. "You aren't alive, and you don't have a brain. You're inside mine."

* * *

It took him a while to wrap his brain—er, his *mind*—around the concept. It had taken me a while, too, when Robert had collected me. This was not something they taught in Sunday school. When you got down to it, most people thought death resulted in one of several options: 1.) Absolutely nothing. 2.) An afterlife of eternal bliss. 3.) An afterlife of eternal suffering. Maybe even 4.) Reincarnation, or 5.) Entrance into a higher plane of spiritual being, or something.

No one ever considered 6.) An afterlife in someone else's brain. But I'm here to tell you, brothers and sisters, *believe*. Amen and Alleluia.

Once Brad was relatively at ease with the concept, the questions poured out of him. "If I don't have a brain, how can I think? Or speak?"

"Because you still have your mind, which is connected to your soul. The brain is nothing more than a muscle. Your mind and soul power it."

"So Plato was correct in the *Phaedo* in that the body is evil and impedes our search for the greater truth?"

"Huh?" I asked.

"I'm only trying to explain what's happened to you."

"Yes, I know."

"Okay, then." I remembered Brad had been a college teacher. Jesus, did I hate academics. Always thinking too damn hard about things, trying to describe the world in the most inaccessible, complex ways possible. I preferred journalism: the pursuit of easily understood facts. Man steals money. Fire destroys building. Mob kills naïve reporter. That sort of thing.

"Okay," he said, running his hands through his hair. "Here's an easier one. Say I walk out of this room, down the steps, through the lobby, and out the front doors of this 'Brain Hotel'. What then? Do I float away and go toward the proverbial light?"

"No," I said. "You'd hit a brick wall. The only way out of here is if I allow you to take over my physical body. Or if this physical body dies."

"Who gave *you* the car keys to this joint?"

"Funny you should use that analogy," I said. "It's how I think of it, sometimes. Anyway, my collector, Robert, entrusted me with the keys. I am behind the wheel, and the sooner you accept it, the better." I thought maybe I was being too harsh. "Don't worry. I'm a careful driver."

"Oh joy," Brad said. "What if I kill myself?"

"You can't. You're already dead."

"Fine. What if I kill my 'mental projection'? Imagine myself to be absolute nothingness?"

"It won't work."

"How do you know?" Brad asked. "You ever want it bad enough to try it?"

This was all going in the wrong direction. Why wasn't Brad looking at the bright side of this whole thing, like I did when I was collected?

"Why are you so intent on killing yourself?" I asked.

"Because I'm looking around here, around this Brain Hotel, and you know what? I notice there's somebody missing. My wife, Alison. Unless you're keeping her hidden away for some reason."

"No," I said quietly. "She's not here."

"I thought so."

I didn't want to go down this particular path yet. I needed him to feel safe, and maybe even enthusiastic about being here. Then we would discuss his wife. And how he was going to help me avenge her.

"Look, let me show you around," I said. "I think you're going to find this place interesting."

Brad sighed. "If you don't mind, I think I'll stay here and try to think myself into absolute nonbeing."

"If you like, you can do both at the same time," I said, trying hard not to sound like a used car salesman. "Our tour begins right here, in this room. At your request, we can craft it into whatever you like—a frontier log cabin, a modern luxury apartment, a country getaway . . ."

"Maybe later."

"Okay, okay. You want to see the lobby?"

"Anything important there?"

"Of course. There's a movie screen that allows you to look out into the real world through the eyes of my physical body."

Brad narrowed his eyes. "What's there to see now, if you're here talking to me?"

"Nothing, I guess. My real body is taking a nap."

"Sounds exciting."

I ignored that. "There's also a microphone on the lobby desk, in case you need to reach me while I'm in the real world."

"It connects to a telephone, or something?"

"No. You speak into the microphone, and I can hear it in my head."

Brad thought about this for a moment. "Doesn't it get confusing? Hearing all those voices?"

"Ah. Which is why there's only one microphone. Want to check it out?"

"Not particularly."

"All right—then how about the restaurant? One of the souls here used to be a gourmet chef for one of the best casino restaurants in—"

"I'm not hungry. Which shouldn't surprise you, seeing that I don't have a stomach anymore."

Christ. This was going nowhere. I took a seat next to him on the couch. For a while, we both sat there, looking at the pale-green walls, scratching our noses, readjusting ourselves on the couch—the usual timewasters. Finally, I said: "Brad, I know this is all a rude shock to you, but time is a factor here. I need to know a few things. Things I'm sure you'll want to tell me. Things that will help make things right."

Brad turned to me. "What things?"

Was this partial amnesia or was he being difficult? "You know. Things about our mutual friends. The Association."

"The who?"

"The organized crime syndicate that operates out of Las Vegas."

"That's what you call it? I guess it's a good enough name. The Association. Why, sure. I kind of like it."

"I'm glad."

Pause.

"Well?" I asked.

"Sure, I could tell you . . . *things*. In fact, I could tell you quite a bit about that particular crime organization."

I set my jaw, waiting for him to fill the silence. Finally, after years of fruitless searching, I would know the truth.

"But first," he continued, "I need you to do something for me."

This caught me off guard. "What?"

"I want you to find the bastards who killed Alison."

"That's what I want, too. Once we nail the organization—"

"No," Brad interrupted. "Not the *organization*. The two individuals. The assassins. The prick who shot Alison in the throat, and the cunt who sliced me up."

In other words, Brad Larsen wanted me to solve his murder.

* * *

Brad insisted on telling me his version of events first. It was fine with me—I'm sure whatever Dean Nevins had pieced together left much to be desired. I poured Brad a glass of Brain Scotch—an approximation of Chivas Regal—I'd brought for the occasion. It was a lesson I'd learned from my reporting days: keep your sources well-fed and well-lubed.

"Sure you're not hungry?" I asked.

He gave me a funny look. "Not much point eating, is there? I'm dead."

"Not true. Life inside the Brain Hotel can be exactly like the real thing if you work at it. Do things as you normally would. This includes eating, drinking, sleeping, shaving, showering, shitting . . . the whole thing. Take it from a man who's been here a long time. It helps." Another reporter's tip: build some "we're on the same team" camaraderie.

In this case, however, it didn't work.

"Do things as I normally would?" Brad repeated. "Let's see. Normally, I'd wake up in the morning and kiss my wife Alison on the forehead. Normally, I'd ask her if she wanted cereal, or something else, like eggs or French toast. She'd have to help me, of course, because I always end up burning the pieces on the stove."

I could see where this was headed, but I thought it best to let him get it out of his system.

"Normally, we would plan our day together—maybe go for a walk, or pack a lunch and walk up the creek bed to read and talk and hang out. Normally, I would kiss my wife, maybe even make love to her, and normally, we'd spend the rest of the day doing simple chores or listening to music or any number of things I can't do right now because you see, my wife Alison, *she's dead!*"

I watched his chest heave and his face disappear into his hands. Somehow, through all of this, I'd forgotten the crime at hand. A man and his wife had been murdered in cold blood.

Why couldn't I be a wee bit more sympathetic? Come to think of it, this was the root of all of my problems with the residents of this hotel. I scooped them up, expecting them to be so full of fire and spit that they'd heap stacks of evidence on my desk and wait patiently as I brought my years-long quest to an end. How arrogant of me.

But I couldn't find a way to articulate this without sounding full of it. Instead, I walked over to the table and freshened up his Brain Scotch, even though he hadn't touched it yet. I freshened my own drink and sat back down. "Tell me what happened, and let's see if we can't piece this together."

This seemed to rouse him from whatever fugue state he'd entered. I thought I heard him mumble, "Okay," but he might have just been clearing his throat.

"The day of the murder . . ." he started, then corrected himself: "murders, I was working on a paper."

"Ledger books?"

"No, a *paper*. A thesis on the love poetry of John Donne. I'm sure you've heard of him."

Only a few days ago, to be honest. Donne was the author of the blood-drenched poetry book I'd found in the Wit Protec house.

"I always worked in the morning hours. It was when my thinking was clearest. I'd read the texts the night before, let them absorb overnight, then wake up and start fresh. I loved our reading time in bed the most. Of course, Alison wasn't much into Donne. I think the book she'd been reading was something by Jacqueline Susann."

Now this Susann woman, at least, I'd heard of. She'd died about a year ago. She was most famous for a novel that became a movie about actresses and housewives taking a lot of drugs.

"Anyway, I know it was morning, because I was working, and I always stopped whatever I was working on by noon to have lunch with Alison. So, it was maybe ten or eleven. Alison was listening to music on our portable radio—the only modern appliance we kept in the house, aside from a refrigerator and a toilet."

Flash memory: the radio, still playing when I arrived at the crime scene.

"I remember her dancing around to some silly ballad from a couple of years ago—"Baby, You're Mine" or something. She was trying to distract me from my work—which I usually hated, but in this case, I couldn't resist how goofy she was being. Pushing her hips into my back, touching my hair . . ."

Brad pulled his drink to his lips and took a sharp, joyless swallow. I knew I had to snap him out of this mood. Fast.

"Do you remember what radio station was playing?"

"Why is *that* important?"

"It's not," I said. "Just another detail."

"I don't remember."

"Okay. Go on."

"Well, this song was playing, and Alison was dancing around, and all of a sudden there was a knock at the door. This is the moment I've been playing over and over in my head these last couple of days. Why didn't I think anything of that knock? After all, I was a government witness, hiding out hundreds of miles from home so that I could stay alive long enough to testify at a federal trial. Why did I think that knock was ordinary, like mail being delivered or the phone ringing?"

I had no reply for Brad. I was about to mumble something stupid when he saved me the trouble.

"I'll tell you why. Because Alison and I weren't raised that way! We didn't have it beaten into our heads from age five that you couldn't trust people! That you wouldn't always have somebody around to protect you, even when they said they were going to! So, for the briefest of moments, I forgot where we were, and I thought nothing of letting Alison answer the door. I went back to a line in my text and started reading again. No, I'll tell you what I had really thought: *Thank God for the door. Now I can get back to work.* Can you believe it? Do you know the selfishness and arrogance it requires to produce such a thought?"

I looked down into my glass.

"Let me tell you—it takes a lot. I was so self-absorbed that it took a full couple of seconds for reality to kick back in, for me to realize where we both were, and what we were doing here, and by then, it was too late. Alison had opened the door. And somebody stuck a shotgun in her face."

* * *

Brad was filled with a combination of self-loathing and anger I'd never seen before, even in the most self-pitying bastards I've encountered. It was as if he wanted to nuke the Earth, then save one last bomb for himself to detonate inside his own broken heart. I could allow Brad to finish his own story here, but it took a while for me to drag it out of him, and I'd hate for anybody to wade through all his psychodrama just to glean a few basic facts. (I know I did.) I wished I could have taped his memory of the murders and played it back in private, so Brad wouldn't be forced to relive it. However, this was not part of the soul-collection deal.

59

According to Brad, here is what happened:

Alison opened the front door the very second Brad realized it was a mistake. The killer pushed a shotgun into her face, and Brad remembers an awful second or two passing before anything happened. It seemed as if the killer hadn't planned to open the door and start shooting. Perhaps he'd wanted to bargain with Brad, or at least make him plead for his life. Perhaps he was shocked somebody had answered the door.

Once the moment of confusion passed, however, the killer fired his gun, and Alison's throat exploded. Brad watched her step back, her knees buckle, her body give out.

"I was paralyzed," Brad said. "None of the images held any meaning."

Fortunately, his paralysis broke, because the killer cocked the gun and swung it in Brad's direction. Through dumb luck, Brad slid from his desk chair to the ground just as a bullet sped over his head and blew out a large portion of the wall behind him. Brad charged the killer.

The killer tried to reload, but was unable to. So he went for a bunt—grabbing the gun with both hands to smash it into Brad's charging body. They collided. Brad spun back into his own desk, collapsing it, papers and textbooks flying willy-nilly around him. He landed on his back. But the killer was thrown off his feet, too, which probably saved Brad's life—there was no time to reload the rifle.

Brad heaved forward once more, as if he were doing a sit-up, and lunged for the killer's legs as he stood up again. The killer went down, but hoisted a punch in Brad's direction; the punch crushed nose cartilage. Brad returned the favor (connecting with the killer's mouth), twice (bony forehead), and a third time (left ear) before the killer swung the base of the rifle up into Brad's mouth. Again, Brad staggered and fell on his back. He spat blood and jumped up instantaneously. Needless to say, Brad was angry. And when it comes down to it, the man whose blood is flooded with adrenaline is going to have the edge. The killer was only in it for the money—otherwise, he wouldn't have allowed Brad any kind of reprisal. Either that, or he was a shitty assassin.

I made some preliminary notes on the killer: *inexperienced, yet solid. Trained in the basic areas. Young.*

Brad hoisted the killer up by his shirt and thrust his entire weight against the nearest wall; it was a spectacular collision, to hear Brad tell it. He put his entire shoulder into it. To follow it up, he pounded the killer's body into walls throughout the living room, then the kitchen. Anytime the killer tried to push back, Brad used his momentum against him, and flipped him into, say, a glass-fronted cabinet, or a Formica countertop. (Which would account for all of the blood-streaked wood and glass found at the crime scene.)

That said, I'm not sure this was the lopsided battle Brad painted it to be. Consider the facts: Brad Larsen is a college professor, and our killer is a piece of Las Vegas muscle. Even the weakest piece of Vegas meat is still pretty damn tough. True, Brad had the adrenaline rush of watching his wife die. Still, I can't believe Mr. College Boy turned into Muhammad Ali, wiping his kitchen up with the killer. I have to believe the struggle was dead even, until it reached the back deck.

The back deck is where everything fell apart. As I understand it, the killer wound up on the ground, and was reaching for a small pistol tucked in the back of his trousers. (Probably for emergencies . . . and hey, this qualified.) Brad saw him reaching for it, however, and kicked the gun out of his hand quicker than you could say, "Die, you scummy bastard."

Gun went airborne; clattered to the wooden slats. Brad nabbed it. Quoted some poetry at the killer.

"It was the last thing I'd read before watching Alison die," Brad told me. "All I could think of through each punch, jab, and kick, were the words: *mark but this flea*. It kept me alive."

Then, Brad shot the killer in the kneecap.

"Right then, I knew what I was going to do," Brad told me. "I was going to take this pistol and shoot one body part at a time. I was going to make this man die slowly, and screaming, in inverse proportion to the time it took Alison to die. I wanted him to reflect on what he had done and let the lesson burn into his soul before he left this world. First, the kneecap—I'd read somewhere that rupturing the knee hurts like hell itself, but is non-fatal. Then a wrist. Then, maybe an ankle. A shoulder. The other kneecap."

Brad never got to shooting the wrist, because behind him—out of nowhere—came a blinding pain in his back, as if God himself had decided to stick a cocktail toothpick through his entire body. Brad dropped the pistol.

He hurled his body around, only to receive a similar shock to his upper chest, right above his heart. *Is this a heart attack from the stress of it all?* he'd thought. *Am I being struck down before I can completely devolve into an animal?*

Not quite. Brad's eyes managed to focus, and he realized somebody was stabbing him.

He lifted his left arm to shield another blow, but the knife plunged right through his forearm. The blade lingered there, caught between the opposing forces of Brad's attempts to dislodge it and the wielder's attempts to draw it back. Brad saw his attacker: a young woman, with red lips. That's all he saw. Call her Killer Number Two.

The knife ripped free and slid back into Brad's left shoulder. Then out again and across his chest, bisecting his right nipple. Down, across three of his fingers.

At this point, Brad did what any sane person would do: retreated. His legs, still fully operational, shuffled him back, out of harm's way, until he tripped over a wooden slat that was a fraction of an inch higher than its companions and crash-landed on his ass. The knife was on him again, pushing into his stomach. Brad rolled and started to crawl forward. Sharp blows hit him in the back, the fury and power intensifying with each strike. Killer Number Two was trying to nail him to the floor.

Brad's salvation: the wooden railing, three feet away. He crawled for it, despite repeated blows. His hand reached the middle rung and grabbed it tight. He looked behind him and saw Killer Number One crawling on the floor, too. Crawling for the gun Brad had dropped.

Brad reached for the top rung, wrapped his fingers around it, and was wracked with the worst pain he'd ever felt in his life. It was as if God had pushed the base of his spinal cord into a food processor. He turned his head, and saw the knife buried to the hilt in his right shoulder. Killer Number Two was walking away.

Brad was able to turn his head once more and saw Killer Number Two bending over to grab the gun Killer Number One was so desperate to reach. He faced forward again and coughed; felt blood dribble from his lips. He placed both hands on the top rung and somehow managed to pull himself up, resting his full bodyweight on the railing. He rolled around to face his tormentor.

Killer Number Two had the gun. She was an attractive blonde. Full red lips, taut face, upturned nose. That's all he registered before . . .

"Cool your tool, fool," she said, then shot him in the chest.

"Are you sure?" I asked Brad.

"That's what she said."

Notes on Killer Number Two: *aggressive female. Young. Very young.*

* * *

With those four words, Brad Larsen took a bullet in the head and flipped over the railing, landing in the muddy creek.

Well, not quite *in* the creek. But close enough. His body flopped in the wet, packed mud. He waited to die, listening to Killer Number Two drag the whining, complaining body of Killer Number One back into the house. Then all was quiet. Leaves in the trees rustled, water gurgled, the occasional vehicle passed by, motor whirring off in the distance.

Brad tried to crawl to solid ground, but the slow, forceful flow of the creek pushed him further and further downstream. In retrospect, the flowing waters probably kept him alive a while longer. He spent the majority of the time flailing around, hovering between consciousness and oblivion, wondering about Alison.

It had to be a special kind of hell. I can only imagine what it would be like to lie there, cut to death, unable to breathe without pain, let alone able to stand up and go back up to the house to find out what had happened. It gave me the chills.

In time, Brad gave up the ghost. He wandered about the site for a while, lost. He saw his dead wife in the front room of the Witness Protection house . . . but he couldn't find her soul anywhere. He wandered to his dead body. He cried, then wandered some more. And about sixteen hours later, I arrived at his side.

"So," he said, lighting a Brain cigarette. "Now you know what kind of monsters you're looking for and what you have to do when you find them."

"What's that?" I asked.

"Put them through the exact same agony Alison and I had to live through."

"Not to be technical, but both of you are dead."

"Ah," Brad said, smiling for the first time since we'd met. "Now you're starting to see the picture."

7

A NEW CASE

So that was the deal. No Association skinny until Brad and Alison Larsen's killers were located, and Brad got the opportunity for a little payback.

Reasoning with him—explaining that crushing The Association was by extension punishing his executioners—wasn't going to ease his suffering one bit. Brad wanted me to deliver the assassins' severed heads on a drinks tray, cups of their blood in drinking glasses nearby.

In other words, now I had a bigger workload than ever.

Of course, if the roles were reversed, I'm sure I would demand the same thing. God knows what kind of punishment he saw inflicted upon his wife's body by those kids. I only saw the aftershocks—bloodstains on a piece of ratty carpet. Maybe that's what made it easier to agree to this whole thing.

I'd been running east on reflex. At the moment, it'd seemed like Las Vegas would be the first place the Feds would be crawling around. But Brad insisted we head back. No doubt his killers had driven out to Illinois, done the deed, then headed back to collect the bounty. And I couldn't disagree with his logic. It was all so damned reasonable it made me want to vomit.

* * *

So, I journeyed back west. Whoever The Association had sent to do the deed most likely lived in Vegas, and now the bodies were stacked up, it was time to head home and collect the reward. Somewhere, I would find two killers living it up. And once I found them, it would be the beginning of the end. For the first time in years—perhaps since Robert first collected me—I felt the warm vibe of optimism.

I drove through the night, routinely looking at my new face—Brad Larsen's face—in the rearview mirror. *I am going to find your killers*, I told it. And I meant it.

Of course, I was being an idiot.

HENDERSON, NEVADA

Eight months later

8

SOUL PATROL

It was a slow night in Tom's Holiday, a bar for the wayward souls at the Brain Hotel. Old Tom had given up eighty percent of his living space to create the joint. He was content to sleep in a small room in the back on a waterbed-style single bed with only a transistor radio and a small collection of Ian Fleming novels he'd once read. Tom's Holiday had daily specials, a decent selection of Brain pub food, and a jukebox that contained every song he'd ever heard. It stopped around 1970, but that didn't bother any of the patrons—only Old Tom. He was forever asking me about new music, urging me to listen to the radio in the real world more often.

"Ya got any new Beatles?" he'd ask.

"Sorry," I'd reply. "I don't think they're getting back together any time soon. Want me to listen to some Wings? They're on tour this year."

"Ah, that garbage. Don't bother. What's Hendrix doin'?"

I didn't have the heart to tell him the news about that one.

Old Tom was one of my first soul collections. He'd been a chef and bartender at a number of casinos, then worked his way up to—then out of—a prime bartending gig at a crooked casino. One ill-conceived wisecrack, and that was it. Some thug made him chug a cocktail of liquid drain cleaner. I'd picked him up, thinking he'd know a shitload of management detail; turns out, all he knew was how to mix a mean Sazerac.

Over in the corner, a group of souls—Old Tom, Doug, and Genevieve (now no longer the only Brain hooker)—were watching an episode of *The Bionic Woman* I'd seen earlier in the week. I was lazing over a tall glass of draft Brain beer, trying to forget everything for a few moments. You spend enough time with a body of information and after a while you start to lose perspective. You start to believe the information is devoid of meaning. You forget why you're looking at the information. You question your role as a gatherer of information. And that's when your world really turns into a pile of shit.

So, there I was, taking a mental-health break, when Brad walked in.

"Hard at work?"

I looked up and smiled. "Collecting my thoughts."

"What's to collect? They're all in those filing cabinets of yours, aren't they?"

Brad was referring to the cabinets in my office. As I've mentioned, all I observed in the real world was instantly transcribed to sheets of paper. Well, not instantly—I had to want it to be recorded, but it was fairly easy, so I kept everything recorded just in case. Soon my office filled up with filing cabinets. I started putting them in other rooms on the floor, and eventually the entire second floor became a massive filing system of the past six years.

"It's not that easy," I explained. "The names of your killers could be printed on any one of those pages. They're probably in file #4,759, page 312. You want to start skimming pages?"

"It's been what . . . eight months, best as I can tell? How far along are you?"

"Very close. It's only a matter of time."

"I've heard that before, in eight million variations."

"What do you want?"

"You know what I want."

True enough, I did. And so long as I was in a truthful mood, I could admit to myself I was nowhere near catching Brad Larsen's killers.

* * *

Robert taught me that you can't count too much on the souls you collect. "The sad truth is," he told me, "ninety percent of 'em you never want to see again."

This was especially true now. Over the past eight months I'd collected five additional souls, which—including myself— brought the Brain Hotel total up to twelve. Three of the newcomers were useless.

Soul #8 was Mort, an accountant who'd claimed he kept books for "organized crime figures," offered to show his books to the cops, but died of a heart attack a few days later. He was a tough collection. Had all sorts of ideas about the afterlife, being

Catholic and all. Association info? Nada. "All I did was crunch the numbers," he said. "Honest. Now you gonna explain to me why I don't see no Saint Peter?"

George, former aide to a corrupt Henderson councilman, was soul #9. I collected him thinking I'd learn all sorts of insider goodies about local corruption. But once inside the Brain Hotel, George refused to speak. All he did was oil-paint Revolutionary War scenes. And he couldn't even get the historical details right—many of the British Redcoats wore Timex wristwatches. He also sang drinking songs to himself, usually loaded on a bottle of Brain gin he'd cooked up in his room. The only Association info he supplied came in the form of parody folk ballads he played on his Brain guitar:

"Their victims, my friend
They're swinging in the wind
Their victims are swinging in the wind."

Useless!

Fredric, soul #10, was not much better. He'd been a bookie when he was alive and stole money from a couple of his clients to pay for his girlfriend's Tijuana abortion. Somebody caught him and chopped off his arms. Inside the Brain Hotel, he replaced them with a set of ripping, hairy guns capable of tearing a Manhattan phone book in half. But he never used them, except to hoist a mug of Brain beer at Tom's.

* * *

On the useful side was soul #11: Lynda, a dead hooker I'd picked up in Laughlin. To tell you the truth, I'm not sure she was killed by The Association. She could have been one of those random dead hookers you run across from time to time. Like Genevieve.

But she did have an important piece of info: the name of the Larsens' killer. "Oh, that would be Ray," Lynda said. "Ray Loogan. He was braggin' about it. Couldn't have been more than twenty-four or twenty-five. He didn't seem to ever have to shave. Guy got iced 'round Labor Day, you said? Had to have been Ray."

I was surprised. This Loogan punk sounded like someone you sent to dislocate somebody's grandmother's shoulder, not take out a government witness five states away. But he must have impressed somebody higher up. This was a great gig for a guy his age—especially if he pulled it off.

Since I had the victim's soul in my head, I can only confirm Ray had been successful.

Lynda went on to tell me that Loogan's bosses had sent along a babysitter named Leah Farrell to keep an eye on him; she had to bail him out of a mess somewhere along the line. (Killer Number Two, most likely.) But Lynda couldn't tell me exactly what the mess was, or if Loogan had been penalized (read: whacked) for it. She'd only heard Farrell had been out of Vegas for months, helping Loogan with unfinished business.

The luckiest acquisition was #12, a soul named Paul After. He was a hired gun who'd been double-crossed and decided to turn state's evidence. The evidence? Nothing as good as what Brad Larsen had, apparently. Just some tax nonsense. Paul thought he could use the cooked books to bargain for higher rates. The negotiations ended when Paul's employer sent a lawyer to the meeting with a semi-automatic pistol. Blammo. That was the end of Paul. And the beginning of our relationship.

So naturally, Paul had good reasons to want to work with me. He wanted his bosses—who I assumed to be The Association— burned like toast. He was also Grade-A professional muscle, unlike the rest of the B-list schlubs I'd been collecting.

* * *

Mind you, these five souls and the tiny bit of information they supplied were the net result of eight months' work. Why so long? I couldn't very well waltz back into Vegas wearing Brad Larsen's face. Once I switched to Larsen's face, my own—that is, the face of Agent Kevin Kennedy—was lost forever. How was I to know Brad was going to hold out on me? To recopy, I would have needed a photograph of Kennedy, and I made it a point of destroying all pictures of myself. Or any of the selves I've been. Not that I was eager to endure the special hell of face-changing again.

So, I hung on the outskirts—shit towns like Laughlin, Cooper's Mill, and Hagertown. I crept back into Henderson for my personal belongings one night in October, and kept them in the trunk of my car. I switched cars three times on the trip back from Illinois; Doug really came through for me. I ended up with a used '72 blue Datsun, purchased legit from a dealer in Flagstaff.

I made it a point never to stay in one place too long. I left a trail only the most dedicated schizophrenic could follow. I even spent a couple of uncomfortable nights in the backseat of the Datsun, in the middle of the cold desert, to stay loose. Okay, maybe I spent those nights in my plush (and seldom-used) king-sized bed in the Brain Hotel while I had other souls babysit my physical body. But I woke up with the cramps and kinks. I think I can claim the hardship.

Why so paranoid? Three letters: F, B, and I. They weren't amused to discover Agent Kevin Kennedy had been scamming the Las Vegas office for months. I didn't realize how easy it was to make the bureau's "Ten Most Wanted" list. I was slightly comforted by the fact that I was wearing a different face; the likelihood of the Feds figuring it out was next to nil. Yet, paranoia still got the best of me. Every time I relaxed with a can of Fresca and a corned beef sandwich, I'd be struck with the horrid feeling that a rogue FBI sniper was yards away, lining up a shot. My cleaned-out skull would be quite a prize in Dean Nevins' office. KEVIN KENNEDY, the faux-gold etching would read. THOUGHT HE COULD SCREW WITH ME—SEPTEMBER 1975.

Meanwhile, the soul of the real Kevin Kennedy, inside the Brain Hotel, never forgave me for ruining his professional reputation. How dare I corrupt his office? How dare I soil the Kennedy name? (I figured it was a cheap shot to bring up Chappaquiddick.)

To further complicate matters, I caught the mother of all stomach bugs in February. Knocked me right out for two weeks straight. It took everything I had to suck down chicken bouillon and stale crackers. I was off real food and drink for another two weeks after, and I still can't look at a boiled hot dog and beans the same way again. Solve a murder case? Heck, I couldn't even solve the problem of how to keep solid food down. There went a month and change.

Brad was becoming increasingly pissed that I was taking so long to track down his killers. When I asked him for the tiniest morsel of Association skinny to speed my search, he refused. "A deal's a deal," he said. "And nothing I know will help you find my killers any faster. Believe me. If I did, I'd do it myself."

After pressing him further, Brad said: "You're thinking too small. This is The Association. They're *everywhere*. New York. LA. Even goddamned Philadelphia." Which was basically like telling me to go look for a needle in a haystack the size of the United States.

So, all told, the hunt for the Larsens' killers was turning out to be quite pathetic, considering a) I knew the killers' names, and b) I had one of the victim's souls absorbed into my own brain.

Plus, I was running out of money.

9

SHERMAN OAKS GOLD

Despite the amazing powers my brain seems to possess—the ability to change my face, collect a soul, inventory and sustain countless unique intellects—I still have trouble managing a dime. To properly conduct an investigation of this magnitude, you need thousands of dollars. Right now, I had a little over $900 in my checking account. My Mastercard was nearing its limit, and this was my fifth card. Not everyone I collected had proper credit. If I wasn't careful, I would have a collector after *me*.

So, sometime around June, I came to the realization that I had to accept some freelance work. Good thing a couple of years ago I'd hung out my own PI shingle under the name

"Stan Wojciechowski" (about as far from "Del Farmer" as you can get) in a variety of outlets—from racing newspapers to legal journals, and eventually as a backup vendor for the internationally renowned Brown Agency in LA. That was a real coup, considering this PI stuff was only a sideline. I've met guys who would sell their left lung to be on Brown's backup list.

No matter the outlet, each call is flipped over to an answering service in Sherman Oaks, California. I called the service every three days to skim through requests—mostly to decline, sometimes to keep certain contacts alive. This time, though, I actually needed something. I had been staying in yet another Henderson fleabag motel and was getting tired of the scenery. I cracked open my last can of Fresca and dialed the phone. The gravelly-voiced girl on the other end of the line answered.

"Hey . . . Mr. Mojo Wojo! How are you, my man?"

"Uh," I said. "I'm fine. I'd like you to list my telephone calls—service requests only, please."

She ran through the job prospects and locations. Between each she paused to audibly pop her gum. I stopped her on the sixth.

"Where was that last one?"

"Philly, Mr. Wojo. This one was passed down from Brown yesterday. An attorney named Richard Gard called, asking if you could fly out there later this week."

Huh. Philly. *Even goddamned Philadelphia.* Isn't that what Brad had said? I wondered if it was a sign.

"Did he mention the particulars?" I asked.

"Just that it's a security consult."

Easy stuff. Lawyers needed muscle every so often. Nothing too strenuous, to be sure. It would give me time to check the city for signs of Loogan, while rebuilding my bank account. "Phone Mr. Gard and tell him I'll be on the next available flight."

"You got it, handsome. Hey—you ever going to take a job out here in LA? I'm dying to meet you in person."

She was forever flirting with me, this Sherman Oaks girl. I didn't understand it. She'd never seen me before.

"You never know," I said.

* * *

There wasn't much to pack—I kept my personal belongings to a minimum. I could fit everything I owned into two cardboard boxes and a large lawn-sized green plastic trash bag. The bag was for my clothes—one gray suit, three pairs of trousers, one pair of denim jeans, four button-down dress shirts, two ties, and enough underwear and socks for nearly two weeks. In one box I kept a Swiss Army knife, two pistols, ammunition, a magnifying glass, a lighter, one four-ounce drinking glass, a wood backscratcher, and other assorted tools of the trade. In the other I kept clippings and notes, as well as a couple dozen favorite albums. The record player was a separate unit with its own cover and handle.

I stored everything else in my Brain library. I knew someday I would have to present evidence to a judge in a court of law, and it bothered me that I couldn't crack open my brain for everyone to read. But I guess when the time came, I could always rent a Dictaphone and hire a stenographer. Maybe even the Sherman Oaks girl would lend a hand. I'd take her out to a beef and beer dance to celebrate.

I chuckled at the thought, then sealed both boxes with large strips of masking tape. I stuffed a stray pair of black dress socks in my trash bag, then spun the bag and twist-tied it. There. Packed.

All that remained was to slip the front desk a final payment, another call to the Sherman Oaks girl to let her know I'd be traveling, a walk to my nearby travel agent to retrieve my tickets, and . . . Oh, yeah. The important business of taking everything else—random notes here and there, doodles, old clothes—out to my Datsun and blowing the thing to smithereens.

Paul After, soul #12, had shown me a neat variation on the Molotov cocktail a few weeks back. Even though I eventually built the thing, I didn't know how it worked. Paul had guided me through, piece by piece, using ordinary items available from any decent hardware store.

It was a flashy way to make an exit, but necessary. This way there would be no trace of me. No trail for anyone to follow. Not the FBI, not The Association, not even my mother, God rest her soul. Everything I owned would go with me to Philadelphia.

I collected a trash bag full of the things I was torching and stuffed it in the trunk of the Datsun. I grabbed my trash bag wardrobe and a box of possessions and hauled them through my motel door.

On this second trip, somebody was waiting on the landing, and it didn't look as if he was there to help with the luggage.

"Hold it right there," he said, leveling a .45 at my chest.

* * *

I didn't recognize him at first. He was a lean guy; dark hair, neatly parted to the right, strong jaw, mirrored sunglasses. He wore jeans and a brown button-down with goofy gumdrop designs on it. The shirt almost negated the gun.

"Whatever you're thinking," he said, "don't."

"I'm not thinking anything." Actually, I was thinking about hurling my bag full of clothes at him, but what would that do? Mess up his hair part?

"Good," he said.

"Can I ask one thing?"

"What's that?"

"Who are you?"

The man half-smiled—that is, one corner of his mouth curled up, while the other stayed put. "Funny. I was going to ask you the same question."

"Look—"

"What I mean to say is," the man continued, "I believe we've already met, but I'm not entirely sure. We're going to go back into your room there and talk about it."

"Where did we supposedly meet?"

"Woody Creek, Illinois."

Finally, it clicked. Special Agent Fieldman. Eight months had aged the guy. Last time I'd seen him he was a junior G-man. Now he looked and talked like Lee Marvin's cocky younger brother.

"Hands on your head, and step back into your room," Fieldman said. "Now."

"I think you've got the wrong guy," I said. "I'm just a traveling man." I'd meant to say "traveling salesman," but I got the Ricky Nelson song in my head by mistake.

He ignored me. "Both hands on your head."

This was not good. Fieldman was wearing those ridiculous sunglasses, so I couldn't use my trusty yank-his-soul-out-of-his-body trick. For some reason, eye-to-eye contact is necessary for soul collection. I'd always wanted to ask Robert about that.

Does this mean we could never collect Stevie Wonder? Not that it would be likely to come up, but it would be good to know.

I was forced into my standard fallback position: surrender consciousness, transport myself to the Brain Hotel, and regroup. Back in Reality, my physical body would collapse, and be at the total mercy of Agent Fieldman. But it would give me some time to think. It was a chance I had to take.

"I don't feel too hot," I said, taking a few wild steps backward and mumbling something else about a lousy open-faced roast beef sandwich.

Fieldman must have smelled a rat because he stepped back, too, and took better aim. That was the last thing I saw before my vision went woozy and I snapped awake inside the Brain Hotel.

* * *

The lobby was deserted, which was not unusual. None of the souls drifted down here unless something interesting was happening in the real world: a soul collection, a fist fight, or a good movie. Especially movies. Last summer, a few of the souls—Doug, Old Tom, and Genevieve—made me sit through *Jaws* four times.

I walked over to the lobby desk and picked up the black courtesy telephone, which sat next to the huge silver microphone. This was my polite way of summoning the souls, you see. I could bark commands like an angry god, but they wouldn't appreciate it. I know I wouldn't.

I dialed an imaginary number for Paul After, happy I had finally collected somebody who could handle this kind of thing. Doug was fine if you were shoplifting or breaking into a car. Harlan was great if you needed someone to eat a large sandwich. But Paul . . . Paul was the real deal.

He answered on the second ring. "Yes, Del?"

"How did you—"

"Who else would it be? Avon?"

"Listen," I said. "I could use your expertise. I've got a real-world situation I'd like you to handle. Come down to the lobby and I'll give you control of my body."

Paul cleared his throat. "Tempting offer, but you're not my type."

"You know what I mean."

"Okay, okay. What's the situation?"

"Uh," I stalled, thinking of the best possible way to put this. Unfortunately, nothing came to mind. "An angry FBI agent has confronted me. To buy some time, I passed out in front of him. He probably has smelling salts under my nose as we speak, trying to bring me round. All you have to do is snap awake, deck him, bind him, gag him, lock him away for a while, whatever. Do your stuff. I'll take care of it from there."

"Do my *stuff*," Paul repeated.

"Can you help or not?"

"It'd be my pleasure, Mr. Farmer. God knows, I don't see any action in this freak motel of yours. I'll be right down."

I was still trying to figure out if Paul was being sarcastic when he appeared beside me. He must have cheated and ported his soul along instead of walking down the Brain Hotel staircase.

"What now?"

"Now all you have to do is step through those doors."

"That's it? You mean I could have left at any point?"

"No. You can take over my body because I'm letting you."

"I hate this place," Paul said, then stepped through the front doors and into the real world.

***

On the lobby screen, blackness fluttered and finally opened up. Light poured in, then adjusted. We were sitting upright. The view snapped to the left, then the right, where Agent Fieldman was sitting on my motel bed. He was pointing his gun at us.

"Good morning," Fieldman said, somehow looking more imposing up on the silver lobby screen. "Have a nice nap?"

The view snapped back to the left again, then right, up, down, and behind. The view wobbled. Angrily. What the hell was Paul doing? Neck exercises?

Finally, a hushed voice: "Goddamnit, I'm handcuffed to a chair!"

Fieldman said, "You are observant, Mr. Larsen."

Whoops.

10

THE THING IN THE TRUNK

Agent Fieldman had grown an attitude over the past eight months. Maybe the experience of having your soul yanked out of your body changed you fundamentally. Made your mind stronger, your senses sharper. Or maybe he had been hanging around Dean Nevins too much.

"So, what kind of drug was it?" Fieldman asked, pacing around the room.

I wanted Paul to follow him with his eyes, but he refused and kept staring forward. I probably should have let him off the hook, stepped back into the body and tried to handle this myself . . . and I would have, had I a single idea on how to handle this. I hoped he was cooking up something good.

Fieldman came back into view. He crouched down and looked us right in the eyes. "I asked you a question. What . . . kind . . . of . . . drug?"

Drug? What in the devil was he talking about? Did he think Brad Larsen was into trafficking? This was getting weirder by the second. And Fieldman's goofy gumball shirt was really starting to bug me.

Paul said nothing. I depressed the button on the silver mike and quietly asked: "Are you okay there, buddy?"

He said nothing.

Fieldman stood up, then chuckled. "I know what you're thinking. You're thinking, I'm going to stay quiet and plead the fifth and wait until some lawyer bails my butt out of this. Right? As long as I keep my trap shut in front of this agent of the law, it'll all be cool. Right? Huh?"

Paul said nothing.

"Well, I've got a surprise for you," said Fieldman in a faux-whisper, as if he were sharing some great secret. "I'm not here as an agent of the law. That's right. I filed form EL-6 last week. Official Federal Bureau of Investigation Extended Leave of Absence."

This time, Paul's eyes twitched to the right. The view on the lobby screen jumped.

"That got your attention, didn't it? That's right, friend. I'm not here as a federal agent. I needed time off from that scene. Needed to catch my breath, take a look around. A mental-health break, you might say."

Couldn't blame the guy.

"I was having too many sleepless nights, too many strange thoughts going through my head. Strange thoughts about a hotel lobby and conversations with a ghost. Maybe you've been there, Larsen. Maybe you know this hotel. Maybe you're this ghost. Are you a ghost, Larsen? Because last time I saw you, you were three shades of blue and wearing a toe tag on your way to the county freezer."

He was right. Brad Larsen's body was deader than Mama Cass.

"And yet . . . and yet, I keep hearing these reports. Brad Larsen spotted near Hagertown! Brad Larsen spotted near Cooper's Mill! Larsen alive and well and bouncing around, buying Datsuns! 1972 Datsuns! Blue!"

Uh-oh. I suppose it wasn't paranoia, after all.

"And all this time, I'm having nightmares and sleepless nights and endless days and horrible nights . . ."

I was right. Having your soul yanked out of your body does change you fundamentally. Not to mention psychologically. If Fieldman kept this up, soon he'd be in a rubber room writing home with Crayolas.

"Because the Brad Larsen I saw was dead and buried, and yet here's Brad Larsen buying Datsuns. So, I'll ask you again, what kind of damned drug was it?"

I wondered what Paul was making out of all of this. I hadn't clued him into my investigation of the Larsen murders. Or the reasons why I was being hunted by the FBI.

I hit the silver mike again. "You sure you're okay? Give me a nod or something, buddy. Let me know you're alive up there."

Fieldman kept on truckin'. "You know what I'm talking about. The mickey you slipped in my coffee. Or should I say the one your buddy Kennedy slipped in my coffee? Yeah, I know all about him, too. The Vegas office had their eyes on him for months. There he was in Woody Creek, cozying up with Agent Nevins, bossing people around . . ."

I/Kennedy did no such thing!

". . . and all the while, trying to figure out a way to cover your tracks. Can I ask how you did it? You find some poor slob who looked a little like you, poison 'em, give 'em postmortem surgery and leave him there in the river? Where did you hide all the while? Did you let your wife die? Or did you kill her because she found out what you really do? Or was she in it from the beginning, and you and Kennedy decided to double-cross her?

"Questions, questions, questions . . . oh, I've got a million questions. I could go on for hours, and rest assured, I will, until every single question is answered to my satisfaction. You wait. You're going to be telling me what kind of underwear your great-grandmother wore before we're through. But don't worry. I'm going to ask you an easy one first. Something you can probably tell me in a few words. What . . . kind . . . of . . . drug?"

I had a question for Fieldman: Why . . . do . . . you . . . keep . . . asking?

He continued as if he'd heard me. "In case you're curious, it's highly effective. Stays in you for months. In fact, it's still probably worming around in my system right now. At first, I thought it was some kind of hallucinogenic, what with all of the out-of-body experiences I'd been having. Acid-flashback kind of stuff. But test after test came up negative—no trace of any known drug in my system—and the nightmares kept coming. All about that goddamned hotel lobby."

So that's what this was about. When I had yanked Fieldman out of his body, he must have endured a serious shock to his system. And now he was after Brad Larsen and Agent Kevin Kennedy to find out what kind of drug we'd given him so he could find an antidote and go back to his calm, pressed-suit and brown-bag existence.

"Larsen," Fieldman said, putting his face within breathing distance of ours. "I'm not going to ask you again."

Paul, piloting our body, didn't say a word.

Instead, he breathed in sharply, then smashed the top of our head directly into Fieldman's nose.

The man's eyes crossed for a split second, then a faucet-strength gush of blood spurted from his nose. Paul stood up—still handcuffed to the chair, as far as I could tell—and smashed our forehead into Fieldman's face again. The agent's legs buckled from under him. He fell to the floor like a puppet with snapped strings.

"I thought he'd never shut up," Paul said, aloud.

* * *

I was relieved, but not as relieved as I should have been. What did Fieldman mean about Alison Larsen knowing what Brad "really" did? What, did Professor Larsen plagiarize a paper back in grad school? I didn't know, but I was sure as hell going to find out.

"Hey. Del."

It was Paul, looking into a mirror. Which, of course, made it look like he was looking down at me from the lobby screen. Somehow, in the few seconds in which I'd turned my attention away from the screen, he'd freed our body from the handcuffs and the wooden chair.

I hit the microphone button. "Great job. You've gotta teach me that some time."

"Which part?" Paul asked. "How to stay calm while being interrogated by an accountant? Or how to break someone's nose with your forehead?"

"I guess both." I didn't like Paul's cocky attitude, but I wasn't in a position to be arguing with him about it now. "Look, there's something important I need to do down here. Would you mind taking care of our pal, Fieldman?"

I thought I'd get a wise-ass reply, but amazingly, I didn't. "My pleasure," Paul said, then turned away from the mirror. The hotel room spun like a wild amusement park ride.

Good. While Paul was busy sticking Agent Fieldman in a closet somewhere, I was going to have a little chat with Brad. I took the elevator up to his floor and walked down his own private hallway, which he had decorated simply—if by simple you mean red velvet wallpaper and burnt-gold trim and baseboards, along with gold-trimmed electric chandeliers with low-wattage bulbs. Was this the Brain Hotel, or Brad's Brain Whorehouse? Well, as I've said before, the residents are allowed to choose their own surroundings, no matter how bad their taste. I guess it could have been worse. I could have killed and absorbed the soul of the guy who invented Tupperware.

I knocked on Brad's door—privacy is everything in here—but got no answer. I knocked again, louder, but again, nothing. I used my mental master key, which was simply me imagining the lock clicking open. Which it did.

The interior of Brad's room was a completely different story. In fact, it hadn't changed a bit since he moved in. It was still the plain-Jane college dorm room template I'd slapped up for him on his first day. Maybe he worked on the hallway for six days, then rested on the seventh.

He wasn't in here, either.

I took the elevator back down to Tom's Holiday. It was the only place souls ever bothered visiting, apart from the lobby.

But Tom's was empty, too, save Tom, who was buffing his bartop with an old pair of Brain boxer shorts and a can of Brain Olde English wax. "Hey there, Del," he said. "What's happenin'?"

"You haven't seen Brad around, have you?"

"Nah. Just me and the wax here. Stopping down later? I remembered a couple, three more songs off that first John Lennon album you might wanna hear."

"Sure, sure," I said, then headed for the lobby again.

As I walked away, I heard Tom moaning, *"Mothaaahhhhh . . ."*

At the front desk, I used the black courtesy phone to open up a line throughout the entire Brain Hotel. I loathed using it, because it seemed to piss off the souls. Maybe it was a reminder this was not Reality, that they were still dead and trapped inside my head. Maybe it interrupted their umpteenth viewing of *Mary Hartman, Mary Hartman.* Who knew?

"Hey, guys, this is Del. I apologize in advance for cutting in, but Brad Larsen, I have an important message for you. Come on down to the lobby as soon as possible."

I hung up the phone and waited. Time passed. Brain dust motes flew through the imaginary air space and attached themselves to the lobby walls. The wallpaper faded a bit, and then faded a bit more. The carpet became desiccated and brittle from the lack of use. The air smelled like it had been sealed in a tomb for a hundred generations.

Brad never showed up.

I turned around to look up at the lobby screen. Paul had our body outside, heading back toward the motel. The ground looked hot. Tiny sizzle lines were rising up from it.

I hit the mike button. "How's it going on your end?"

The view on the screen jolted. "Shit, Del! Don't do that!"

"Sorry." I was becoming a real apologist lately. "What's going on?"

"I've got everything packed in the Datsun, and I set the timer. There's a cab waiting around the front for us. By the time I sit our ass down in the backseat, the Datsun will be nothing but flaming embers."

"Excellent." I still couldn't believe what an amazing asset Paul was turning out to be. Me? As much as I take pride in my professional abilities, it's safe to say I'd still be handcuffed to that chair, trying to trick my way out of the situation.

"By the way, where'd you stash Fieldman?"

"The trunk. Where else?"

My blood turned to fizzing Pepsi in my veins. "The trunk?"

"Yeah, the trunk."

"The trunk of the Datsun?"

"You have another car you're planning to blow up?"

11

SUPERNATURAL DISASTER

Without another thought, I whipped myself through the front doors of the lobby and regained control of my body. I'm sure being jerked away from the controls wasn't a pleasant sensation for Paul, but I didn't give a hoot at that particular point. Paul had planned to kill Fieldman without a second thought. While I may be many things to many men—rogue agent, crappy detective, soul collector—I'm not a killer. At least, not when I can help it.

I recalled, with a shudder, my command to Paul to "take care of him."

My vision swirled for a few seconds, and I felt my soul ooze back into the confines of my physical body. My skin was sweaty, my muscles fatigued. Paul had kept us busy. I spun around and saw the Datsun parked about a hundred yards away, near a group of dirty boulders. I started running for it.

"Paul," I said aloud.

Nothing. My heart started to smack against my ribcage. My lungs informed me that I was running way too fast for my own good. I didn't care.

"Paul!" I yelled.

His words spat out in my skull. *Don't go back there! You're going to kill us all!*

"How long we got left on the timer?" I wheezed.

No time, goddammit! Turn the fuck around!

"How long?"

Paul didn't answer. Maybe he went back to his room to say a few prayers. It wasn't a bad idea.

After what felt like a mini-marathon, I reached the Datsun and accidentally slammed into it. That's it, I thought: ka-boom. The second death of Del Farmer, once again by flaming automobile. Mercifully, though, the car only bucked on its suspension. My hands flittered around the trunk uselessly for a few seconds before I realized I needed the key. I patted down my pants pockets, then my shirt. Flat.

"Paul, where are the keys? Where are the car keys, damnit?"

A quiet voice spoke in my head: *I threw them in the trunk.*

Perfect.

Ordinarily, I would have found myself in a state of absolute despair—the kind that leaves you no other option but to piss your pants and start barking like a dog. Or running away from the car as fast as you can, forgetting about all this "morality" bullshit and catching a cab outta here. But I was moving along with such a fevered inertia that I bent down, snatched a rock from the ground, and started pounding the rock on the keyhole of the trunk.

Predictably, it didn't do a thing except chip the paint.

Still, I struck it again and again, thinking that every blow would be it: Ka-Powsville. I kept it up, like that crazy ape from the opening scenes from *2001: A Space Odyssey*. I wished I had a bone. I'd fling it into the air and all of a sudden "The Blue Danube" would be playing and I'd be aboard an interplanetary Pan Am ship flying to the moon. *Da-da-dadada* . . . THUMP-THUMP! THUMP-THUMP!

Suddenly a gunshot rang out, interrupting the peaceful strains of Strauss. The bullet whizzed past my right ear.

I stumbled back a few steps, then dropped to the ground. Then, another shot. I looked at the Datsun, and sure enough, there were two fresh puncture marks by the keyhole. When the third shot rang out, it was clear what had happened. Paul had clocked Fieldman and dumped him in the trunk along with all his belongings . . . including his gun. I guess he hadn't counted on him waking up anytime soon.

The fourth was a charm. The slug shattered the lock, the lid flew open, and Fieldman popped up like a Detroit Dracula. His eyes adjusted to the harsh sunlight—he didn't have those stupid sunglasses on anymore. He wasn't too blind to see me, though. The me who Fieldman thought had smacked him around and put him in the trunk.

"Hold it right there," he said, aiming the gun at my chest.

We'd come full circle.

"Getoutofthetrunkandrun," I said, still breathless. "Bombin-thecar. Runnow. Getawayfromthecar." I took a few steps back, by way of demonstration.

"Don't move," Fieldman said. After all of this, you'd think he'd go and take a shot at me already. In his mind, I had a) risen from the dead, b) given him a strange hallucinogenic that turned his life into a surreal hell for eight months, c) broken his nose, d) knocked him unconscious, and then e) stuffed him in the trunk of a crappy used car. Most people would have stopped at "a," you know? Not Fieldman. He was a federal agent ready to die on his vacation, and he still wanted to arrest me.

I heard strange clicking sounds. I didn't know bombs from boobs, but something told me this was the sound of Paul's homemade device getting ready to blow. There was no time for further argument.

I looked at Fieldman. Thank God he wasn't wearing those sunglasses.

* * *

The explosion was everything I could have hoped for: hot, bright, and loud, as if the veined fist of God had come down from the heavens to wipe the pathetic Datsun off the face of the earth. The blow knocked me off my feet, slammed me into the hard dirt, then rolled me clear back across the ground a few yards. Tiny pebbles cut into my elbows and ass. I hurt like hell, but after a few tentative breaths, I knew I'd live. And so would Fieldman, in a manner of speaking.

I closed my eyes, tuned out, and went to the Brain Hotel to check on Fieldman's soul. When I got to the lobby, though, there was no sign of him.

I went back out through the lobby doors and back into Reality. The pain hit me as if I'd experienced it all over again. Slowly, I pulled myself to my feet and started waving my arms around, trying to clear the smoke. I approached the burning wreckage and saw what I thought used to be Fieldman's body, hanging over a piece of metal I suspected had been the rear bumper. Or maybe it was the other way around.

I coughed and took a few steps back, trying to take in the picture. His soul *had* to be around here somewhere. After a few hurried minutes of looking, I started to worry. Robert had told me souls *always* hang around the flesh for a while. Even in cases of total vaporization, a soul will lurk around the sizzling droplets for a while before seeking the Great Beyond. Shit, I'd been dead for six years, and I still hadn't sought the Great Beyond. I'd been too busy.

If Fieldman wasn't out here in Reality, that left only one possibility: he was somewhere in the Brain Hotel. It was unlikely, though: I can always tell when I take on another resident. Every soul collection leaves me feeling wiped out. I felt relatively normal at the moment, considering I'd been Reality/Brain Hotel hopping, running around like a fool, and beating my Datsun with a rock.

"You are looking for me, Collective."

My head snapped in the direction of the voice. It was Fieldman, all right. Standing where he wasn't standing a second ago. However, it wasn't exactly Fieldman. His image was blurred, as if he had been shot by a 16mm camera at the wrong speed.

"That you, Fieldman?"

The Flickering Image of Fieldman chuckled. "I haven't heard that name in . . . *a while.* If you like, you may call me Fieldman. Though I have long since forgotten to think of myself by that name."

Okkkayyyyy. Clearly, Fieldman had lost two things in the Datsun explosion: his physical body *and* his mind.

"Doubting my sanity, Collective?" Fieldman asked. He started walking toward me. His image cleared up a bit. Maybe someone was adjusting their dials. Fieldman was wearing a long robe, adorned with the same drippy gumball design his last earthly shirt had. And sandals. I hated guys in sandals.

"Why do you keep calling me that? Don't you know who—" I stopped myself. Of course, he *didn't* know who I really was.

"I know who you are, Del Farmer."

He knew my name. He seemed to be able to read my thoughts. Fieldman had died and come back as the goddamned Buddha.

"You have many questions, Collective. Allow me to answer some of them for you in a speedy fashion, because although I exist out of time, you are still trapped in its boundaries, and right now, as we speak, several law enforcement officers are coming this way to investigate a fiery disturbance, the same disturbance that ended my life as Agent Fieldman and began my quest out of time, out of this physical plane. I died an agent of the law, and an agent I continue to be, although the laws are different, as is the agency."

"I thought you were going to do this in a 'speedy fashion'?"

Fieldman's eyes narrowed. "At the moment of my death, you tried to absorb my soul into your Collective in advance of an explosion. My soul was caught between those two violent and competing forces."

This was the first thing that made any sense. I knew I'd grabbed hold of Fieldman's soul before the bomb went off, but my hold weakened. I'd mistakenly thought it meant he was safely tucked away in the Brain Hotel. Apparently, I was wrong.

"In short, I am no longer slave to linear time. I am here with you now to assist you with your murder investigation."

"Wait . . . you want to *help* me? Why?"

"The murders of Brad and Alison Larsen will become extremely important in the near future."

"How could you possibly know that?"

"Were you not listening to the part about me being free from the tyranny of linear time?"

"You're saying you know the future."

"Yes. And on that note, you really need to starting running now, because your cab is ready to leave."

Fieldman had lost me again, but the last bit made sense. I started jogging back toward the motel, praying to God—or Buddha, for that matter—the hack driver had decided to wait this out, despite the explosion and the wailing of police sirens, which were now becoming audible in the distance.

Don't worry, Collective, a voice spoke in my head. *I'm your backup.*

Great.

* * *

Bless the higher powers: the hack Paul called had stayed put. I mumbled an apology, stuffed my belongings in his trunk, and scooted over into the backseat. I slapped a $50 bill against the Plexiglas partition and asked to be taken to the Las Vegas International Airport, TWA terminal, pronto. The squad cars and fire engines zoomed past us, spinning into the ground behind the hotel.

"That's not about you, is it?"

"Of course not," I said, slapping an extra $20 on the glass.

"I didn't think so." The cabbie pulled us out through the same dust the cops had stirred up and sped on toward Las

Vegas. I took a peek at his license on the dash in case I had to remember it later. STEPHEN M. KNIGHT, it read. RED OWL COMPANY. As it turned out, I wouldn't have to remember it: I arrived at the terminal in plenty of time for my flight to Philly, and if Mr. Knight ratted me out, I never heard about it.

* * *

As much as I'd hoped against it, I discovered Fieldman was still with me. He was in the airplane seat next to me, taking in his surroundings with a look of total bemusement. When I closed my eyes to port myself to the Brain Hotel, he was in the lobby, waiting for me. *Interesting*, he'd say. *This resembles a beloved movie theater from your childhood.* Then he'd pop back into the seat next to me and entertain himself with the seat belt for a while.

Fieldman was the only soul, it seemed, who could check himself in and out of the Brain Hotel at will.

Fieldman was #13, God save us.

PHILADELPHIA, PENNSYLVANIA

Several hours later

12

LOVE CITY

I hailed a cab at Philadelphia International and handed the driver the address: 1530 Spruce Street. The Sherman Oaks girl had found a place for me. A friend of hers at the Moore College of Art knew a building that catered to college students and other transients. No year lease required; you could pay by the month. Since it was June, the end of the school year, there were plenty of furnished rooms available.

The building was quite nice, but old. A stone date-marker read "1870," and it looked it. Perhaps the most recent renovation had been the row of mailboxes in the lobby. As promised, the landlord was waiting outside for me with my keys. He didn't speak much English—or else he didn't care to. I handed him an envelope containing $350—security deposit and a month's rent, up front. He handed me two keys: one for the front door, one for my own apartment. The front door was tagged with a green plastic overlay and a tiny, yellowed sticker that said LOBBY in shaky capital letters. Just in case I was confused. The landlord left without a word.

He is concerned you are a serial killer, Fieldman said in my head.

"Good. Maybe he won't bother me about a late rent check," I said. "Now, if you don't mind, I'd like some peace and quiet."

Every Collective needs their rest, Fieldman agreed. *We will speak again.*

Oh, I was sure we would.

I pushed all my things inside, then carried my wardrobe (i.e., my plastic trash bags) up to my apartment, and prayed nobody would steal my boxes while I was gone. I keyed in. The first room was tiny—a stove and sink shoved into one corner, a desk and chair in another, and a battered houndstooth couch placed beneath two greased windows that, if cleaned properly, would afford me a great view of a gray brick wall. NEWLY RENOVATED, FURNISHED STUDIO APARTMENT, RITTENHOUSE SQUARE VICINITY, HISTORIC BUILDING. Yeah, Washington slept here all right. And left his crap all over the place.

I opened a door leading into the bedroom. It was furnished with a toilet, bathtub, sink, and mirrored cabinet. Confused, I went back out into the first room and looked for another door. There wasn't one, except for the one through which I'd entered. After some poking around, I learned that the scratchy-looking couch was also a day bed. How efficient—a living room, dining room, kitchen, study, and bedroom, all in one low-priced space! Only now did I realize why the landlord never gave me a tour. The walk upstairs would have taken longer than the tour itself.

I went back down to the lobby and thought about leaving, but instead opted to carry my two cardboard boxes up to my fully furnished closet. Halfway up, I caught my reflection in the glass covering a fire extinguisher. It shocked me, even after all these months. Brad's face was rugged, yet boyish. Nature's way of saying, *I am harmless, but please do not touch*. This face, I remember thinking, will serve me well during this investigation.

At this particular moment, however, it did not. Halfway up the second staircase, I met a woman wearing a college sweatshirt and faded jeans. She was carrying a shoulder bag stuffed with papers and books. "Pardon me," I said, as mechanically as possible.

"You're pardoned," she said, smirking. Her eyes went to my shoes and back up. "You need a hand with that?"

"No, I'm fine. Thank you."

She skirted to one side, and I mimicked her, unintentionally. We repeated the mimic. She started laughing. I frowned.

"My name's Amy Langtree. I guess you're moving in."

Yes, but my friends call me Move. I thought about saying it out loud, but it was probably best not to start a conversation. "Yes. Uh . . . I'm Del. Del Winter." This was my new alias. Sure, it wasn't too much of a stretch from my real name, Del Farmer. But I found it useful to keep "Del." *You* try keeping a dozen people in your head straight, and then talk to me about names, okay? I needed all the psychic anchors I could get.

"Great name. Sort of like Del Shannon, right?"

"Sort of," I said, trying to squeeze past her. "Only it's Winter."

"Aren't you going to shake my hand?"

I started to shake, but one of the boxes slipped, and a semi-auto clip slid out of the top. Damn it. I quickly dropped the box and scooped it up.

"Del, you need help." Amy grabbed the first box and started up the stairs. She looked back at me, smiling. I looked up and returned a queasy version of a smile.

"No lip. C'mon. What apartment number?"

I told her, full knowing this was not going to sit well with the other souls.

* * *

One thing I may have failed to mention about my Brain Hotel residents: they tended to be cooperative, just so long as I didn't appear to have a life outside of my job. The minute I tried to resume a normal life—settling down with a nice girl, finding a job with benefits—they were all over me.

Oh, the souls had it good. No puzzles, no worries, no bills. They could lounge in their quarters, or eat and drink to excess, or read books and paint. The only thing I ever demanded was a bit of their time (no more than twenty minutes, usually) every so often to ask a few questions. Most of them led their own lives in their Brain Hotel rooms, and rarely bothered to ask me for anything. It was like being the president of a small company; I only dealt with a select few employees, and the rest . . . well, the rest did whatever they did and didn't bother telling me about it.

But the ones who paid attention—man, they could give me trouble. And one who was starting to pay more and more attention to my real-world activities was Paul After.

I knew he wouldn't take kindly to Amy Langtree.

Amy kneed the door open and walked in. I followed, hunched over, still trying to casually stuff ammo clips back into the box. She dropped her box on a table in the corner, careful not to knock over the telephone that sat there.

"What do you do for a living?"

"Living?"

"Yes—your job?"

"My job?" I repeated.

She squinted at me. "Let me guess. You hang out all day mimicking people's actions and speech."

I told her my new cover. "I work for the Philadelphia Electric Company." Well, at least it was a chance to try it out. See how it worked on a civilian. Somehow, I didn't think the residents of the Brain Hotel would buy this as an excuse to talk to her. If anybody happened to be in the lobby screening room at this particular moment, I was sure to hear an earful when I returned to the hotel later.

Amy nodded and walked over to me. "You in the collection department?"

"Huh?"

A clip I'd forgotten about was sitting on top of the box I was holding. Amy picked it up and pointed it at my face. "You no pay, I blow brains out?"

"Oh," I said. "Oh, no no. Hah. Hobby. I mean, it's a hobby of mine. Guns." I stared hard at her. "Keeps nosy neighbors from asking too many questions."

Amy's eyes widened for a moment, then she laughed. "Damn, Del, you do have a sense of humor. A sick sense of humor, but I'll take it. I was beginning to worry."

I smiled—uncomfortably—then turned to drop the box. I could feel Amy giving me the once-over. What was it with her? Most women, upon meeting a strange man carrying a box of firearms into his tiny studio apartment, would spin on their heels and hit the road. Fast. But not her.

"What kind of guns do you have? I used to have a cop buddy who showed me quite a few of his police-issue numbers. You got single or double action?"

Paul was going to *hate* this line of conversation. Nice cover, Del, he'd tell me. Why not give her a tour of the Brain Hotel while you're at it?

"Amy, this is not a good time. I'm not feeling great, and I've got to finish—"

"Yeah, yeah, you're getting settled. Speaking of—where's the rest of your stuff? Need any help?"

This time I was prepared. I'd planned the story in advance: I had moved with some work files and necessities. The electric company was having my furniture and personal effects sent later. Of course, I didn't own anything else; I made a mental note to pick up a few pieces of junk to avoid suspicion.

Amy seemed satisfied with my explanation. "I guess I'll take a rain check."

"On what?"

"On the gun talk." She whipped out a felt pen from her backpack and started to write on the top of one of my boxes. "Here's my number. I'm right upstairs. Nice meeting you, too, Del."

"Nice . . . you, too."

I showed her to the door, then turned around to expel the air from my lungs. I looked around, pressed my palms to my eyes, then walked into my new bathroom.

I uncapped a bottle and dry-swallowed two Bufferin, cupping water from the faucet. I looked at myself.

New friend? a voice in my skull asked, more than a twinge of sarcasm in it. I recognized that voice. At least it wasn't Fieldman again.

With Paul, I had to be careful. He was still sore about the whole dead Fed/trunk mix-up—especially when I blamed him for the creation of Linear Time-Free Fieldman. But it was important to keep him happy, to maintain his enthusiasm for the investigation, since he was one of the few useful souls I had. Besides, I couldn't go around pissing on everybody forever.

"Look, Paul, I made her go away. You saw that, right?"

Yeah, I saw. I saw you flirting like mad.

"Point is, I made her go away."

I made her go away, he mocked. *Come on. If you want to be serious about your investigation, it's important you don't get involved . . . with anybody. Raises too many questions.*

"Don't worry about it."

If you want action, use one of the Brain hookers. I've gotten used to them. Genevieve is especially accommodating.

The phone rang. I went back into the non-bathroom room and answered it.

"My name is Richard," a voice said. "I believe you are an associate of a man named Stan Wojciechowski. Are you available to speak this afternoon?"

"Of course."

"Meet me at the Rittenhouse Hotel, Room 1223, at four p.m. You won't require anything. Just yourself. Is that clear?"

"Sure. See you."

I hung up. Actually, he'd be seeing Paul. I must have spoken it out loud, because Paul responded in my head:

What was that?

13

PORTRAITS OF THE ARTISTS AS YOUNG MEN

Here was my problem: I hated freelance work. Great money for usually minimal labor, but it was too much of a distraction. Too much additional information got in the way of my real investigation. After careful consideration—about ten seconds' worth—I decided to enlist Paul After. He would play the part of hired dick, leaving me free to get a fix on Brad Larsen's killers. I figured he would enjoy the taste of bodily freedom; I'd have a chance to kick back and do some real work.

I would always be in control, mind you. I could watch what was happening from the movie screen in the Brain Hotel lobby. And if Paul did something to jeopardize the mission—or my physical body—I could crack the reins, drag his soul back to the hotel, and carry on myself. Of course, to the casual observer, my body would fall unconscious, maybe even lose control of its bodily functions. This was not something I liked to do often.

* * *

As I thought, Paul agreed to take the case for me. He complained about it at first, but I knew he wouldn't turn me down. He'd enjoyed his taste of freedom back in Henderson too much.

Paul dressed my body in gray pants and a white ribbed undershirt. Then he slicked back my hair and shaved me. Nicked me twice.

"There's something I've been wondering, Del," he said, looking into the bathroom mirror. "Why do you look exactly like me?"

"I don't," I said, speaking into the lobby microphone. "You're seeing your own face. Happens a lot at first. In Reality, we're wearing the face of a recent murder victim. I'm tracking down his killers."

"Why wear the guy's face?"

"I've found it can help speed the investigation."

"Who was he?"

"A man named Brad Larsen. He was also set to testify against your former employers."

"Was he a good-looking guy?"

"Don't worry. The villagers won't come after you with torches and pitchforks."

Paul squinted. "If you say so. But it's still damn weird. All I see is me."

"It happens to everybody. It's too much of a shock to see your own consciousness in another man's face. Or so the theory goes. I saw myself for a long time until I came to terms with everything."

Paul grunted and dabbed his/my cheeks with a hand towel. He finished dressing us in a white shirt, red necktie, and gray suitcoat—the most stylish items in my limited wardrobe. I could sense Paul hated it, as if he were forced to wear his older brother's hand-me-downs. But until we received our first paycheck, there wasn't much we could do about it.

"Interesting choice," spoke a voice behind Paul, in the real world. It was Fieldman, whose image was distorted by the rays of sunlight peeking through the curtains. "Not everyone would put that ensemble together."

"Can't you shut him up?" Paul asked me.

If only.

* * *

We arrived early, so Paul took the opportunity to stroll around the square for a few minutes. Rittenhouse Square was a well-heeled neighborhood, despite the scruffy kids in dashiki shirts playing beat-up guitars in the park. Giant apartment complexes, hotels, and office buildings lined the four sides of the park, and everybody and everything seemed to gravitate toward it, being the only patch of green for blocks and blocks. William Penn may have had a brilliant plan in mind when he first cooked up the city grid, but he didn't give much thought to green open spaces.

Soon, it was time for our appointment, and I surrendered control of my body. Watching Paul operate my body was an education. Every motion was studied, whereas mine were automatic, unthinking. Take entering the hotel. I would have marched right up the front desk, asked for Richard Gard's room, then taken the elevator to the correct floor. A straightforward, let's-go-to-work approach. But not Paul.

Paul walked into the hotel bar first. Slowly, as if he were too bored to be doing anything else. The bar was right off the side of the lobby; a dark, oaky-looking room. While I didn't exactly know what Paul was thinking—it was more like I possessed deep intuition about Paul's intentions rather than direct knowledge—I knew he was checking for signs of Gard. Why would Gard be here and not upstairs? Good question. It's not one I would have immediately asked.

Paul walked directly to the bar and took a seat. He looked at the bartender, then to the guy at his right. Sweaty, young, in a very fashionable tweed suit, though wrong for this time of year. Blonde hair falling in every direction but the correct one. He kept looking at the door, waiting for people to pass his line of vision.

Finally, Paul tapped him on the shoulder. "Mr. Gard."

The man started, then wiped his brow with a cocktail napkin and recovered. "Mr. Wojciechowski."

"No," said Paul, "I'm his senior associate. Paul After."

They shook hands. I received a sensory flash: *sweaty palms*. Ugh.

"Mr. Wojciechowski is seeing to some urgent business in Nevada," Paul explained.

Good boy. Keep the famous Mr. W. shrouded in mystery. Clients loved that.

"I understand." Gard took a drink, then seemed as if a light bulb had gone off in his thick blond skull. "How did you . . ."

Paul finished the sentence. "Know you? Come, now. I assume you're going to pay me a lot of money to predict what's coming next."

Damn. Mr. Mofo Disco Detective.

Gard seemed impressed, too. "Care for a drink?"

"In a moment," Paul said. "First, I'd like to know why you are down here, in this bar, instead of upstairs in the room number you supplied my associate. Seems like you're up to more than sneaking a peek at the hired help."

"I admit, that was part of it. But there's also bit of preface to your job. The clerk at the front desk was supposed to send you over."

"What preface?" Paul asked.

"Before you meet Susie, I wanted to make this perfectly clear: no matter what I say upstairs, no matter how aloof I may seem, your loyalties will remain with me completely. You will run every single decision by me. You will not move a finger without my knowing about it. Everything begins and ends with me."

Paul nodded.

Seemed fair to me, too. Gard was footing the bill.

"Upstairs, you are going to meet a woman who is my mistress. I demand complete discretion as well as respect in this regard. She is going to ask for your assistance. You are going to give it. You are also going to give her the impression you are working for her, not me."

Paul smirked. "I'm to win her confidence. And, of course, I'm to report everything to you."

"You're quick," Gard said.

And you're a sweaty goofball.

Paul glanced at himself in the mirror, as if he could hear me. Could he?

"Now how about that drink, eh?" Gard asked. "Take a few minutes, then come upstairs as planned. I'll introduce you and you can begin your assignment." He placed a hand on Paul's back. An uncomfortable jolt went through both of us. "Henry! Give this man whatever he likes."

A pug-nosed, white-haired man in a bow tie raised his head.

"A Shirley Temple, please," Paul said.

"A hard-boiled man like yourself?" Gard laughed.

Paul didn't answer the question. He told Henry not to forget the cherry. Gard shook his head.

"Oh, by the way." Gard fished a check out of his suit pocket and placed it on the bar. "For today's meeting. I'll mail a check for double that every week, as agreed."

Paul didn't look at the check. I wanted him to, but I couldn't exactly force his eyes down to the bartop. "Thanks."

Gard was left holding the conversational bag, so he decided to leave.

There was a lot to learn from Paul.

* * *

I tuned out while Paul was enjoying his Shirley Temple and wandered back to my office. I could have ported myself there, but that kind of thing became disorienting after a while. The more the Brain Hotel seemed like real life, the better.

I poured myself a glass of Brain Chivas Regal and read through a notebook of some Association notes from last year. The notes were perfect; exactly as I'd recorded them months ago. But the Chivas was only as good as I remembered it.

After a while, the notes all seemed to blur together. A lot of numbers, a lot of places, a lot of words and letters. It started to bore me.

I made my way back down to the hotel lobby in time

for Paul to meet Gard's mistress up on the screen. It was not unlike watching a movie, especially when our new client entered the scene.

"Susannah Winston, Paul After."

There was a pause. A long, awkward pause. Hell, I was getting ready to say something when Susannah finally broke in.

"After what, Paul?" she asked, smiling.

"Charmed to meet you, Ms. Winston."

I noticed Paul's hand lingering on Susannah's. Mine would have, too, believe me. I tossed back another gulp of Brain Chivas and took a closer look.

Susannah Winston had chestnut hair, fashionably bobbed to a sharp point on both sides of her prettily squared jaw. Her nose was slightly upturned, as if to clear way for her lips—full and dark red. A man in his twenties would consider her the antidote to marriage: one single, sensuous reason to stay single forever. And a man in his thirties or forties would think of her as a luscious packet of instant infidelity. Richard Gard looked to be pushing forty.

Susannah was much, much younger. She had large, round blue eyes and a mouth that curled upward like a smile, even when she wasn't reacting to anything. Even doing something as mundane as lighting a cigarette. I could detail the physical attributes below her neck, but it would be redundant. I could see the death-drop curves beneath those polyester slacks as clearly as if she were wearing a bikini.

"What can I do for you?" Paul asked.

"I used to date the wrong kind of boy, and now one of them wants to murder me," she said, then wrapped her lips around her cigarette.

Richard looked away, as if he didn't hear. Instead, he asked, "Anybody up for a drink?"

Susannah looked at Paul. "I'll bet you're a gin-and-tonic man, aren't you?"

"Just tonic," Paul said. "No ice."

Good boy. I'd warned him about boozing it up on the job in the real world.

Susannah waited until Richard had returned with the drinks—plain tonic for Paul, two gin and tonics for Richard and Susannah. Apparently, these people were big on gin. Me? I couldn't stand the stuff—always gave me a wicked hangover the next day. Then again, this was probably because I only used to drink the cheap stuff.

The three made their way to the living room and sat down—Paul in a plush loveseat, Susannah and Richard on a long spare couch without any extra pillows.

"I haven't even told Richard the entire story, to be honest," Susannah said. "I wanted both of you to hear everything. I'm sure it hurts him as much as it hurts me."

Richard heard that, all right. He glanced at Susannah, gave her a warm, large smile, then looked back down at his drink.

"I'm from a small, yet substantially wealthy family from the suburbs of Boston," she said. "My father made his fortune after World War II, when he invented a military tracking device that, to this day, is considered state of the art."

She let that sink in and continued. "I grew up in splendor, was sent to private academies. Smith College, eventually, where I majored in Victorian literature. A colossal waste of time. All of it. And I don't say that lightly. All I wanted was a real education—one that would teach me the way the world *really* worked. That's what I needed. Not emerald-studded bracelets and pretty pink dresses.

"I received that education soon enough. The year after I graduated Smith, I spent a week in New York City with some of my classmates—courtesy of my father, of course. We stayed at the Royalton, had our pick of restaurants and Broadway shows, four-star everything. It was a perfectly miserable trip."

"Yeah, I hear *The Wiz* is a real nightmare," Paul said.

Richard's eyes narrowed. "Now look here . . ."

"No, it's all right," Susannah said. "I guess it does sound like a pathetic sob story. Poor little rich girl doesn't get her way. But you haven't heard the part that makes me cry, Mr. After. At least allow me that."

Paul nodded deferentially.

"One night, my girlfriends and I decided to see the seamy parts of town, the kind we'd certainly never see at Smith. We took a cab down to the East Village and walked into a jazz club. I met a boy there—his name was Chris. He was skinny, his clothes were ten years out of style and his fingernails were dirty, but I let him buy me a drink. To be honest, it was exciting."

"And sure to anger your parents," Paul said.

Susannah looked down at her shoes. "Precisely. I was looking for a different kind of education, and here was a man who presented himself as the crash course. So, I never went back to Boston. I moved in with Chris—who turned out to be a pot-dealer, a television repair shop janitor, and sometimes, when he was in the mood, a novelist. Of course, all I focused on was the novelist part—even though he never let me read a word. For a sheltered Smith girl, he was Jack Kerouac. Until he raped me."

I'm sure she had been saving this for the right moment. Both Paul and Richard did the exact same thing: lowered their drinks and averted their eyes, as if ashamed for the entire male sex.

"Oh, he made such a fuss about apologizing, blaming the drink, his frustrations with being unknown. But nothing could explain away the act. The first chance I had, I ran to a nearby diner and called my father to beg his forgiveness and ask for train fare home. But my mother answered. It turned out I was too late."

"He came looking for you?" asked Richard.

"No. He'd already dropped dead from a stroke."

Susannah took a sip of her drink. I noted how much care she took not to leave any of her lipstick on the glass. Must be hard to drink that way.

"When I arrived home, I found my mother had pulled a Sylvia Plath."

Paul and Richard said nothing. They lowered their heads even further.

"But then I discovered Dad had forgiven me, in his own way. Weeks after I'd told him I was staying in New York, he had his will changed, and I soon discovered I was a half-million dollars richer."

"That was all he had left?" Paul asked. "For an inventor of something as important as . . ." He faked a pause, as if struggling to remember. He was trying to make her give away an extra detail.

It didn't work. "No, that was all," Susannah said, and took another clean sip from her glass. "The government basically stole the patent, and probably gave him a million to shut him up. Part of me didn't even want to take the money—I didn't enjoy earning it through my parents' death, or for that matter, that my father had earned it inventing a tool that sent thousands to their deaths in Vietnam."

"The guilt must have been awful," Richard said.

Thank God I wasn't the one conducting this case. I couldn't imagine spending any more than twenty minutes with this drama queen.

Paul said, "And you took the money."

Susannah shot him a pair of icy daggers. "Yes, I took the money. I had nothing. And I wasn't going to refuse my late father's apology."

"Was that necessary, Mr. After?" asked Richard.

"I'm sorry if I offended either one of you," Paul said. "I'm simply trying to establish motive." He looked directly at Susannah. "Besides, I think I know where your story is headed. Out of the blue, your East Village friend catches wind of your windfall and takes the next cheap bus up to Boston to try for a second chance at love. With a fist or a pistol, if necessary."

"No," said Susannah, looking pleased with herself. "I never saw the boy again."

"Then who's after you?"

"Oh," she said, then laughed to herself. "You thought the man after me was . . . *him*? Please. No, no, Mr. After, I didn't have Richard bring you all the way from Los Angeles to protect me from a scummy painter boy. We've hired you to protect me from a professional killer."

Boy, I thought. Professional killers were everywhere this time of year.

* * *

"Come again?" Paul asked.

"Of course, I didn't know he was a pro at the time. He was all fancy French wines and exotic meals at first. He told me he was an international banker. Only later did I realize his most recent target had been an international banker. That's how he knew so much about the lifestyle. He was—is—a professional chameleon."

"What's his name?"

"The name he used? Roger Adams. I'm sure it's fake."

Paul took the opportunity to stand up. I was suddenly thrown off by the sudden change of perspective. Even flashed up on the screen of the hotel lobby, sudden motion always gave me a touch of vertigo.

"Ms. Winston, can you tell me anything about the daily schedule of this Adams? I happen to know a great deal about these types of men..."

Understatement of the year!

"...and it would help to understand his habits."

"I didn't see him often enough to learn a routine. You see, I've been traveling for a while. I mean, was. Travel brought me to Philadelphia, and to Richard."

The sap smiled as if this were some sort of personal achievement.

"Right after my parents died, I decided I wanted to see the world. I met Roger months later, in Paris, while I was staying in a small artists' tenement. The rent was cheap, and the conversations—the ones I understood, at least—were phenomenal. Everyone I met was either a novelist, or a painter, or a graphic designer..."

Was there a pistol in this hotel lobby? I asked myself. Could I put myself out of my misery now?

124

She went on at length about the wonders of café life, and how she was completely bedazzled by the Great and Powerful Roger Adams, and what they ate for dinner (shark), and what they drank afterward (vodka gimlets), and what pretentious poetry they talked about (Auden) . . . To his credit, Paul let her ramble. I guess he didn't want to insult her again. Or maybe she lulled him to sleep. Her beloved Richard Gard, I noticed, was looking droopy around the eyes. Paul waited until she talked herself dry before nudging the conversation back toward the topic at hand.

"And you saw him only once in Paris?"

"Yes, but we met up many, many times afterwards. He traveled a lot on business and I found myself tagging along. It was fun and it gave my traveling a kind of purpose. I felt alive again. Until reality reared its ugly head."

"When did you first realize?" Paul asked.

"When I found the gun in his suitcase, and the dossier."

Ah. Now here's where Ms. Winston was tripping herself up. And I didn't need Paul's expertise to know it. Pro killers didn't carry a pistol, singular; they carried a portable arsenal. Knives, clips, guns, poisons, knucks, the works. And a dossier? Yeah. Unless it's tattooed onto their lower intestine for emergency reference, all the pros I've encountered never kept written info on their person. It was memorized or locked away in a safe location.

Of course, Paul knew it, too. I could sense him smirking. "A dossier?"

"Yes. Photographs, addresses, social security records—everything."

Paul nodded. "Where were you when you made this discovery?"

"In Dublin. I'd been dying to go ever since I read *Portraits of the Artists as Young Men*. I've long loved Joyce—and art history. Especially the chapter about Picasso."

"Ah, yes," Paul said. "It's a classic."

My God. Who the hell did she think she was fooling? One look at Richard Gard supplied my answer. Gard wouldn't know James Joyce from a Rolls-Royce.

Then again, I wondered if Paul would.

Susannah continued, "We stayed at The Westbury, of course. Roger slipped out for a couple of paperbacks for the plane home, and I was bored sitting in the room all by myself. I let my eyes wander."

Richard Gard suddenly spoke up. He'd probably been dying to talk for the past ten minutes. "And that's when you found the gun?"

"And the dossier?" Paul added.

"Yes." Susannah paused for the requisite amount of time. "I didn't know what to do. Part of me wanted to play the innocent and ask Roger about the things I'd found when he returned. But then the sane part of me took over. I knew he'd kill me once I'd found out. Then I heard the room key turn in the lock."

Richard actually winced.

"It was Roger, of course. I slid the files back into his briefcase and nudged the briefcase off the side of the bed, praying it wouldn't make too loud a noise, or flip over and spill its contents. But thankfully, it didn't. Just one thump, which the sound of the door closing again completely covered.

"I asked Roger if he'd found anything good. He told me, 'Nothing.' Then he asked me what I'd been up to. I said,

'Nothing.' There was an uncomfortable moment between us. I knew he sensed something, so I tried changing the topic. I told him I wanted to go downstairs for a drink, maybe buy a couple of magazines. He told me no. I said, 'What do you mean, no?' And he repeated himself. 'You're not going anywhere.' So, like any sensible woman, I told him he could fuck off and I started to walk past him. He punched me in the face."

That seemed to impact Paul and Richard as well. As much as men didn't like to be told stories about women being raped, they sure as hell didn't like to hear about men slapping women around. It was an indictment of the whole gender. By mere virtue of having a penis, we belonged to the guilty party.

"I was stunned. Before I could scream out or cry for help, he hit me again, slapping me hard across the face. I could hardly breathe. The next memory I have is of Roger pinning me to the bed, his thick monkey fingers wrapped around my throat, threatening to kill me if I ever walked out on him again."

Then the eruption of tears began. "I don't know what you must think of me," she said. "Oh wait. I know. You must be thinking, 'What kind of girl would get herself involved with the same kind of trash, over and over . . . ?'"

Richard went to her and started to rub her back. "Believe me, Susannah," he cooed. "I don't think any of those things. I've heard far worse stories in my time."

"None like this." Susannah buried her face in her hands. "I'm sorry . . ."

"Sorry? God, why are you sorry?"

"For me. For my past."

Richard put down his drink and rested his hands on her shoulders.

Paul cleared his throat. "Go back for a moment. What happened after he hit you?"

"He took a shower." Susannah sipped her drink. "Right then, as if nothing had happened. I couldn't take that abuse anymore, boyfriend or not."

"Then what did you do?"

Susannah paused. "I decided to run."

"Go on, baby," Richard said.

"I . . . I rushed out with all my things, but stopped at the pile of his clothes, the ones he'd taken off before his shower. And I know I shouldn't have, but I . . ."

"But you . . . ?" Paul prompted.

Susannah's eyes turned his way. "I took a pack of hotel matches and set his clothes on fire. He was always bragging about his stuff. He treated his goddamned shirts better than he treated me."

Richard looked at her hard. "Which is how the room caught fire, right?"

"The room caught fire?" Paul asked.

"Yes," Richard said. "That much, she'd told me. He died in a fire."

"God as my witness, I didn't know! I didn't know!" she cried. "When I saw on the news later about the fire . . ." Susannah took another sip and stared off as if she were watching the broadcast again. "I knew he was dead."

"So, the guy who sent you the note can't be your ex, can he?" Richard asked.

"He can't be . . . but what if he is? Oh, God, Richard, this man is a murderer! He didn't tell me he killed anyone until after we got to Europe! He said it was going to be our honeymoon!"

"Note?" Paul asked.

I wondered if this was how super-lawyer Richard Gard introduced exhibits in the courtroom. I knew who I wouldn't be calling when it came time to bring down The Association in federal court.

Richard walked over to his briefcase and removed a thin sheet of paper from a manila folder. He handed it to Paul. It was incredibly flimsy and glossy—a photocopy.

L—
You're dead.
All my love,
R

"This is not very specific," Paul said. "Sure it's not a prank?"

"No," said Richard. "We're not. But I'm not ready to take any chances."

"Who's 'L'?" Paul asked.

"Me," said Susannah.

"Oh. It's Susannah with an L?"

She scowled. "No. It's a stupid nickname he gave me—lemondrop. My sweet and sour lemondrop, he'd always say." She looked away, covering her face with a tiny balled-up fist.

Richard walked over and sat down to hug her. "Don't worry. Shhh. I'll take care of everything."

"He's going to kill me, Richard."

"No one's going to kill you."

Susannah broke the hug. "You don't know. You don't."

"Shhh. Nothing's going to happen to you."

Susannah resumed the hug, and behind his back, with tears running down her face, smiled. "You're too good to me, Richard."

I couldn't glom a vibe from Paul. He was trying too hard to be his noncommittal, professional self. But I did catch a glimmer of a thought: *I can't believe I'm watching this*. Or it might have been: *I can't believe I'm involved in this*. Or, quite possibly: *I can't believe a word of this*.

"She's lying, you know."

I spun around. Fieldman had been standing in the Brain Hotel lobby, watching the scene with me. He had a knack for sudden appearances. I should have told him to go back to Vegas to start his own show.

"Which part?" I asked. "The rich inventor father? The Greenwich Village artist-rapist? The international hit man?"

"No man named Winston ever invented anything for any branch of United States military during the twentieth century."

"Maybe the government can keep a few secrets. Even from you."

"Not likely. You want to know what is in the tap water in 1976? What the Air Force *really* found in Roswell, New Mexico? Why the United States government invented static cling?"

"Stop," I said. "Please. I'm only keeping an eye on Paul to make sure he knows what he's doing, then I'm going back to work."

"Ah, your quest for the Nevada crime syndicate. The entity you refer to as The Association."

"That's right. Aren't you supposed to be helping me with my case? Isn't that what you told me back in Henderson?"

"Yes, I did say I was here to help, but not with that particular quest. You are wasting your days with that, Collective. The musical genre known as *disco* will outlive your Association."

"Disco is all over the radio, in case you haven't noticed."

"I am absolutely amazed at how little you absorb, Collective. I'm not sure how your delicate sensibilities are going to survive the Sex Pistols or Guns N' Roses."

I'd had enough. "Are those supposed to be musical groups from the future? What, is it a rule that you have to name yourself after a firearm? And stop calling me 'Collective.' You make me feel like an accountant."

Fieldman shook his head and faded away.

* * *

I rejoined the conversation already in progress. Richard was back from refilling drinks. "Sweetheart, why don't you fill in the gaps—you know, some physical description?"

Paul smiled. "Anything helps."

Susannah caught herself staring at Paul but recovered nicely. She started to plow through the information as if she'd been up all night practicing. "Roger is a short guy with a Napoleon complex. Last time I saw him—this was five years ago, now— he had short-cropped hair. Very Italian-looking. I used to go for that sort of thing when I was young."

"Distinguishing features?"

"He had these deep-set eyes. Almost looked like they were black. A wide smile . . . and an awful limp."

"A genetic marvel," said Richard, chuckling.

"He was once shot in the kneecap."

Paul asked, "Anything else?"

"He's very nondescript. People used to say he looked like somebody they knew."

Paul studied Susannah, who narrowed her eyes.

"So, what can I expect from you, Mr. Paul After?"

"I find your man and have a nice chat with him. Maybe we'll compare dossiers or talk about firearms."

"And what if he doesn't want to have a nice chat?"

"He won't be able to chat with anyone," Paul said. "Ever again."

Uncomfortable pause. They all looked at each other. It was too much for Richard. He was probably imagining his disbarment hearing.

"Pardon me," he said. "I have to visit the boys' room. Please make Paul at home, will you, sweetheart?"

With that, Richard left. Susannah decided that making Paul at home entailed standing up, slinking across the carpet and taking a seat next to him.

"Have I ever seen you before, Mr. After?" she asked.

"I wouldn't think so."

"You look familiar."

"I shouldn't. I'm not from around here."

"Neither am I."

She took a drag from her cigarette, then blew smoke. "I suppose people tell you that you look like somebody they know all the time."

"Not usually."

She paused. "You're a hard one, aren't you?"

Paul shrugged.

"I like that," she said. "I honestly do."

Susannah stared at Paul for a while, not sure of how to place him. I tell you, the man was a Grade-A professional. I'm not sure a usual member of Stan Wojciechowski's crack detective team—namely, me—would have been able to face this task unmoved.

She tried a different approach: Big Boss Woman. "How many hours you going to devote to me?"

"As many as it takes."

"That's not an answer, Paul. I enjoy details."

"I enjoy working alone."

"I'll need you whenever Richard's not around. Days mostly, when he's at the firm. And some nights."

"What do you mean, need me?" Paul asked.

As if on cue, Richard returned from the bathroom. "Well, are we happy, Susannah?"

"I'll need a schedule," she said to him. "I need my freedom."

"Of course," Richard said. "Paul, you can start being Ms. Winston's guardian angel tomorrow morning. I'll send a car for you."

"Whoah," Paul said. "What is this? Some kind of fraternity prank? If you want a babysitter, I'll give you the number of my eight-year-old niece in Toledo."

Richard's eyebrows lowered—undoubtedly, his patented kill-a-jury-with-my-sincerity look. "But, Mr. After, this *is* the job. Until you find this madman, she's going to need some protection. She's quite safe here in the hotel—I've seen to that. But I need someone to be with her when she's shopping, or having lunch out in the city, or even walking around Rittenhouse Square."

"How many hours are we talking?" asked Paul, forcing every word out of his lips.

"As much as she needs," he said.

Paul finished his drink then stood up. "I've heard enough."

Damn! I ran over to the lobby microphone and nailed the button. "Easy there, Paul. Take it easy."

"This is a bunch of crap," he muttered, mostly to himself, but still audible.

"What?" barked Richard.

"Hey!" I yelled. "What the hell are you doing?"

Paul stood still for a moment, thinking it over. I'd like to think it was my stern voice that kept him from flipping Richard the bird and storming out of the room. But most likely, Paul realized that without this job, we would be homeless. Brain Hotel and all. He didn't strike me as the type that enjoyed rooting through garbage cans for dinner.

"This tonic," Paul said. "This tonic is crap."

"But it's Schweppes!" Susannah protested.

Richard ignored her. "Do we have an arrangement, Mr. After?"

"I suppose I'll be seeing you tomorrow morning, Ms. Winston," Paul said.

"As if it's a bad thing?" Susannah asked. "Richard, I'll show Mr. After to the door. Could you refresh my drink? No ice this time."

"Sure, my peach." He looked at Paul. "So, we're square?"

"As a box," Paul said.

In the hallway, Susannah looked at Paul, then finally touched his cheek as if she were blind and trying to see with her fingertips.

Richard called from the other room: "You want ice, sweetheart?"

"No, I don't, sweetheart," she called back, rolling her eyes. She looked at Paul. "I think you're going to like the time we spend together."

Paul didn't say anything.

"Did you ever meet anyone who reminded you of an ex-girlfriend, Paul?"

"Pardon?"

"And feel you want to fuck that person because they looked—perhaps even vaguely—like someone else?"

"No."

Susannah smiled.

"See you tomorrow, Ms. Winston."

14

DRINKS AT TOM'S HOLIDAY

"My God, is she something," I said, speaking into the lobby microphone.

I must have scared Paul. On screen, the perspective snapped to the right.

"What? Oh. You. Nice fucking job. I thought you were a private detective, not a babysitter!"

"Funny, it didn't seem you minded the assignment too much a few seconds ago."

"Screw you. You saying I can't handle her? Jesus Christ— I'm doing your job. Your incredibly pathetic job."

I waited a moment to let Paul realize how ridiculously he was acting. "Have you calmed down yet?"

"Get out of my head," he said. He continued walking, then suddenly stopped and looked deep into a mirror. It gave the chilling effect of him looking directly at me, sitting in the Brain Hotel lobby. I wasn't used to it.

"What's wrong?" I asked.

"Do you know this Susannah Winston from somewhere?"

"No," I said. "Not exactly my type. I like my women educated and truthful. Why do you ask?"

"She said I looked familiar. Hence, you look familiar."

"But don't forget, we're wearing the face of a dead man. It's highly unlikely my client ever met this fruitcake."

"I suppose," said Paul. "God, everything's so fuzzy. Sometimes I lose grip on who I am. You kept me in that room for so long I don't know what's up or down. I mean, I could have been married to that nightmare, for all I know."

"Not likely," I said. "You're an assassin from Las Vegas, remember? It doesn't leave much time for a personal life."

"You know, you could let me out more often. I feel like I'm going crazy in here, sometimes."

"Welcome to life after death, Paul."

Without warning, another voice spoke up. It was Fieldman. He was standing next to me in the lobby, worming his way to the silver mike.

"Paul," he said, "it's possible you're experiencing a retroactive memory."

"Stay out of this," I warned.

Fieldman stuck his tongue out at me. "All this time you've been with the Collective, you haven't heard a rational explanation for your unusual abilities, have you?"

Paul asked, "I suppose you have one?"

I couldn't believe this. A mutiny, right in the middle of an assignment. "Do yourself a favor, Paul. Tell him to crawl up his own thumb."

"The Collective here runs the show without the slightest idea about how it all works," said Fieldman. "I, however, have a theory."

"You do?" Paul asked.

Fieldman cleared his spectral throat. "All of us—you, me, and Mr. Farmer here—are trapped in a soul nexus of the deep future. A future so distant, even I am unable to see it. And in this future, we are long dead. So right now, we are merely recreations of our former selves, resurrected by computers from the far future. But our computer-generated simulations are blurring together by accident—I suspect we're still in an experimental stage, and the thinkers who have brought us back are unable to give us proper boundaries. It's a glitch that will soon resolve itself."

Paul nodded, as if he understood perfectly. "Fieldman?"

"Yes, Paul?"

"Lay off the LSD."

Paul turned his attention to me. "Let's go have a drink, Del. We've got some arrangements to make."

* * *

After laying my physical body down for a rest back at 1530 Spruce Street, we met at Old Tom's. Paul and I walked into the bar, waved hello to Tom, and parked ourselves in one of the faux-leather-padded, oak-tabletop booths along the right wall. We both ordered a drink—Brain Chivas and a Schmidt's chaser—then got down to business.

Paul wanted to lay down some ground rules; it was how he'd always worked, he said. He told me he could deal with existing in someone else's body, and he could even deal with living a solitary life in his Brain Hotel room until needed. But one thing Paul could not deal with was being unable to control the assignment.

"You want me to do the best work possible?" he asked. "Fine. Let me do the work. I don't need a straw boss. I don't even need the occasional piece of advice. Let me do things my own way."

A reasonable request. However, I had to lay down some ground rules of my own.

"One," I said. "The Association investigation is top priority. If I need our body, goddammit, I'm taking our body."

"Even at the risk of abandoning our one paying client?" Paul asked.

"Paying clients are good for one thing and one thing only: cash. If we're forced to, we can find cash somewhere else. But a missed opportunity to collect evidence against The Association can never be regained. Every day that ticks by with The Association still in power is one less day the American public can feel safe." Sure, I was laying it on thick, but the situation warranted exaggeration. I had to tame this hired gun before he did something regrettable.

"Two, you surrender the body when I say. No fights. It's useless anyway, and it only pisses me off."

I looked at Paul to gauge how pissed off he was getting. It didn't seem to faze him. Maybe to him, this was merely a business conversation. I used the silence to take a sip of the Brain Scotch. Much better than the stash I had in my office—

after all, this was Scotch how Old Tom remembered it, not me. God, to think of the years of sweet, drunken bliss that man had seen.

Paul interrupted my reveries. "I understand. And now I want you to promise me two things. One, when I ask you to tune out, you tune out and trust me. I promise not to compromise the investigation one bit. Hell, I want those pricks to pay for what they did to me as much as you do. But I can't function knowing that you can storm in at any second. I'm a human being, man! I have things I need to take care of. There's stuff in my brain I need to work out on my own. In the real world. Not in here. I have to know I still exist."

Jesus. This was the closest thing to a buddy-buddy talk Paul and I had ever had. I wanted him to elaborate on the things he needed to "take care of," but I didn't want to stop him when he was on a roll. I nodded.

"Okay. Secondly, when it comes time to take down the Man, you let me take my pound of flesh. I've been dreaming about it for a long time now. I wish I'd had the balls to do it before, when I had the chance."

I didn't know what Man Paul was referring to. But I played it cool, letting him think I did, and agreed to both his demands. Yes, I should have asked him, point-blank, who the Man was and finally started to piece things together. Was the Man this JP Bafoures? What was his real name? Where did he operate in Vegas? But the moment I admitted I didn't know much, I'd lose Paul's respect. I'd lose him.

"The Man will be yours," I said. Then, scrambling to think of something neutral to say: "I want justice served." I made a mental note to bring up the Man in the future. Subtly.

There was a song I didn't recognize playing on the jukebox—a male and female duet, something about them having "the time of our lives . . . never felt this way before." I noticed Fieldman sitting in the corner, drinking something clear like Fresca, and munching on a basket of popcorn. I didn't have any proof, but I was convinced he'd been messing with the jukebox.

We finished our drinks and left the bar.

15

FIRST DAYS ON THE JOB

The rest of the day was uneventful except for the note I found taped to my apartment door. It was from Amy Langtree, saying she'd stopped by to borrow a colander. I should have found her persistence annoying and intrusive, and I should have done something blunt to stop this whole thing from blossoming. Like, bought a cheap wedding ring from a pawn shop and started flashing it around, or asked her where I could score good dope and a blow job, or started babbling and drooling in her presence, or picked at my nose or ears, whatever.

She was clearly fixated on someone who was not me. I was wearing a dead man's face, for goodness' sake. We'd barely spoken a dozen sentences to each other. My soul clearly predated hers by a generation or two. And now she wanted to drain her spaghetti with one of my kitchen utensils?

Still, Amy Langtree could be useful. She was a local. She lent me the appearance of normality. If I took the time to develop this friendship, and there was ever trouble down the line, she would be an important character witness—could perhaps buy me enough time to make an escape. I started thinking about how to ask her out for something non-threatening, like lunch, or a walk through the historical sites. Something like that wouldn't necessarily lead her on.

Then I remembered, this all had been decided for me: Paul needed to use my body most of the time. Clearly, I had to cool things off even before they began.

***

There were other things to work out, too—things like financial priorities. Until Gard's first check cleared the bank, we had a little under $200 on which to live. I thought we should spend a bit on foodstuffs—hot dogs, bologna, bread, cans of vegetables and soup—and hang on to the rest. But Paul insisted we go out and buy a new suit. "You want to show up as a representative of the Brown Agency wearing these costume-shop specials?"

"We're not from the Brown Agency," I said. "We're freelance."

"Okay, then we'll look like shabby freelancers." Paul was in control of the body and was looking down at me in the bathroom mirror.

"What's shabby about my gray suit?" I asked. I'd bought it from a consignment shop in Sherman Oaks seven years ago. Top of the line men's fashion—a real dandy. I didn't care for the atrocities I saw in men's magazines these days.

Paul sighed. "Where do I start? It's about as hip as an elbow. It has lapels skinnier than David Bowie's ass. It has tapered cuffs, for Christ's sake. I've beaten people up for less offensive things than wearing that suit."

"Granted," I said, "it's a bit conservative. But do you think our client will give a shit?"

Paul stared at me.

"Okay, she probably will. But where are we going to find the money? Until our first paycheck clears . . ."

"Use the two hundred dollars we've got stashed away at Girard Bank."

"And in three days, when we're starved for a nice piece of meat, we won't have a coin to our name."

"The check will clear by then."

"I never trust banks."

Maybe I was worrying too much about the money, but I'd never dipped this low in my life. In Nevada, there'd always been a quickie nudie photo gig or an unpaid hotel bill to earn me enough cash for the week. Here in Philly, I didn't know a soul. I'd placed my entire financial future in the hands of a philandering lawyer.

Plus—and this is embarrassing to admit—I was hoping to spend some of my dwindling funds on a couple of new albums. I was tired of the music I'd already listened to over and over in my head. It was useless to count on the radio—it usually took a few repeated listenings for a tune to stick, and have you ever tried to break through those listener request lines? I'd have more luck taking down The Association with a weapon found in a Cracker Jack box. Music was one of my passions; work was bleak without it. But could I tell Paul that? No way. In the real world, a new suit mattered much more than a new Bread album.

Of course, it turned out not to matter. Paul went out and bought two suits for the bargain-basement price of $160. I don't know where he bought them—or if it was entirely legal—because I woke up from a nap and walked downstairs to the lobby to find Paul modeling one of them in a mirror. That is, watching myself on the Brain Hotel lobby screen, modeling one of them.

I ran to the silver microphone and pressed the button. "What the hell do you think you're doing?"

I startled him, and it ruined his necktie knot. "Hey—whoah!" he shouted, and spun around, reaching for a gun on his hip that wasn't there.

"It's me. Inside."

Paul exhaled. "Damn it, I told you not to do that."

"Call it landlord's privilege. You and I need to talk."

"About what?"

"The threads."

"Hey, I'm trying to do our job. I deposited Gard's check in our bank account, and went out and made a business purchase. You didn't expect me to go out and babysit our client dressed in one of your goofy numbers, did you? Dead or not, I've got a reputation to protect."

"How much money do we have?" I asked.

"Seventeen bucks. And speaking of which, you shouldn't let our finances dip so much. It's bad for appearances. What if I need to buy our client a drink?"

This was rich. Tough Boy here blew our last couple of Franklins on a new suit, and he was lecturing me on fiscal responsibility. I didn't know how to respond without losing my temper, so I didn't.

"I need the body back, Paul."

"Right now?"

"Yeah. I've got something important to do. You know I can kick you out in a heartbeat, but I prefer to be an adult about it."

Paul sighed and tightened our fists. "Fine." He closed our eyes. I slid into the body and opened them. Immediately I felt the coffin-like suit envelop me. The image in the mirror didn't help, either. God, the lapels on that suit. Enough to rest a cup of coffee and a large Danish on. And these flared pant legs? I'd hate to have to chase somebody down in this thing. Awfully tight in the hips, too. This was why I stopped reading the fashion pages in *Esquire* back in 1968. Ever since I'd died, menswear had taken a definite turn for the strange.

I pulled the new suit off and changed back into a comfortable pair of slacks and a casual shirt. I combed my hair back down—Paul was forever combing it back in the mother of all pompadours—and checked my wallet, which was left on the desk. Sixteen bucks, the liar. I searched through the new pants pocket and found another dollar.

I left the apartment and bought a big fat Philadelphia-style hoagie—oil, mayo, prosciutto, provolone, onions, peppers, the works—as some weird form of revenge. Cost me $2.95, not counting tax. I should've had a Yoo-hoo while I was at it.

If we were going to spend all our money, I was going to enjoy some of it.

* * *

Paul, the eager beaver, arrived early for his first day of work. He'd woken up earlier than I—even souls need rest—and, as a result, I awoke to the dim awareness that my body was making a pot of coffee. I wandered down to the Brain Hotel lobby and watched Paul on the screen.

"Ugh," I said. "I hate coffee."

"Good morning to you, too," Paul said. "I hope I'm not being presumptuous, but I do have a client to start protecting this morning."

"Yeah, yeah. Some advance notice would have been helpful—you could have left a wake-up call at the front desk."

"Sorry. I'll try to remember."

It didn't sound like he meant it.

"I'm not trying to be a hard-ass, Paul. I just don't like somebody else controlling my body while I'm not awake. First, you sneak off to buy a couple of suits, and now you're waking up my body without me knowing it. I'd like you to ask first."

Paul sneered at me in the reflection from the toaster. He buttered a piece of slightly blackened toast.

"Go ahead. Make all the faces you want. All I know is if we don't start making some cash, this operation is going under. Then who'll be buttering your burned toast?"

Paul had no rebuttal. He ate three slices, half a grapefruit, and an apple before buttoning his shirt, putting on his new jacket, and leaving for work. I walked over to Old Tom's for a plate of Brain steak and eggs and a Brain Bloody Mary to fortify myself for a day of intense research into the Larsen murders.

* * *

I spent about ten minutes shuffling through some notes in which I thought I remembered Philadelphia being mentioned. There were a billion avenues to explore: I could line up my Association organization chart again, and look for any Philly connections/birthplaces, and then check it against back notes. I could look for previous mentions of "Ray Loogan" or "Leah Farrell." I could sort through a filing cabinet for notes I'd previously considered irrelevant, hoping to glean a usable fact from the endless pages of black type. But, to be honest, I found myself completely drained of ambition.

I was curious to see what was happening with Paul. It's odd—for the past eight months I'd wanted nothing more than to devote my waking hours to the Larsen murder investigation, to finally be done with it. The very moment it became a possibility, I found myself distracted by a meaningless babysitting case.

I walked down to the Brain Hotel lobby and stared up at the viewing screen. I was just in time to catch Paul walking into Susannah's hotel lobby. It was a weird effect—like one of those mirror images inside a mirror image.

* * *

Paul started toward the elevators, then noticed our client was sitting at the bar. He looked at our watch: 8:15. A bit early to be tossing them back. And especially dumb to be tossing them back out in the open.

"Hello, Ms. Winston," Paul said, touching her shoulder.

She flinched. "Fuck!" She spun around. Her lipstick was smudged on a corner of her lower lip. There was also a small black pistol in her right hand.

This was another chance to see Paul operate like a pro. Without a word, he snatched the piece out of her grasp. I don't even think she knew what had happened until she looked down at her hands. Paul took the seat next to her and slid the gun into his jacket pocket. "How's breakfast this morning?"

"Jesus . . . don't do that!"

"Do what? My job?"

"I was having breakfast."

"You could be dead right now."

"It's only scrambled eggs."

"Funny. Can we go somewhere private?"

"I'd like to finish my meal, if you don't mind."

"I'll have room service send it along. With a couple of extra Bloody Marys." Paul put his hand on her back. "Come on. Let's go."

Amazingly, Susannah placed her fork on the plate full of eggs and stood up. Paul asked the bartender—"Satchmo," he called him—to send food and a pitcher of Bloodies up to Ms. Winston's room. I realized what he was doing. If he was forced to lead this lady around on a leash, now was the time to take up the slack.

She pouted the entire way to her room.

* * *

Susannah and Paul reached her apartment. It was different from the one we'd all stood in yesterday. This was on a much higher floor and was a fully furnished apartment. Gard must have rented one of the basic, traveling executive rooms on the lower floors for the meeting in case I—or Paul, that is—turned out to be an unsavory character.

The apartment was different from anything I'd seen before. Down deep, it was a perfectly respectable, tasteful hotel suite. But it had been augmented in every imaginable way. For starters, clothes blanketed every available surface—skirts, frocks, blouses, stockings, even undergarments. The place was one big closet. The remaining spaces that weren't covered in expensive fabrics were occupied by a hospital library's worth of magazines—movie and celebrity-type rags, as well as a bunch of paperback romances. One doorway was draped with a hanging bead door. There were two earth-green beanbags tucked away beneath the garments. I couldn't smell anything standing in the Brain Hotel lobby, but I'd bet the air was thick with stale incense.

Paul held out his lighter for her. She scowled at him, then dipped her face toward the flame.

"Something wrong?" Paul asked.

She didn't say anything. They entered the living room. She closed the door behind him. Then she walked away and sunk herself into the hotel-supplied couch. I could tell it was the hotel's, because it was one solid color. "Go ahead. Make your speech."

"No speech. Just a few rules. For one, you tell me everything. Where you're going to be, how long you intend to be there."

"Even before I pee?"

"Even then."

"What if I can't predict how long it will take my urine to leave my body?"

Paul ignored her. "Rule two. When I'm not with you, you stay inside this room."

"Or unless Richard takes me out to dinner."

"Obviously."

"Although," Susannah continued, "I'm not sure what he could do to protect me. I mean, he's not you."

Paul ignored that, too. After a few moments of heavy silence, Susannah asked, "That it? Two eensy-weensy rules?"

"That's it."

"Okay. I have a few eensy-weensy rules of my own. Whenever we're out, I'm going to introduce you as my cousin. No one needs to know anything; no one is to infer anything. I have a reputation to protect in this town. Understood?"

"I'm a professional, Ms. Winston."

She ignored him. "Is-that-un-der-stood?"

"Yes, my massah."

"Repeat it."

"It-is-un-der-stood." Paul stared off, out the window to the skyline. "You know, for a minute there last night, I thought we'd both get along."

Susannah looked at him coldly, then broke into a smile. "I like you, Paul. However, image is very important."

"Oh. Am I the disreputable type?"

"That remains to be seen, young man." There was a hint of a smile on her face.

"I seem to make you nervous, Mrs. Robinson."

"Nothing makes me nervous, silly boy."

There was an uncomfortable pause. Again, I couldn't read Paul's mind, but I was sure he was waiting for Susannah to take the lead. I know I would. Maybe he could get away with earning a paycheck by hanging out in an air-conditioned hotel room all day, eating room service meals and swapping cheap paperback novels back and forth. Then again, I'm sure Paul doubted it could be that easy.

"So," said Susannah. "What should we do?"

"What do you normally do?"

"My everyday routine, you mean? Oh, nothing much. Eat breakfast, read the newspaper, shop, get high, polish my toenails, and try to avoid death."

"Very funny."

"I'm sorry, Paul. I didn't plan any serious activities for us today."

"You don't have to entertain me."

"Still, I'm being a poor hostess."

My God, I thought. Was this an assignment or a first date?

"Do you blow grass?" Susannah asked.

"Only when I'm cleaning my lawnmower."

Susannah laughed and seemingly let down her guard. Along with her polished Smith speaking voice. "Man, you're a trip. Hey—what do you say we get drunk?"

To my surprise, I heard Paul respond: "Sounds like a fine idea to me."

* * *

Now this was real trouble. Let me take a moment to explain why.

Whenever I took my alcoholic pleasure inside the Brain Hotel, there were no worries. Inside, there was no such thing as a hangover. Unless, of course, you insisted on one, for reality's sake.

But whenever I (or, whoever happened to be in control of the body) drank real alcohol, all kinds of bad things started to happen. Brain plumbing started to go. Brain toilets backed up. Brain walls tremored and sometimes even disappeared. Some personal Brain effects would suddenly vanish, too. I've had problems with sensitive case files going missing. I'm not sure if it was the impact of alcohol on the normal processes of my physical brain or if it was completely psychological. Either way, it was a miserable experience for all involved.

What—you thought I drank Fresca for the taste?

This, of course, I'd only heard secondhand. I've never been inside the Brain Hotel when the physical brain became intoxicated. But I'd heard the complaints for weeks. I had to warn Paul.

* * *

Paul called room service and ordered a bottle of Tanqueray, a bottle of tonic, a bucket of ice, half a case of beer, a couple of bottles of soda water. I couldn't believe it until I saw it being delivered only minutes later, despite it being 9:30 in the morning.

"Paul," I said into the lobby mike. "I have to speak with you."

"What can I mix you?" Susannah asked up on the screen, wheeling the cart into her living room.

"Right now," I insisted.

"A gin and tonic, please, heavy on the gin. Excuse me a minute, will you?"

"Of course," she said.

Paul walked us into the bathroom, closed the door, flicked on the light over the mirror and stared at himself. "What is it?" he whispered.

I carefully reminded Paul about the personal dangers of alcohol consumption. He sighed, then shook his head.

"What do you think I am? A rube? I wasn't planning on drinking."

"Then what's the gin for? Window-washing?"

"Alcohol is a social lubricant. If Ms. Winston thinks I'm intoxicated, she'll relax and become intoxicated, too. Most likely, she'll pass out and I'll have the rest of the day to kick back and relax."

"How professional."

"Hey—you have your ways of running things, and so do I. Now if you're through with the AA lecture, I have our client to attend to."

"Cheers," I told him.

I flipped off the lobby mike and watched Paul turn away from the mirror and flick off the lights. He walked back into the living room where Susannah was waiting for him with a drink. "Here you go," she said. "Bottoms up."

Tough assignment.

I tried going back to study my Association notes, but the thought of what was happening in the real world kept me distracted. In the end, I retreated to Old Tom's for a Brain drink. Fuck the Fresca.

16

DÉJÀ RENDEZVOUS

The first week continued in a similar vein. Paul would jerk me out of my slumber, having already seized control of my body, and I'd be forced to wander down to Old Tom's for a morning pick-me-up. Tom made a mean order of scrambled eggs and greasy, fatty bacon, along with a big tumbler of cold tomato juice. However, I started to miss waking up in Reality. Damn—after a few days, I realized I missed taking my first morning leak. A Brain piss didn't cut it. Someday, I was sure, some psych researcher would confirm that the male urination ritual set the tone for the day to follow: a healthy, horse-powered piss would indicate a take-charge day, while a sporadic, split-stream piss would indicate a day of indecision and discontent.

Lord knows what a researcher would think of a piss in one's own mind.

Most of the residents in the Brain Hotel didn't bother installing a bathroom in their quarters. I was one of the few; I aimed for verisimilitude whenever possible.

While Paul spent the day with Susannah drinking (or faking it), shopping, or watching movies at one of the many theaters within walking distance of the hotel, I'd be organizing Larsen murder evidence. I needed to see everything laid out in front of me, so I spent a lot of time re-reading and underlining the daily accounts stored in my numerous filing cabinets. It was amazing how fast my files ballooned—every second I spent in Reality translated into a sentence or two—sometimes even a full paragraph, depending on the metadata (did the subject's pulse spike? Did they avoid my gaze?) my brain had absorbed while investigating in the real world. Already, there was a folder full of notes from Paul After's case. Incredible, the Brain storage system.

"Which, of course, lends credence to the fact that you are one self-contained mega-speed processing computer from the future," said a voice. Fieldman. Uninvited as always.

"The human brain can't handle all of this information?"

"No, a human brain certainly can. Just not in this orderly system. The brain links information casually, not logically. A heard song can instigate an emotion which in turn instigates a memory. In here, you have no songs. You have no emotions. You have, simply, notes you can look up in alphabetical order."

"I like things simple. Before you go interpreting the filing cabinets as a sign of me being a dead piece of machinery, don't forget all the improvements I've made to this hotel over the years." It was true. Robert had been a complete slob. When I was absorbed, everything was spread out and random in a vast desert of the mind. The place looked a lot like the outskirts of Vegas. Anyway, I spent most of my time creating a logical space for my soul to inhabit, and it wasn't easy.

Fieldman frowned. "Don't go bad-mouthing your precursor. You never did understand his system, did you? He had music..."

"Wait one second," I said. "You didn't know Robert. He was gone years before you came floating into the picture."

"Remember: I exist out of linear time," Fieldman said. "Robert understood how the Brain worked. You only *think* you do."

"Don't you have a mission to complete or something?"

"I do. Which is why I worry about you."

* * *

Every so often in that first week I'd tune back in to Reality to see what Paul and his client were up to. Then I'd go back to work. Which wasn't going all too well, to be honest. Nothing at all seemed to connect Ray Loogan or Leah Farrell to the city of Philadelphia. There weren't even any Loogans or Farrells in the phone book.

I'd only get my physical body back at odd, random times—whenever Gard could excuse himself from his wife to spend a couple of hours knocking boots with the mistress. Largely, I used the time to do some minor housekeeping, go for a walk, check the mailbox. I received a notice from Girard Bank three days after Paul started his assignment. Apparently, Gard's check had bounced, and the bank had charged my account a $20 penalty, which dipped it below the $50 minimum. I had three days to correct the situation or my account would be dropped.

Bounced? Back in Henderson, this kind of thing was unheard of. If someone were to bounce a check on me out there, I'd have bounced something heavy off his head. But I couldn't do that now—Gard was our sole employer. I had to remind Paul to call Gard the next day, first thing. This matter could be handled delicately. Quickly.

And it would seem like every time I did have possession of my body in the real world, I'd run into Amy Langtree in the hallway. It never failed. I'd dash out for a package of cheap hot dogs and a loaf of bread and there'd she be, asking where I was headed. "For a walk," I'd tell her, trying to avoid eye contact.

"Can I tag along?" she'd ask, all perkiness and smiles.

"Well, I have an errand to run first. It's a real tedious one, too."

"Oh. Okay. Some other time?"

I hated like hell to lie to her, but it wasn't as if I had a choice. "Sure."

Then she'd walk away, and I'd feel like the largest heel in the world.

* * *

I was reading through some of my notes and drinking a tumbler of Brain Scotch when I felt the vibe. It's hard to describe—kind of like déjà vu, but in a more immediate and pressing way. Not the slow wonderment of *Gee, I feel like this has happened to me before.* This was more like, *Holy shit, this is happening to me again.* Something was going on with Paul. I ran from my office, down the hallway and front lobby stairs to take a peek at Reality.

Reality was me/Paul in a cab, riding in the backseat with our client, Ms. Winston. She was wearing something cut exceedingly low in the front. I could do nothing but gawk. Then my view was snatched away.

Paul had turned around. Through the rear window, I could see that another cab had gunned through a yellow light and was speeding right for us.

"Is your ex-boyfriend a cabbie?" Paul asked.

"No, why?" asked Susannah.

"Driver, slow down. Now."

The driver obeyed, and the cab almost overtook us, but slowed down at the last minute.

Oh boy. When Paul was right, he was right. Something weird. Though I couldn't believe Ms. Winston's ex-nutcase had found her so quickly. The cab pulled up next to us, and a face appeared in the opposite window, on Ms. Winston's side. A young face; deep-set eyes, full of a weird mix of fear and rage.

Paul drew our gun and shoved our client down to the seat.

The guy in the other car rolled his window.

Paul started to roll ours.

I tried to send out a shrieking telepathic message: "Whoah, Paul! What the hell are you doing? Cease and desist! Cease and desist!"

Then I heard our pursuer call out: "You're a dead man, Larsen!"

The rear passenger window shattered first. Glass showered over us and our client. Paul ducked, then spun his head back. I could see the exit hole in the window closest to us. Missed us completely. And then another shot. Paul looked over the edge of the seat. Our cabbie's head exploded all over the front windshield.

Now this is horrible to admit, but at that very moment I was glad Paul was in control of my body. I'm not exactly sure

I would have been able to control the contents of my stomach and/or bladder at this particular moment. Instead, Paul started to return fire, pumping the trigger more times than I thought necessary. I couldn't see if he hit anything, but our pursuing cab veered out of control and screeched to a halt. We rocketed past.

It occurred to both of us at the same time. Our driver's brains were dripping over the front of the moving vehicle.

"Paul," Susannah moaned. "What's going on?"

But Paul didn't say anything. He lunged our body through the tiny opening in the Plexiglas partition. We weren't svelte enough to clear it—I could sense the edges of the partition digging into our sides. I didn't feel any pain; Paul took the full hit. But I'm sure I would discover bruises later. That is, if my body left this taxi in one piece.

Then I saw what he was going for: the cabbie's jittering, dying leg. He squeezed through another inch and pounded our fist into the cabbie's thigh. The legbone connected to the footbone, the footbone connected to the brake pedal. It was as if our taxi had driven right into a brick wall. Our body was forced through the partition up to our hips; our client hit the back of the driver's seat with a dull thwacking noise. And, as if to add insult to grievous injury, the cabbie's broken head pushed through the remains of the windshield.

I'm sure Paul was feeling a tremendous amount of pain, but all I could see was blue vinyl taxi seat. Then, as Paul wriggled our body free, I saw a dead body, the torn roof of the cab, then finally our client, peeking up from the backseat.

"That's disgusting," she said.

Paul reached behind the dead body, opened the door and slid us out. I momentarily thought of trying to absorb the cabbie's soul, but then realized he would do the investigation no good—unless, of course, I wanted to sleep for the long drive back to Las Vegas. Besides, I could sense Paul was in no mood for a demonstration in the art of soul collection.

He looked at Susannah. "Stay here and keep your head down."

She nodded.

Paul started walking us, cautiously, to the other cab.

* * *

By now, a crowd was beginning to form—as well as confused, backed-up traffic. I suppose there wasn't usually this much excitement in Center City Philadelphia. Hell, there wasn't usually this much excitement in my life, and it's safe to say I didn't lead an average, milquetoast kind of existence.

Our would-be killer started to step out of his cab. There was still a gun in his hand. I couldn't believe how young he looked. Young, bewildered, and full of righteous hatred, all in the same facial expression. This guy had the face of a third-grade bully—right after you've kicked him in the nuts with a pair of steel-tipped work boots.

A woman emerged from the driver's seat. She took one look at us, then wrapped her body around the guy, pushing him back against the cab.

"Ray! Stop!" she cried out.

"I've got to finish this!" he shouted.

"There are too many people!"

"I'm gonna fucking do this!"

Ray lifted his gun and pointed it at us, but his woman reacted fast: she cracked a blackjack over his head. Without a retort, Ray's body went limp. The woman caught him under

161

the arms before his head could slam into the ground. It was quite touching. It almost made the smack on the head seem affectionate.

By now, we were yards away. Paul lifted our pistol and took careful aim at the woman's chest. I could see by the sight on the pistol he was aimed perfectly. "Don't move," Paul said.

The woman looked up at us, and gave a weak smile. "He wasn't being paranoid, after all."

"What?" Paul asked.

Then I felt another vibe, clear as day. Paul knew this woman.

The woman used the momentary confusion to wrap her hand around Ray's. She pointed his gun at us. "Let's both walk away from this."

My God, Paul *did* know this woman. But wait a sec—*he was wearing Brad's face!* She knew Brad Larsen, too. Of course. Every assassin knows the victim, down to the last detail, right?

And wouldn't you know it—Paul lowered his gun for her. "How are you mixed up in this?" he asked.

"Isn't it obvious?" the woman asked. "Ray blew it, and I flew in to make everything all nice again. I didn't know how badly he'd blown it until this very moment. You're still alive. And so is that bitch!"

"What do you mean?" Paul asked. "What the hell are you talking about?"

"You're still breathing. And unless you want to change that, we're both going to walk away from this and sort business out later."

Paul stood there and watched, slack-jawed as a mental patient, as she shoved our would-be assassin into the backseat of the cab, then slid herself into the driver's seat and closed the door. Then she fired up the engine and sped past, her eyes fixed on us the entire time.

* * *

Time out, I thought. I seized Paul away from the controls of our body for a moment and placed him in a corner of the Brain Hotel lobby. I opened my physical eyes and saw the cab turn a corner and disappear. It was weird, being in the real-life scene after watching it on the Brain lobby screen. Like stepping into a movie after you've been watching it for a while.

I turned around and saw Susannah peeking out from the cab window.

I closed my eyes and yelled for Doug; he answered immediately. I quickly laid it out for him: "You're going to wake up in downtown Philadelphia. Walk over to the brunette sitting inside the cab. Her name is Susannah. She's been through a lot. Comfort her until further notice."

"You got it, dude," Doug said. I was impressed. It was a lot for him to absorb.

We swapped, and I found myself back inside the Brain Hotel lobby. I walked over to Paul. "Start talking, tough guy."

Paul glared at me. "Don't you do that again!" He rubbed his eyes. "Man, that hurts like a mother!"

"We haven't got all day, Paul."

"I know, I know. Look—I knew that woman. She's somebody important from Vegas. She's tight with the Man."

Again with this Man. "Who is she?"

"I can't name names, but I know she's a player. That's the only reason her boyfriend walked away with his heart still in his chest."

There's a beautiful tremor in the brain that comes with complete, stark understanding. Like the first time you grasp algebra, or perhaps learn the theory behind a musical scale. I had the pieces floating around in my mind, but it took until this moment for them to congeal into something solid.

"What's her name?" I asked, even though I already knew the answer.

"Her name is Leah Farrell."

Leah. And Ray. Ray Loogan.

"All right, Paul, I'm going to be straight with you. A while ago I mentioned that I was involved in a side project—a murder investigation. I didn't bring it up much because I didn't want it distracting you."

"You'd better start talking, chief," Paul said.

"Okay, okay." How to put this? "You know the face we're wearing?"

"The face of the murder victim, right? You told me that. But how does he know Leah Farrell?"

I laid it all out for Paul exactly as Brad Larsen had, including the bits and pieces of evidence I'd glommed for the past eight months. Paul nodded along.

"But the weird thing," I continued, "is that this Leah Farrell chick knows our client Susannah, too. Do *you* recognize her, Paul? Ever seen her around Vegas?"

Paul shook his head. "Don't you think I'd have told you if I did?"

I paused to plan our next move. "Look—let me take it from here. I've got a lot of strange shit to sort out."

"Be my guest," Paul said. "I'm only in this for the babysitting."

* * *

I resumed control of my body to find my tongue in Susannah Winston's mouth. Quickly, I broke the embrace. Her eyes were still closed.

"Godsorry," I stammered.

Susannah's eyes fluttered open, dreamily.

"Why are you sorry?"

"I'm not . . . I'm not being professional," I said. Damn that Doug. I'd told him to *walk over* to the brunette, not *deep throat* the brunette. I made a mental note to chew him out later.

She started to fix my shirt collar, but I gently nudged her hands away. "Ms. Winston . . ." That's it. Keep it professional.

"Susannah," she reminded me. "It's Susannah, Paul. Man, you save my life, and then you call me by my last name?"

"Sorry. Susannah. My mind is in a different place." Damn. I didn't sound one bit like Paul. That sounded like me. No-frills, basic, just-the-facts me. I could tell that *she* could tell, based on the expression on her face.

Time for a subject change. "Never mind. We should get out of here."

The cops showed up. They noticed the cabbie with the missing head. But they didn't notice Susannah and me, walking arm in arm, down Market Street, as if strolling the shops. Susannah had thought to grab the shopping bags out of the cab—a sure sign of a criminally devious mind. There was more to her story than a chance encounter with an ex-hit man lover.

This was going to be tricky.

17

CHRISTMAS MISTRESS

Paul agreed to conduct the meeting so I'd be free to observe and take notes inside the Brain Hotel lobby. He chose a bar not too far from Gard's Center City office (and, as it turned out, our Spruce Street apartment). McGlinchey's seemed to be the kind of place where patrons minded their own business. And from the look of the dust and funk on the walls, everybody had been left alone since the last centennial.

Paul took a green vinyl booth on the left side, which gave him the perfect vantage point to catch Gard when he came in. He ordered a draft of Schaefer and a tumbler of tonic water and ice to diffuse the beer, which came to a grand total of eighty-five cents. I liked the place already. I had to return here when I was in control of my body again.

Gard seemed completely freaked out. I was sure he'd walked by this place a million times and never given it a second look. Now that he had, he was sorry. He slid into Paul's booth and ordered a gin gimlet from a waitress who wore a tube top and didn't appear to shave her armpits. Gard shuddered.

"I don't have much time," he said. "What's going on? Where's Susannah?"

"Over at Nan Duskin, shopping," Paul replied. "I made it clear to the owner that Ms. Winston was not to leave until she had spent an appropriate amount of money. I needed to speak with you alone. We had an incident this morning."

At this point, the waitress slapped Richard's gimlet on the table and asked him for ninety-five cents. Some of the drink dribbled over the sides of the glass and pooled on the table. Richard put the five back in his wallet and started fishing for a single. After an uncomfortable length of time, he gave up and forked over the five. "Here. Keep the rest."

Then, to Paul: "What kind of incident?"

"Ms. Winston's ex-boyfriend took a few shots at us while we were in a cab. Our driver got his brains blown out. On the bright side, we didn't have to pay the fare."

Poor Richard went white. "My God. He is real."

"Real and connected to an unsavory crowd. Turns out, Ms. Winston was not exaggerating—'Roger' does indeed work for a criminal. But his name isn't Roger, it's Ray— Ray Loogan, and the criminal operates out of Nevada. I'm familiar with them, having worked in the Las Vegas area for some time."

"My God," Richard repeated, then proceeded to drain half his gimlet.

"That's not all. He was with an associate of this criminal—a woman named Leah Farrell. Which means if she's with Ray, chances are this criminal from Las Vegas is very interested in your Susannah."

"Can't I ever pick 'em without complications? If they don't have bruiser ex-husbands, they're tied to the mob. Jesus H. Christ—I'm too old for this bullshit."

Paul said, "Maybe you should consider fidelity."

"What?"

"Nothing. But I need to know more before I can bail your pinstriped ass out of this."

Richard considered this for a moment. Even from my vantage point in the Brain Hotel lobby, I could practically see his wheels spinning. *Can I wrangle out of this now and ignore her, or will she come after me? Is paying for more protection worth a thrice-a-week screw? Should I have her killed?*

"I'll tell you everything I know."

"Great. Another gimlet, Mr. Gard?"

* * *

Predictably, Richard had met her in a bar: the Crab Club on Second Street in Old City, the newly minted historical section of the city. The federal government had poured a ton of money and concrete into the area—formerly a slum—to be able to host President Ford for the Bicentennial in the actual historical environs without having to chase away winos and junkies every two minutes.

They met December 23, 1975. Richard had been at his firm's office party, which spilled over into the bar at Harrigan's

Saloon, near Market Street, then the Crab Club. He was intoxicated, but by no means devoid of his lawyerly charms. Susannah had introduced herself when he bumped into her to order another martini. Richard soon abandoned his buddies, called his wife in Lower Merion to tell her he was taking a room in town, and took Susannah to "drop her off at her apartment." As it turned out, there was no need for Richard to rent a room. Upon sobering up the next morning, Richard found himself in a tricky Yuletide situation. As fate would have it, Susannah Winston was a far cry from the acne-scarred, flabby-thighed bimbo from the steno pool he usually landed. No, she was an amazingly young, amazingly beautiful woman who was alone for the holidays, orphaned, and in dire need of companionship. She also gave the most "mind-numbing" blow job Richard had ever received.

Now, this was a fact I could have lived without knowing. But as Richard told this part of the story, I caught Paul conjuring scenarios and images, involving him and our client. They flittered by the lobby screen almost too fast to catch. Almost.

Richard spun this wild tale of a lost case file and the urgent need to replicate the documents on Christmas Eve: *No, honey, I don't work for Ebenezer Scrooge, but I do try cases in front of him, and if I don't have this case file together by noon tomorrow . . .* blah blah blah. And on Christmas Eve, instead of being home with Elaine and his twin boys, he ended up drinking milk and eating the slightly burned cookies Susannah had baked. He even darted out to a shop on the square to buy her an impromptu Christmas present of emerald earrings—using the firm's petty cash account, of course. Susannah returned the favor by numbing his mind yet again.

Again, more images from Paul: red-and-green felt, pine needles, Santa Claus, lips. I was going to have to watch this situation carefully. Perhaps take more drastic measures.

Richard realized how simple it would be to care and feed a mistress. Fact, Susannah Winston was independently wealthy—no clumsy requests for cash for a manicure, or a new bra. Fact, she had her own apartment on Rittenhouse Square, not five blocks from the firm. Fact, she didn't give a damn that he had a family. Fact, she could give the most mind-numbing...

"I get the picture," Paul said.

"Right." Richard's face was blushed, and he was working on his fourth gimlet. He didn't seem to remember he'd been pressed for time. In fact, he didn't even seem to realize he was talking out loud.

Susannah had supplied the same autobiographical details she had Paul: rich family in Boston, generous trust fund from inventor father, bad taste in men. She also told him she came to Philadelphia to see the Bicentennial. She figured it would be the chance for a rebirth, right along with the 200th celebration of the nation's birth.

And then, the note from Roger Adams had arrived. The rest was recent history: a teary confession of past wrongdoings, a desperate plea for help, and no way for a man with even the thinnest fibers of self-respect to wriggle out of the obligation. Richard had to help his mistress. He called the biggest agency in the country, the Brown Agency, for that help. Best of all, he could expense it.

Gard looked around for his briefcase. Ah yes, there it was. Right next to him in the booth. Absent-mindedly, he rubbed the condensation from his glass, then turned to gather up his things.

"Before you go, there's one more thing. Mr. Wojciechowski had a call from his accountant yesterday. It seems there was a problem with my retainer check."

Good boy, that Paul. I knew I could count on him to talk cash. It was the one part of the investigatory business I loathed.

"What kind of problem?"

"The kind where it fails to clear."

"What?"

"Now I'm sure it's a mix-up, and I'm not the kind to suspend services for lack of payment. We're both adults, beyond that petty nonsense. I would like a new check that can be cashed by noon tomorrow."

Richard frowned. "Ah, those bank assholes. Always screwing things up . . . yes, yes, of course, Paul. I don't know what to say. I can give you a check right now. I'd walk with you to the Girard Bank, but it's out of the way and I really have to—"

"Tomorrow will be fine."

And with that, Richard excused himself and left.

* * *

"Now we know two things," I told Paul from the Brain Hotel lobby mike.

He looked down at his reflection in the pint glass, which made it seem like he was staring right at me from the lobby screen. "What's that?"

"One, the man who hired us is an aging jerk who enjoys blow jobs way too much."

"C'mon," Paul said. "How much is too much?"

"Two, our client's story has evolved over the months. She's gotten ambitious."

"Yeah, I was thinking the same thing," Paul said. "One minute, she's knocking around Philly for kicks, the next she's planning a grand rebirth. It doesn't fit."

"Third . . ."

"I thought you said we knew two things."

"Now I'm theorizing."

"Oh. Please continue, then."

"Third, she's somehow connected with Ray Loogan, who killed our fellow Brain Hotel resident, Brad Larsen."

Paul paused to mull it over. "Kind of makes you wonder how you got called in on this case, doesn't it?"

"To a point. Our 'Stan Wojciechowski' is a backup vendor at the Brown Agency, and Brown is the best there is. They're the Pinkertons of the seventies. It's no wonder Gard called them, and they decided his rinky-dink babysitting gig was something for a freelancer, not one of their own boys. Very well could be a coincidence."

"Sure. And my mother was Betsy Ross. She used to sew me diapers made of rejected American flags."

He was right. There was something I was missing. "What are you saying?" I asked. "The Association set this up? Why? What's the motive?"

"The Association?" Paul shook his head. "Oh, yeah. That's what you call it. No, I don't think it's something the Man would pull . . . I mean, it's too damned indirect. He's usually blunt, to the point. Unless . . ." He snapped his fingers. "Wait a minute . . . unless he's somehow on to your investigation, and connected it to the name Stan Wojciechowski."

"I see where you're going," I said, "but it's impossible. Wojciechowski is a name I use for my freelance business. I purposefully kept it that way so the money stays clean. Or, I should say, Association-free."

"Stan has never done a little digging for your investigation?"

"Not a single shovelful."

"Well, we've got to resolve this one way or the other. I don't think approaching our client point-blank is the way to do it, though."

"I agree. Better keep this particular part of the investigation in-house for now. I'm thinking of grilling Brad Larsen."

"Sounds perfectly groovy to me."

A tap on Paul's shoulder interrupted the conversation. The view on the screen snapped up to the greasy, tired face of our waitress. "Can I get you and your imaginary friend anything else?" she asked.

"No," Paul said. "We're fine."

Then, to me: "You know, we've gotta start having these little conferences inside the hotel from now on."

18

CASE SOLVED

Hours later I was sitting at Brad's table in his Brain Hotel room. I purposefully chose his room—spare as it was—to make him comfortable. If he was going to freak out and start foaming at the mouth and hurling profanities, better he do it in here.

"I have something important to show you," I said. "Something you've been waiting a long time to see."

"You do?" he said, a spark of hope in his eyes. It was the first time he'd resembled a living person since I'd absorbed him eight months ago.

"Yes." I slapped two photographs on his kitchen table. They were photos of Ray Loogan and Leah Farrell, extracted from my Brain footage of the cab scene. Years ago, Robert had graciously shown me a way to burn a memory onto a sheet of Brain film, then develop it. I'd never thought the skill would come in handy. What did I know?

"Well?" I asked. "Anything?"

Brad's face shifted slightly.

"It's a simple question," I said.

Brad nodded. "Yes. That's him."

Finally. Confirmation after all these months. We had our killer. It was a matter of time before we reeled the bastard in.

"What about the woman?"

"I don't think so," he said after a long pause. "I mean, could be. She attacked me from behind, you know."

"But it's possible?"

"I don't know. Like I said . . . maybe."

Brad didn't seem terribly excited about the case being solved. It was all he'd talked about for months: *find my killers.* Well, break out the cake, ice cream, and candles—I'd finally found the bastards. And the most Brad could do was nod?

Maybe he was confused. I tried it again. "Are you sure these are the people?"

Brad's eyes slowly lifted from the photographs and zeroed in on me. "Of course I'm sure. This prick shot my wife in the throat. You don't think I can remember his face?"

"I don't doubt it, Brad. But you don't seem particularly happy about it."

"There's nothing happy about looking death in the face. You of all people should know that. You do it for a living. Are *you* a happy man?"

I decided to change the subject. I slapped a third picture—a photo of our client, Susannah Winston—on the table. "Do you recognize this woman?"

Brad gave it a once-over, then shook his head. "Nope. Should I?"

"You haven't seen her here anyway? Even recently?"

"No, I haven't."

I didn't think Brad hung out much in the hotel lobby—otherwise, he would have seen thousands of hours of Susannah's face up on the screen. But it was worth a shot.

"So, as far as you know, she's not a member of The Association?"

"Again with your Association." Brad smirked. "Nice try. But I've told you already. No information until I'm able to take a hot steaming piss on our killers' graves."

"Wait a minute," I said. "You're admitting it's possible you do know this woman? Are you holding back something?"

"Sure, it's possible. But not in this case. Look: I don't know this woman."

There was a knock at the door. I was startled. Another knock. It took me a moment to realize it came from Reality, not the Brain Hotel.

"You'd better answer it, Del," Brad said. "It's probably your girlfriend. I'm going to spend the rest of my day wallowing in some personal misery, if you don't mind."

* * *

I assumed control of my physical body and stood up from the couch. I answered the door, and sure enough, it was Amy, holding her hands behind the apartment wall, out of view. "Surprised?" she asked.

"Yes, very. Uh . . . Amy . . ."

"I brought you something."

I shook my head and spread my hands as if to say, *You shouldn't have*, but Amy insisted. "It's a housewarming present. Come on, close your eyes."

"Okay." I took a few steps back, then closed my eyes. "Come on in." Involuntarily, the Brain Hotel lobby started to materialize, but I squeezed my eyes tighter and wiped it away. What was that about? Normally, I had to make the effort to port myself to the Brain Hotel. Maybe I hadn't snapped out of it completely.

"Where's the TV?" Amy asked.

"I don't have one."

"Oh. Thought I heard voices."

God, I thought, horrified. Was I broadcasting that conversation? Sometimes the other end of the Brain Hotel conversation would slip through, like a mumble, creeping out of my physical body. Yikes. I heard the door close, and sensed Amy walking to my right. A paper bag rustled on the floor.

"Well?"

"Wait a minute . . ." she said. "Okay. Open up."

I did. And I saw a small gray rat running around on my hardwood floor. No, wait; it wasn't a rat. It was a kitten. A tiny gray kitten with white paws. It darted forward, to the beat-up houndstooth couch, then sunk its claws into the side and hoisted itself up to a cushion. "Surprise!" Amy laughed.

"It's a cat," I said.

"Whew! What a relief. For a moment there, Del, I wasn't sure if you'd be able to identify basic animal species."

"Why did you bring me . . . a cat?"

"Face it, champ—you're lonely down here, all alone with your ugly couch and rusty toaster. Everybody needs someone to come home to."

The cat dug its claws into the couch and pulled them back. I heard strands of material strain and pop.

"Hey, kitty," I said, trying to be a sport about the whole thing, despite visions of Cat Chow and kitty litter and turd logs dancing through my head. "Come here. Pss-wss-wss-wss. Come on, girl."

"Boy," Amy said.

The cat took one look at me and froze. An anguished chirp issued from its lungs, and it quickly lunged for the hardwood floor, scratched its nails in a frenzied attempt to run, and squeezed itself beneath the couch.

"Well, that was charming."

Amy smiled. "Oh, he's scared."

"I've never had a pet before. I'm not sure I know what I should do."

"You seem like a natural. And besides . . ." Amy turned around to open the paper bag she'd brought along with her. "You've got enough supplies to last you at least a couple of months." She pulled out two bags of Cat Chow (can I call it, or what?), a bag of litter, a tan plastic box for said litter, and a miniature rubber brush—pink.

"What's that for?" I asked.

"To groom him, of course."

We looked at each other, then said at the same time:

Me: "Do you want a drink—"

Amy: "Hey, I was wondering if—"

I waved. "No, you first."

"Really, you go."

"I was going to ask if you wanted a drink."

"Water, please." She started to laugh. "I was going to ask you out to dinner."

I walked to the kitchen without another word. Amy waited a few uncomfortable seconds, then stood up and walked into the kitchen area. Why not? The case was as good as over. Paul was soon going to recuse himself from his babysitting gig. Soon, if I could help it. We'd find Loogan and Farrell, do a little soul collecting, and fly back to Vegas. There was no reason in the world not to have dinner with a beautiful woman.

I filled up her glass with tonic water and a wedge of lemon and walked it back out to her. Then, simultaneously:

Amy: "I've gotta go."

Me: "I'd like to go."

"Right," Amy said. Her eyes narrowed. "Wait. Go where?"

"To dinner," I said.

"You...oh, okay. Great. Uh, I'll give you a call later this week?"

Boy, she stammered worse than *me* in a tight spot. "There's no need to call. How about tomorrow night? I'm off work." I wasn't sure, but what the hell. I had to reclaim my body wherever I could. Besides, I had a feeling we wouldn't be employed by Richard "Suck Me" Gard much longer.

"Sounds great," Amy said.

Moment of awkward silence.

"I'll come up for you," I said.

"Great. Enjoy your cat."

"I will. If he ever crawls out from under the couch."

Amy left my apartment with the strangest smile on her face. Strangely enough, I smiled, too.

Hey! yelled a voice in my head.

I said nothing. I didn't want to talk to Paul right now.

You don't have any "nights off." You've got a job to do.

The phone rang.

Oh, I'll get it.

Instantly, my vision went black and woozy. I was being sucked down into the lobby of the Brain Hotel. Ordinarily, I would have fought it, but I was too shocked it was happening in the first place. A tenant, taking control of my body . . . without asking? What the hell was this hotel coming to? Robert would have never put up with this kind of crap.

Up on the screen, I watched Paul answer the phone. Smug, arrogant prick. I'd given him too much power as of late, and he was taking it for granted, getting too comfortable flipping in and out of the real world as he pleased. I was going to have to crack down hard on that guy, let me tell you. But for the time being, I just watched.

"Hello?"

There was a pause. I couldn't hear the conversation, but three guesses.

"I'll be right over." Paul hung up and put a jacket on our body.

I slammed the lobby mike button with my palm. "You're not going over there, are you?" I asked.

"It's my job, remember?"

"Not anymore. We're off the case."

"As of when?"

"Right now. Call her and tell her you quit."

Paul didn't say anything. He kept combing our hair.

"Look—you knew this day would come. Your time with our favorite oral gymnast is coming to an end. The case is over.

We're only two quick soul collections away from leaving this damned city."

"And I think Susannah can help us do that."

"How? With more lies? It's not as if she's going to suddenly say, 'Whoops, I'm sorry, I've been lying to you all this time. Here's the real scoop!'"

"She's of more use to us alive than dead," Paul said.

"Who said anything about killing her? I want you to quit."

Paul didn't answer. He walked over to the phone, picked it up, and spun out seven familiar numbers. She answered on the first ring.

"It's me," Paul said. "I need to ask you a favor."

Favor? I thought.

There was a short pause. "Just some time off tomorrow evening, for a few hours." A short pause. "Nothing to do with you." A longish pause. "I need this, Susannah." An even longer pause. "Of course I do." A short, staccato pause. "I'll be with you all day Friday. And all night. Through the whole Best of Philly party." An amazingly long pause. Flowers wilted, generations passed, time flowed like a river of maple syrup ... "Don't worry— I'll protect you," Paul said, and finally hung up the phone.

He walked into the bathroom, splashed some cold water on his face, then looked into the mirror. "How's that for a Solomon-like compromise? You happy now?"

"You get Gard to pay us," I said. "Then I'll be impressed."

19

MACHO CHEESE

I spent two hours preparing for my first date in over six years. Of course, that last date didn't count. It'd been before I was absorbed from the dead. I was interviewing a female source for a personal finance article I'd been writing. My suggestion was to go out for drinks to talk—I knew this place in the center of town with a cheap drink special: a double shot of whatever liquor for the price of one. At the time, I'd been fond of gin and tonic. Unfortunately, the place got away with their rock-bottom prices by serving rotgut liquor. Two glasses had me ready to crawl under the table and eat crumbs.

And my source? A short-haired, bee-stung-lipped, four-eyed cutie. She was ready to crawl under with me. I remember stumbling out of the bar, not one important question asked, and heading to a restaurant I knew, hoping some food would sober us up. It didn't, of course, because we ordered drinks first and forgot about the food. We left, but not before my little Deep Throat grabbed a basket of peppermints and flung them into the air. They flew all over the bar area and rained on the ground. I apologized like mad, and she laughed and tugged my arm and pulled me out of there.

We ran into a colleague of mine on the street—a cub reporter out double-checking a few facts for a Henderson nightlife roundup—at which point my source wrapped her legs around me and started kissing my neck, all in the interest of embarrassing me. Of course, it worked. We ended up in the community park, watching people and sharing a bottle of red wine I'd bought from a grocery shop on the way over. This was when she confessed to still being married and vomited on my lap. "Sweet Pea" was playing on some radio in the background. Within seconds, I felt sobered up and utterly convinced this sick woman was not my "Sweet Pea," and that she was still somewhere out there, waiting to be found. I helped her up, cleaned her face the best I could in a public bathroom, brought her back to my apartment, and laid her to rest on my couch. In the morning, I felt how cheap the gin had been. Damn cheap. You shouldn't have been allowed to give that swill away. My brain was split in half. And then her husband showed up to pick her up, because she'd called him in the middle of the night. It was an uncomfortable morning, to say the least.

Did that qualify as my last date? I don't think so. Needless to say, I was woefully out of practice.

I showered once and tried on a few different variations of the pieces of clothing I owned. Nothing seemed suitable, all of a sudden. Had I gone through life this long with such a shabby wardrobe? God, why hadn't Paul pulled me aside sooner? I got so sweated up I had to shower again.

Finally, I decided on the most conservative outfit I could have put together: a pair of black slacks and a blue button-down shirt. If only I could have taken Amy Langtree on a date in the Brain Hotel, I could have invented any suit to wear, taken her to any fancy restaurant I dreamed of . . . But no. This had to be real. Times like these, I didn't envy Paul one bit.

In the real world, I needed money to spend on a date. Since Paul had left me with a little under twenty bucks—and Gard's check had failed to cash, as of the panicked phone call to Girard Bank first thing this morning—I'd been forced to bring a bunch of my beloved records and a watch I didn't wear to a pawn shop, which earned me twenty-four dollars. Grand total: forty bucks. An amount I prayed was enough for a night out on the town. Again, it had been quite a while since I'd done this sort of thing. Last time, the drinks had been amazingly cheap.

* * *

Amy and I sat down at a table in a ridiculously ornate Mexican restaurant, both wearing hats. She'd picked the place—only a few blocks' walk from our apartment building. Two oversized margaritas sat in front of us. A salsa version of "I Fought the Law" was playing in the background. My collector, Robert, would have been mortified. It had been one of his favorite songs.

"I came here last year for my birthday," Amy said. "I should say, my friends dragged me here for my birthday. Or maybe it wasn't this place. It looks different. There are a million of these places all over, I guess. By the way, when's yours?"

"My what?"

"Birthday, silly."

"Are you asking me my sign?" I asked, with faux suspicion.

Amy laughed. "Yeah, I guess I am. And in the interest of full disclosure, I believe in horoscopes, astral projection, ghosts, and fate. Don't worry. I won't ask the year."

"I'm a Gemini," I said. "Sign of the twin." I wasn't lying—merely understating.

"I'm a Pisces," Amy said. "A pair of fish. That's a kind of twin, isn't it?"

"Kind of." I looked around, then touched the brim of my sombrero. "You know, I feel kind of stupid in this hat—"

"C'mon, Del. You look *muy* cute-o."

"I don't feel *muy* anything."

"Trust me. You're essential cuteness."

We both took a sip of our margaritas. I knew I had to take it easy, lest I hear about it from the boys in the Brain Hotel later. But the damned thing tasted so alive, like biting into a fresh, ripe lime followed by a river of tequila. Old Tom's margaritas couldn't hold a candle to these.

I stole a glance at Amy. *She* was "essential cuteness." Her smile had this sweet, slow way about it—the kind of smile only a few lucky men see every day of their lives. I've always considered marriage to be a sort of lottery and considered myself not to be the gambling type. There was too much to lose. And the odds were too staggering to overcome. Yet, here I was, sitting with the female equivalent of a thousand dollars a day for life. For a few moments, with the combination of her smile and the tequila, I forgot about the Brain Hotel and everything. It was easy.

"What are you thinking?"

Whoops. She'd caught me staring. "Nothing," I told her. But I meant: *everything.*

Amy looked to the side and nodded to a small man in a chef's uniform standing in the kitchenway.

"Amy?"

"I'm sorry," she said. "Something caught my eye."

I craned my head around as an army of restaurant staffers came marching out of the kitchen with a lit birthday cake, clapping their hands as they chanted: "Happy, happy birthday! Happy, happy birthday! Happy, happy day, Del Winter!" They stretched the word "Winter" to eighteen full syllables.

My jaw dropped. "You've got to be kidding."

"I wasn't around to celebrate your last birthday, so here," Amy said. "We'll celebrate it now."

I smiled in spite of myself. "Amy . . ."

"Actually, it's a big scam. They never check IDs or anything. I just like to get the free dessert."

The Casa Tequila staff surrounded the table, smiling and clapping and singing in manic Spanish gibberish. Finally, the flaming cake was lowered to the table and it was revealed to be not a cake, but a plate of blazing nachos. A staffer in the middle whipped out one of those new, instant-printing cameras. Amy saw her chance, grabbed me by the shirt collar and pulled me into camera range.

"Say nacho cheese!" she shouted.

I was aghast. "Amy!"

The flash popped and I was temporarily blinded. I lowered my head. In fact, I kept my head lowered until the staff dissipated. Amy placed a finger beneath my chin and raised my head.

"Honestly, you looked cute."

I finally looked up, smiled grimly, then took a long, thoughtful sip of my margarita. A sip or two had brought me into this fugue state; it took another to snap me out of it. What was I getting myself into? Where the hell was the investigation headed? Was this what I considered "doing my job"?

"I'm sorry," she said. "You look annoyed."

"No, no. It was sweet. But I'm not big on pictures."

"Why not?"

"I don't show up well in them."

Amy smiled. "Are you a vampire, Del?"

"What?" Then I got it. "Oh, no, no. I'm not photogenic."

"I think you are. I would love to see some pictures from your childhood."

I looked down at the table.

"My family wasn't big on pictures."

"Oh, what a shame," Amy said. "Well . . . *Del*. We'll always have the Casa Tequila."

I smiled again. Again, in spite of myself. Our food arrived. We ate, had some pleasant, meaningless conversation. I promised myself not to be that stupid ever again.

That promise was forgotten after the second margarita.

* * *

We arrived back at 1530 Spruce a bit more intoxicated than when we'd left. I pushed the elevator button, she pushed it again, and then I pushed it, and she bolted up the stairs, and I followed suit, laughing all the way.

Amy ran to my door, then turned around and braced herself against it. "If you want to go home, you're going to have to get through me first," she said.

"I can be a pretty rough customer. You might not survive the encounter."

"I can handle more than you think, mister."

I was tempted—hell, my insides were practically burning up. This was everything I shouldn't be doing with my time on Earth, which was probably why I wanted to do it. Suddenly, I was overwhelmed with the need to grab Amy and smother her lips and press her body back against the door, fumbling blind with the key as I probed deeper . . .

No. Wait. Horrible idea. No telling when Susannah would call, asking for her babysitter to run over to Rittenhouse Square. What if Amy was inside when that call came? What would I tell her then?

Then I had a better idea: we would go to *her* apartment.

I touched her cheek with my palm. She smirked, but quickly melted her lips into a fake grimace and bared her teeth. "Come on, soldier. Let's see what *you're* made of."

My index finger brushed her lower lip. I leaned in close. "Not here," I whispered. "Let's go upstairs."

Amy jerked her head back. Unfortunately, she didn't have much room to work with, and her skull bumped against hard wood. "Ouch. What did you say?"

"I want to see where you live," I said, as casually as possible. "I want to see what you're made of."

"No, no, no," she said, sliding away. "We can't. My apartment is a mess. I couldn't have you up there now. Besides, we're right here at your apartment. Only a few feet away from your couch."

She had a logical point, but something seemed odd—why couldn't we go up to her place? Was *she* hiding something?

"I feel as if you have an unfair advantage," I said. "You can tell a lot about someone from their personal belongings."

"Del, you don't have much stuff."

"True, but . . . but I haven't seen anything of yours."

"You can see all you want," she said, and raised her hand to unfasten a button on her blouse.

It was certainly not the reaction I'd been expecting. Amy was definitely trying to change the subject. Whenever a woman starts to unbutton herself in a public hallway, you know a subject is about to be changed. But as much as I wanted to abandon myself to the moment, I couldn't. Nagging suspicion had freaked me out. No matter that *I* had something to hide—I couldn't get past the fact that Amy did, too.

"Amy, it would mean a lot to me."

She froze at the sound of her name. Then she rebuttoned and took a few steps away. "I'm sorry, Del. I can't."

"Why not?"

"I'd better go now."

"Wait . . ." What now? Keep her talking. Keep it light.

"I want to know more about you. You're not storing dead bodies in your apartment, are you? Heck, so what if you are. I've seen 'em before."

Amy was silent. She wouldn't look at me.

"I know they decompose awfully fast, and there can be quite a stench, but it's not a problem. We can buy a few of those room air-fresheners, and—"

"Del, if you're not going to invite me in, I have to go," she interrupted.

Now I felt like a bigger jerk for even joking. But I couldn't cave in, either.

"I guess you'd better go, then," I said.

Amy locked eyes with me, and I thought I saw a teary glimmer of hurt in them. She turned and walked down the hallway, then up the countless flights of stairs to her mystery apartment.

This was for the better, I told myself. I was merely avoiding something that would eventually cause me pain.

Then I felt a sharp, hard jab to my right temple.

20

SHOT CONTEST

"**D**on't move. I can squeeze this trigger before your piss hits cloth."

A female voice. A bit coarse, but syrupy beneath. A seductive combination. However, I was in no mood to be seduced. Again.

I swung my fist around to where I guessed her nose would be. I was a few inches off. My knuckles slammed into her temple. She yelped. I spun around and launched a fist into her face, and another one to chase it down. I don't mean to sound like a jerk, but for me, that old rule about never hitting a woman goes right out the window when the woman is packing heat. Sure, maybe she was holding the stem of a toilet brush to my forehead, but

I didn't want the benefit of the doubt to earn me a trip to the city icebox.

As it turned out, there was no need for me to be worried about offending her delicate sensibilities. The polecat whipped her pistol right across my nose, snapping it out of place. She followed up with another crack, this time to my temple, then jabbed her knee into my gut. She knew how to put her weight behind it, too. I collapsed to the floor, not knowing what to start complaining about first. I felt gunmetal slip between my teeth and push against the back of my tongue.

This was not good.

Trying to form words around the business end of her pistol, I managed to say: "Before you blow my brains out, can I ask who you are?" It came out with less clarity than I'd hoped for.

"Shhh," she said. "Not a word."

"Sowwy," I said, before I could catch myself. Whatever this was about, I sincerely hoped Amy was long out of earshot. There was still a chance I could explain away my odd behavior from a few moments ago. It would be a bit tougher to explain this.

"Where are your keys?"

"Ugh-ufh," I mumbled.

She took the pistol out of my mouth and pointed it at my Adam's apple. I took the opportunity to swish my tongue around. Uck. The taste of gunmetal was hard to lose.

"I'm not going to die in my own apartment. I pay too much rent for something like that." If my assailant came here to kill me, it would have happened already. Whoever this was clearly wanted to talk.

"You *can* feel this gun in your neck, right?"

"Yes, I can. Look, spit it out. I haven't got all night."

I heard her sigh. Not to sound sexist or anything—I know women today have this whole "libber" thing happening, but the fact remains I know how to defuse a hostile female. It was the affectionate ones I had trouble with.

"All right, Paul. I came here to talk."

Did I call this one, or what?

"Okay. Talk."

"Not here." She nudged the gun into my head. "Over there. On the fire escape."

I walked over and through the door like a compliant puppy. Then I turned to face the woman. Of course. The murderess Leah Farrell. I hadn't had the chance to fully study her during our recent encounter in the middle of Market Street. She was a handsome woman, despite beady eyes and lips that were a shade too thin.

"You know why I'm here. I want to know the new score. If you can satisfy me, I'll let you continue breathing for a while."

"Ooh, let me satisfy you," I said.

Leah didn't seem to enjoy the crack. "Who's the bimbo?"

"Now that's not nice."

She poked the gun into my throat again. "Answer, please."

"She's nobody. She's a neighbor who's got the hots for yours truly."

"Hmm. I'd bet she'd be real disappointed to discover you're screwing another chick."

"And who would that be?"

"Don't play dumb, Paul. Ray told me everything. Of course, everything up to a point. That's why I'm here. I want to know how the two of you did it. Most importantly, I need to know if you two got authorization from the Man."

Now I had no choice but to play dumb. Authorization? The Man, once again? I can only assume "the two" she was referring to was myself and Susannah Winston. Here was my chance to figure out the connection. If I didn't receive a bullet in the head first.

"Yes," I bluffed. "We had authorization."

Leah's face collapsed like a condemned building. "I can't be*lieve* it! All this time . . . What was the deal? He give you double what he promised Ray?"

I noticed her pistol arm droop a bit. Keep her going, keep her going.

"I don't know. What did he promise Ray?"

"Far above the standard. He said it was almost too good to be true."

"Come on. How much?"

She looked at me and spat it out. "Half a million."

I whistled. Probably not the coolest thing to do, under the circumstances.

"What?" she asked. "They offer you the same thing?"

Had to think fast. Why would I whistle if my own fee was double? "No, they didn't," I said. "My offer was generous, but certainly not one million dollars."

"I don't understand it," Leah said. "Why all this hassle to bump Ray out of the picture? He was nothing."

"You two seem to be getting along famously."

"I'm a babysitter. You should know that." Then, logic must have set in. "Wait . . . wait . . . this still doesn't fit. Why did you fake your own death, only to meet up with Ray's tramp later?"

Now I was completely flummoxed. I could barely keep up with the conversation as it was, let alone try to fake a rationale for something I obviously didn't do. Did Brad fake his death? Of course not. He was dead when I found him. The idea was ridiculous. Yet, this was the course I'd steered myself into, and I was stuck driving it. That is, if I didn't want to arrange accommodation in the Brain Hotel for a hot spinning bullet.

I tried the usual way out: abrupt subject change. "Don't call her that."

"Are you going to tell me different? Come on, you don't think Ray was the first to have the little cooze. Besides, does Lana know you're diddling the girl next door?"

"Girl next door" obviously meant Amy; Leah must have seen us together, waited for her to leave, then sprung on me like a viper. But who the hell was Lana? I took a chance and closed my eyes for a second. The Brain Hotel lobby fizzled into view. I ran to the front desk and snatched the courtesy phone from its receiver. "Paging Paul After," I said. "Paul, we've got a Grade-A situation here, boy. Request immediate assistance. And I mean pronto, Tonto."

When I opened my eyes, I found Leah studying me way too carefully.

"Maybe it's you who's falling apart, tough guy," she said. "You don't look too sure of anything."

"I'm in more control than you could ever hope for," I said. That was good. Bravado. Keep her guessing.

Meanwhile, during a long blink: *Paul! Damn it, Paul, get down here now!*

"Which one are you fucking? Miss Sweetness and Light? Or the Vegas slut?" She accented the word "light" by poking the pistol into my head.

"This isn't about sex. This is about Ray."

"Finally, we're talking business. So, tell me. How is this about Ray?"

"Ray's done some very bad things, Leah. Some people want to see him pay."

"What, because he ripped off the Man? Is that what you're going to tell me? Because forget it. He's already told me about it and it's nothing. Repeat—nada. He wouldn't have him killed over something as stupid as a slot machine jiltz. Try again."

Bluffing my way through a conversation was never my forte. Which is not exactly something to be proud of, considering my line of work.

"No, I'm not talking about the slots. Something worse."

"Well, what?"

I didn't say anything. I closed my eyes.

* * *

As if through divine intervention, Paul came walking into the Brain Hotel lobby at that exact moment. He looked sleepy. "You wanted me for something?"

I vigorously nodded my head up and down. I couldn't say anything for fear it would be mimicked by my lips in the real world, and confuse the hell out of Leah. Instead, I gestured with my arms: *take my body, please.* Paul shot me a dubious look, then walked through the lobby doors anyway.

* * *

In the real world, Leah saw my eyes open back up.

Paul felt the gun at this throat. His first thought was broadcast loud and clear in the lobby: *You're a real asshole, Del.*

"Well?" Leah asked, jabbing the pistol forward.

I ran to the front desk and snatched the microphone. "Okay," I rushed. "Explain what Ray Loogan could have done to deserve a hit. She thinks you and your client double-crossed them at some point."

"What?" I wasn't sure if Paul was talking to me or Leah.

"Are you stalling?" Leah asked. "Or are you screwing with me? Because if so, we can end this right here . . ."

"No, Leah—I'm sorry," Paul said, feeling his (our) broken nose. "You must have hit me harder than I thought."

Good, good. I felt my own nose in the Brain Hotel. It was hurting, too. I must have carried the pain back with my consciousness when we made the switch. Weird how some things linger with you.

"Forget that for a second," Paul said. "Let's get something straight, here and now."

"What?" Leah asked.

"All I'm trying to do is stop you killing my client."

"Your client?!" she screamed. "You mean, the same client who sliced the shit out of you back in Illinois?"

I froze. God in Heaven. Was Susannah Winston—or whoever the hell she was—Ray Loogan's accomplice? No, no. Brad identified his killers: Ray and his woman here, Leah Farrell. There was no reason for him to lie about it. Bringing his killers to justice was the only thing he lived for. Or sort of lived for. But why was Leah lying about it, then?

"I don't know what you're talking about, Leah," Paul said, honestly.

I picked up the lobby microphone once again: "She's obviously confused you with Brad Larsen. She and Ray were sent to kill him."

Squinting, Leah slowly let the pistol drop to Paul's chest. "You really don't, do you?"

"My client's name is Susannah Winston. I was hired to protect her from a crazy ex-boyfriend. Then, out of the blue you and Loogan show up, shooting at us, and here we are, tangled in this crazy mess in my apartment hallway."

Leah looked doubtful again.

"All I remember," Paul continued, "is getting fished out of some muddy creek, taking a few months to recuperate, then swinging back into business for myself, as far away from Vegas as possible. I was running out of money, and needed some before I could even think about my next step. Life's changed a lot for me since the last time we spoke."

"I'm sure," Leah said.

Even looking at her through the view screen in the Brain Hotel lobby, I could see the wheels spinning in her head.

"So, you don't even know . . . what is it? Susannah Weston?"

"Winston."

"You're saying you don't know this Susannah Winston's real name, do you?"

"No, I don't. I've never met her before this job."

Leah smiled, then leaned back and eased up on the pistol. I half expected Paul to smack it out of her hands and punch her in the face, but he didn't. He eased back into a more comfortable position on the floor.

"Obviously, we need to compare notes." Leah stood up and brushed the wrinkles out of her pants. "I think we need a change in venue. Is there a bar nearby?"

"Yes, on the northwest corner of Fifteenth and Spruce."

"After you."

Leah stuck her pistol beneath the flap of her purse—which contained nothing, I later learned, except a stiletto and extra clips—and kept it trained on Paul the entire way downstairs and across the street.

Thank God Brad Larsen was nowhere near the Brain Hotel lobby to catch this scene. Oh yeah, Brad? That was Paul—a former assassin who's in control of our collective body—going out to have a drink with the woman who knifed you to death. Only, we're not real sure; it might have been *Paul's client* who knifed you to death. That's why we're all headed out for a drink.

* * *

Unfortunately, the bar on the corner wasn't a quiet neighborhood dive. It was a bona fide chic Center City café, complete with *Philadelphia* magazine review ($$$$!) plastered, lacquered, and hung on every available piece of wall space. At least it was nearby. Paul and Leah took a booth near the back, away from most of the trendy diners eating their plates of bluefish and foie gras. Between Paul's obviously broken nose and Leah's fresh cheekbone shiner, they didn't need any additional attention. She ordered for both of them—oversized shot glasses full of Jose Cuervo, with two Schmidt's chasers. "Next round, leave the bottle," she told the waitress.

Leah turned to Paul. "This is how it works. For every piece of information I offer up, I want you to down a shot of booze."

"Why?"

"Don't forget, I know who you are. And you know who I am. That makes us both smart. I need you dumbed down for a while."

"I can be dumb all by myself."

"Drink up, tough guy. There's two to start, and then we commence our business. If we reach a satisfactory conclusion, we both walk out of here alive."

Paul had nothing to say to that. Better to get it over with, I guess he figured. He drained both shot glasses.

* * *

Inside the Brain Hotel, I felt the walls tremble.

* * *

Paul cleansed his palate with a gulp of beer and a couple of complimentary oyster crackers from a wooden bowl on the table.

"Susannah Winston's real name is Lana Lewalski," she said. "Grew up in a shit town not far from Vegas, and as soon as she was old enough to bleed, she and her slutty little ass were slinging vodka and tonics in the nickel casinos. That's how she met Ray."

"I don't suppose her father was an inventor for the US Army?"

"Boy, she's a weird bitch. She tell you that?"

Paul ignored the question. "So how did this Lana entangle herself in the Man's business?"

Leah wasn't going to be tricked into spilling the goods that easy. She poured Paul another Cuervo. "To your health."

"This is silly," Paul said, frowning. "I have legendary tolerance. You could confess the world's secrets and have to start making shit up before I even feel a buzz."

"Then there's no problem, right?"

Paul drained it. Despite his bravado, it hit him deep. Hell, *I* could feel it. The lobby walls turned pale for a second, *on second thought* my seat felt like it was going to crash through the wall

200

wallflowersincollege punch bowl I was afraid to make a single move. BBBBBBut it held . . . the only thing I ever wanted from life was a woman to love me like a man . . .

Holy shit, I thought. It's happening. The walls are breaking down.

"Good boy. All I know I learned from Ray. I've come to trust him over the last seven months."

"Grrranted."

"Well, Ray was proving himself to the Man, doing jobs here and there, mostly as muscle to scare distributors behind on their payments."

"Yeah. We all start out that way."

"But you never ran into Ray, did you?"

"I was top floor. I never met any of the Man's little people."

"Which makes it all the more odd that Ray received the contract to kill you."

Paul's eyes narrowed. "Kill me?"

Again, I was forced to remind Paul, via Brain lobby mike: "She's talking about Brad Larsen. She thinks you're Larsen." But a bit of static cut into the message: *Talking about my g-g-g-g-generation . . .* "You are Larsen . . ."

Leah smiled prettily and tipped the Cuervo into the drinking glass once again.

Paul sighed; tossed it back. A couple of phones at the front desk started to ring; pissed-off tenants probably complaining about a sudden lack of basic services. Amazing how people can forget where they are sometimes.

"Yeah—*you.* I mean, here was Ray, a nobody, handed half a million bucks to whack one of The Association's top turncoats. Even Ray knew it sounded odd. On one hand, it sounded like the deal of a lifetime. On the other, it sounded like a way to take out the arrogant freshman. A reverse hit, and the beauty is, nobody pays a dime."

"Ray shows up, and I'm sure to kill *him*."

"Correct. Ray decides to take along his girlfriend—one Lana Lewalski. Right there should have been the clue: this guy ain't pro yet. You never bring an outsider along for any job, let alone a career-maker. But Ray had it all planned out: drive out, spend a few days studying up, make the hit, split, have the rest of the payment wired out to him, and spend a few days kicking around the East Coast. Lana, apparently, wanted to be in Philadelphia for the Bicentennial."

Major click. Even Paul shuddered, and it wasn't from the tequila. It was the same damn thing Susannah had told Gard.

"What'd he tell her? It'd be a great family vacation?"

"Well, it could have been," Leah said, "except that the happy couple's first stop was at an abortion clinic. Talk about killing two birds with one stone."

Paul didn't laugh. "How did you get involved in Ray's mess? You find yourself feeling bad for the sorry prick?"

Leah took a small sip of her beer, then raised her fingers like a peace sign. "That's two questions."

Paul swallowed a sigh. Leah poured him more tequila. Up to the brim. "Go ahead. Trust me—you're going to need it."

"Take it easy, Paul," I tried to warn him. But it was no use.

It took three whole gulps to finish it. Now that wasn't fair— it was clearly more than two ordinary shots. I wished I could pop out of Paul's head and call a time out.

The viewing screen started to wobble at this point, and the audio crackled in spots. I was confident it would all hold up at some basic level; after all, this whole framework *I'm in no hurry to disgrace myself in front of your father* had been constructed by my own brain power, and I was *Call a seven, c'mon goddamnit, call a seven or I'll start worshipping the Devil, let's go* the equivalent of a public utility. It was the individual users I was worried about. The last thing I needed was *grapes never taste right in this friggin' fridge. I like 'em cold and crisp. In this damn thing, they might as well be* a mob of angry and confused souls stomping down here, demanding to know why entire pieces of their rooms had suddenly swirled away *the best one is the one about the bookworm who works in a bank, and seals himself in a vault right before the big one hits* like a cigarette butt in a flushed toilet. That's how alcohol fucked with the brain. How else can I explain it? But oh, God, **GOD, GOD!** The voices!

"I was thinking you'd be able to tell me," Leah said.

"I tollld you," Paul said. "I doan remember a damn thing."

"Oh, yes. That's right. Let me give you Ray's version, then. He tracks you down easily enough—the Man bought the address from a Wit Protec flunky. Woody Creek, Illinois is where they stashed you. You remember that much?"

"Yeah," Paul lied.

"After a couple of days of recon, Ray decides to make the push. He goes right up and knocks on your door. Talk about brass ones, huh? Figured you'd expect every other approach except that one. You open the door, one trigger pull, and it's all over."

Paul nodded. I think, mostly to avoid Leah hearing the slur in his speech.

"Only, the door opens, and it's not you. It's some woman Ray's never seen before. You remember getting married, Paul?"

"Uh-uh."

"Well, that's one mystery solved. She was a hooker."

"Must've been."

God, please don't let Brad Larsen ever read a transcript of this conversation. What if his thoughts were leaking through? And what if it worked both ways? I stumbled forward and, after some grappling around, found the lobby mike. "Paul, listen to me. You have got to *Kill the tramp where she sits. Go ahead. Stab her in the eye with the fork on the table* find a way to stop drinking."

Damn these voices!

"Anyway, Ray freaked out and fired anyway, and nailed the bitch in the throat. Which gave you enough time to charge him. Ray couldn't get a shot; you two tumbled around and somehow scuffled about on the back porch. You took a pistol from Ray's belt and plugged him in the leg."

"Hmmm." Paul's eyes lingered on the tequila bottle, kind of a like a condemned man gazing at the guillotine.

"You thirsty? All this macho talk make your throat dry?"

Paul shook his head.

I grabbed the lobby mike and tried to pep-talk him through this. "Hang on, buddy. You're doing *nothing about the situation. Stab her in the eye stab her in the eye stab her in the eye* good. We've almost got what we need to know."

"I'm hanginnn on," Paul said, out loud.

Oh no! What the hell was he doing?

"All thisssounds familiar to me," Paul said.

"Be quiet, Paul! She *put a bullet in her tits put a bullet in her tits* can hear you!"

"Oh, is it all coming back to you?" Leah said, one eyebrow tilted to heaven. "I thought it might. Maybe you'd like to start explaining some things to me, then."

"I know who you are," Paul blurted, slur gone.

"Introductions have been well established, I think," Leah said.

"Paul? What the hell are you doing?"

"It's nnnot me," Paul said like he was speaking underwater.

Then, in a voice as crisp and vibrant as a new day: "No, you don't know me, Leah Farrell. I came after After. *But I know you.* And you can rest assured I'm going to destroy you for helping the man who killed my wife."

Oh boy. Clearly, we had another soul speaking through our physical body. It was easy to guess who. But how? And from where? And what the hell was he doing, scotching the very investigation he hired me to conduct?

Leah, for her part, looked unnerved by this whole turn of events. She probably expected Paul to loosen up, maybe even surrender a few details to help sort things out. I'm sure she didn't expect this . . . calamity.

"What do you mean . . ." she asked, "*wife?* You weren't married."

"True enough; Paul was never married. But I was. To a beautiful, selfless, endlessly giving woman who wanted nothing in life but to appreciate beauty and art and raise brilliant children."

Had there been any doubt about the identity of our mystery caller, it was gone.

"Who the fuck are you?" Leah asked.

"I am going to be the last voice you ever hear," Brad Larsen said. He reached forward, grabbed the bottle of Cuervo, poured himself a healthy drink, sucked it into his mouth, then sprayed it all over Leah's face.

Of course, I only heard this last part by remote; I was running through the Brain Hotel—half faux-running, half porting my soul—racing toward Brad Larsen's room. I kicked open the door just as Brad was simulating his boozy raspberry—the one our body was acting out in real life. "Brad, goddamn it!"

There was some kind of metal gizmo wrapped around his head, with tiny wires and rubber patches attached to his forehead and temples. He was moving his right arm forward, and grabbing an imaginary object that rested on an imaginary table right in front of him. Brad's eyes slowly opened, and he smiled. "And now we light the match . . ."

It didn't take long for me to figure out what he was going for. I leapt forward and slapped his head with my open hand. Stung the hell out of me, but at least it succeeded in dislodging the gizmo. I grabbed it with my non-throbbing hand and yanked it free. It made tiny *pop! pop! pop!* sounds.

Brad yelped, "Hey!"

I looked at the limp collection of metal and wire and rubber in my hand. It was like nothing I'd ever seen before, not even beneath the hood of a foreign car. But I had to ignore it. Punish now, sort it out later.

I closed my soul-eyes and sent Brad to the interrogation room with the houndstooth couch.

* * *

However, back in Reality, the damage had already been done. Leah slapped a pile of twenties on the tequila—probably leaving a 300 percent tip in the process—and led Paul outside with her pistol shoved into his spine. Poor bastard didn't know what the hell to think—one moment he was tying one on, the next somebody was taking over his voice box, and the next he was being shoved out a front door with a pistol in his back. I'm sure the ordinary Paul After could have handled worse, but then again, this Paul After had been through the Play-Doh Fun Factory I call my brain and wasn't entirely sure of his own existence.

She nudged Paul into an alley right next to the restaurant. He stepped around a trash can, and she followed. I could sense that the place stunk to high heaven—city alleys in the middle of summer were never choice locations. The fact that it even registered in Paul's booze-addled mind was worthy of note.

"Okay, stop right there."

Paul turned around, trying his damndest to stay upright.

"I knew you weren't Paul," Leah said. "The Paul I knew wouldn't let a woman bully him into a silly game of drinking for information. The Paul I knew wouldn't have let me anywhere near his real apartment. So who the fuck are you, huh? And how do you have Paul's face?" She nudged the gun into Paul's forehead to accent that last word.

Paul looked up at her. I thought he was going to either giggle, vomit, or both. But what he did next surprised the hell out of me.

He smacked Leah's gun away. It fired into the brick wall behind him. He made a fist and launched it into her stomach. Leah bent in half. She started to scream, but Paul punched her again before she could. She collapsed to the ground in a very unladylike manner.

Paul stood up, and his balance wavered. He took a few steps back into a wall, then slid down it. "I doannnn know."

And then he passed out.

* * *

The voices stopped. The Brain Hotel solidified.

I'm not sure how to explain it, since there was precious little blood running through our alcohol system. Maybe the effect was dependent on consciousness; maybe the infrastructure of the human brain simply can't handle reality, multiple sub-personality consciousness, and a lot of booze. Or maybe punching a woman in the gut was enough to sober anybody up.

At any rate, it was time to check on our boy. I don't know how he corralled the mind power to focus for those few key seconds, but sweet Alleluia, he did. I ran back into the hotel lobby and found Paul on the floor. He had staggered back in from the real world, but couldn't make it any further. His soul was wasted.

"You'd better take over, Del," he said. "I'mmnot feeling too good."

"Take it easy, buddy. I'll handle it."

I ran out the front doors. *Whoah.*

The real world wetbrain stupor hit me like a tidal wave. It's one thing to gradually become drunk over a series of cold mugs of beer, or even from a few shots of whiskey spaced over the course of an hour. It was another to inherit the wind all at once. I needed to pass out somewhere safe.

But I had to do something with Leah first.

Leaving her in this alley meant she'd only wake up in an hour or so, then come back up to my apartment and try to kill me. I doubt there would be any lengthy conversation then, either. I could kill her and absorb her soul, but I felt like I had enough balls to juggle at the moment without a dead body to hide—and God forbid that she and Brad started comparing notes inside the Brain Hotel. The best idea was to keep her out of the picture for a while. And the best way to do that?

Doug came down to the lobby in record time. He took over the body—"Whoah, Reality is more of a rushhh than I remember," he said, then set off to score a dose of horse. It wasn't difficult; this was Fifteenth and Spruce. When he returned, Leah was still passed out in the alley. Doug strapped her arm up tight, then gave her a nice clean shot to oblivion. She resumed consciousness for a horrible second, eyes spinning, then suddenly focusing on her arm, and I swear she knew what was happening to her for a second before she was gone. He shoved the rest of the goods into her pants pocket, then surrendered the body to me.

I shoved a dime into a phone, called 911, gave a location, then finally staggered back to my apartment. It was time for me to pass out.

21

TOILET, CAT

I'd almost keyed into my apartment when a familiar, annoying voice started talking to me.

"While you were playing around with the ladies, I discovered some grim news," said Fieldman. I could see his image in the brass door knocker plate on my apartment door. He loved to project himself into the oddest of places.

"I'm in no mood."

Instantly, his image appeared in the hallway with me. "Well, get in the mood, Collective, because my former employers are on to you. They've got your picture, they've got your alias. It's only a matter of time. And time is something you don't have."

I unlocked the door and kicked it open. Fieldman followed me inside. I closed the door and threw my jacket over a chair. "How do you know all of this?"

"I have my sources. As we speak, the FBI is running your picture through a series of tape files they have. In addition, your photo is being sent to every branch office from here to Seattle."

"And where did the Feds find this picture?"

"I do not know yet. The search request issued from the Philadelphia branch, which in turn, came from a request from the Philadelphia District Attorney's Office."

Richard. Had to be. Calling in a favor from a lawyer buddy. But why would he suspect anything? Why would he check up on me now? *Because you're a thug from Las Vegas who is babysitting his twenty-four-year-old mistress, that's why.*

"You'd better come into the Brain Hotel. I'll show you."

Grudgingly, I sat down on the couch and closed my eyes. Bad move.

* * *

I stepped through the front doors to find Brad, who had somehow freed himself from his houndstooth prison. Up on the screen was Fieldman, looking down at me. He hadn't followed me down into the Brain Hotel.

"All right," I said. "What's the deal?"

"I was merely wondering what you plan to do next," Brad said.

"Go upstairs and sleep for a couple of days," I said truthfully.

"About my case, I mean."

"I see," I said. "Well, before you started screwing around with me and the hotel, I was planning to find your killers, kill them, and

211

absorb their souls for further questioning. Then you were going to give me the information you promised and we were all going to head back to Las Vegas to finish this thing, once and for all."

"I don't think so," Brad said.

I didn't understand. Wasn't this what he'd wanted for the past eight months? Justice, revenge, heads on sticks, et cetera?

"In fact," Brad continued, "I no longer wish to retain your services. You might step into something you shouldn't and make a mess for the rest of us."

"This is true," said Fieldman, up on the screen. "You're in way over your fractured head."

Suddenly, my vision blurred to the right. Everything in front of me suddenly brightened and dissolved into a burning trail of light. Soon, I wasn't able to see any shapes at all. Just bright, spinning globs of pulsating matter. My eardrums popped, as if I were underwater. My God—had the jerk managed to lace my Brain Scotch with a tablet of LSD when I wasn't looking?

Voices: *Here he comes.*

Yes. I can see his shape . . .

Then, in a flash, the world re-formed around me. Only I wasn't in the lobby anymore. I was standing in my Brain *office* with Brad and Fieldman, who was holding what looked to be a television remote control box.

Fieldman smirked. "I bet you're wondering how we managed to drag you up here against your will."

"No," I said. "I'm standing here trying to imagine what it's going to feel like."

"What *what's* going to feel like?" Brad asked.

"What it's going to feel like when I eject both your sorry souls into my bathroom toilet."

This cracked them up. Knee-slapping and everything. I made a note to myself to work on my threatening, tough-guy voice.

"You're no longer in charge," said Brad, chuckling one last time before wiping his eyes. "Tell him, Agent Fieldman."

Fieldman started pacing around me, his clunky gizmo trained on me. "You forget that I know your secrets, Collective. Using the processing power given to each Brain Hotel resident, I invented this—a device that can take your soul and drag it around. Eject it into whatever *we* want."

"I'll mention it to the Nobel committee." What was this confrontation about, anyway? An extra closet or two in their apartments? "Why are the two of you so eager to drag me around? Because I don't have Brad's murderers hung by their thumbs yet?"

Brad sighed and waved his arms around. "God, you can't see *anything*, can you? For such a supreme being, you're painfully, stupefyingly, pitifully *ignorant*."

That was nice. I'd never been called a supreme being before.

Brad continued. "We've been planning this for months now—almost as long as you've been conducting your so-called 'murder investigation.' And all the time you thought you were in control. Ordering us around. Barking questions at us. You have no idea how weak you are."

"Don't bother explaining to the Collective," interrupted Fieldman. "His mind is far too closed to comprehend."

"I suppose you're right," Brad said. "Go ahead and zap him."

"Destination?" Fieldman asked.

"Oh, why don't we use the man's suggestion?"

A smile lit up Fieldman's face. "You are serious, aren't you?"

This talk was getting loopy—not to mention, personally destructive. I had to flex my muscles now or forever hold my peace. "Paul?" I shouted. The more muscles the better. "Hey, PAUL!"

"He's not going to answer," said Brad.

"Oh," I said, with as much braggadocio as I could muster. "He *will*."

"No . . . he won't. Because *I'm* Paul After."

I gave him the same kind of look you'd give someone who's declared himself the Prince of Mars.

"You don't believe me," said Brad. "And to tell you the truth, I wish it weren't true. But Paul After is undeniably me. Or me, that is, until approximately eight months ago."

"It is not worth explaining," said Fieldman.

"Sure it is," Brad said. "It'll give him something to think about when he's hanging out with the Tidy Bowl man for the next fifty years. You see, Del, I used to be an extremely disreputable man. Started out doing small-time jobs for the New York Mafia, then headed out West to make my fortune. Which I did, through a number of businesses. A few of them you even wrote about, back when you were a reporter."

"I don't remember writing about any Brad Larsen."

"Not by name, you didn't."

"What are you talking about?"

"Let's put it this way: if you hadn't come along and collected my soul from the muddy waters of the Woody Creek, there would be no Association left for you to chase."

I stared at him, slack-jawed. "That's not poss . . ." I started to say, but then couldn't think of anything.

"Starting to get it? *I am your fucking Association!* Just me . . ."

214

Possible? Certainly. What kind of evidence did I ever have? Only bits and pieces. I had put the picture together. I had assumed a massive criminal organization pulled the strings. I had never dreamed one man could do so much.

"But I'm drifting from my original point," said Brad. "You see, the key was having two separate lives, so utterly distinct that one could never, ever, lead to the other. In one life, I was Brad Larsen, college professor in training, with a Masters in seventeenth-century English Literature, and working toward my doctorate at the University of California, Bakersfield. I was married to the beautiful Alison Larsen, nee Langtree, and we lived in a gorgeous two-bedroom bungalow three blocks away from campus. She was a hairdresser. And she never asked where all the 'grant money' came from."

I interrupted—merely to inject myself back into the flow of things. "And in your other life, you were this JP Bafoures, bloodthirsty crime boss, willing to kill anyone—man, woman, child—as long as it put dollars in your pocket."

"I only killed two women," Brad said. "And never children."

"So, I'm to believe you've been working the Susannah Winston case? In effect, babysitting your own murderer?"

"Not exactly," Brad said. "This Paul After is not technically me. He's a fragment of my own psyche, sheared off the moment you absorbed my soul."

"Not possible," I said. "I absorbed him months after I absorbed your soul."

"No, you only *thought* you absorbed him then. It was a fabricated memory we put in place months ago."

"I can explain this, Collective," said Fieldman. "Your programming—that is, the processor that is your mind—

is only equipped to handle one identity at a time. Once it encountered Brad, who had a brain disorder known as a split personality, it did the only thing it could: it assigned them two different identities here in your hotel."

"Paul even gave himself a new last name," said Brad. "Bafoures became After."

"Understand, Collective?" Fieldman asked.

"Thank you, Mr. Wizard," I said. This dude never gave up. "If he's a separate identity, why can't he leap to my defense right now?"

"Simple," Brad said. "Fieldman *erased* him."

"You erased him?" I didn't know whether to believe him or not, but at that point it didn't seem to matter.

Fieldman walked up to me and softly applied his hand to my cheek. "You've had enough suffering for one lifetime. It is time to rest."

"How can you 'erase' a soul?"

Fieldman held his gizmo up to my face and tapped it with his index finger. "I'll show you."

And then it was over.

* * *

I spent an agonizing length of time outside of any physical form. (Only later did I realize my "trip" had only taken a fraction of a second, and I'd spent twenty hours trying to piece my mind back together.) I didn't appreciate what I'd had until it was rudely snatched away from me. For years, I'd had the companionship of other souls, whenever I wanted it. I had a building full of unique individuals, each with stories to tell, emotions to vent. And, during those same years, I had souls to reach out to.

Now, all that was gone. The only physical sensation left was tumbling: endless, nauseating tumbling. No sense of up, down, left, or right; no depth. It was like being jettisoned into outer space, only without the blessed quick death of decompression and body implosion. This tumbling went on forever. Every time I tried to figure out how they'd done it, how they'd wrenched my soul from its home inside my brain, I'd start to spin more violently, unable to think on an intellectual level any longer. I would have vomited, but I feared I'd spend eternity spinning in an ocean of my own bile and whatever my last meal happened to have been. No . . . must stop riffing on food and drink, I thought to myself. Me? Who was me, anyway?

And then, as quickly as my spinning hell began, it ground to a halt.

A sturdy, white porcelain halt.

My God, I realized after a few moments. *My name is Del Farmer, and my soul is trapped in a toilet.*

* * *

I knew I was a toilet just as you, sitting there, know you are a human being. There is an undeniable, irrefutable awareness of self.

Frankly, I was amazed how fast my soul adapted to its new prison. And what is a flesh-and-blood body but a prison? I was aware of my functional parts just as a human being is aware of his arms and legs. The core of my being was a wide, deep bowl, but I could feel extensions reaching deep into the floor, down into the great and ancient sewer system of Philadelphia itself. Somewhere along the way, my self faded. What used to be my left arm was now the flushing mechanism. It made perfect sense; I'd always been left-handed. I didn't seem to have a right arm or hand equivalent, but my sense of "face" sure had found a new home. It was the seat and lid. Those diabolical bastards.

Sure, I'd always joked about sending arrogant souls to a city trash can, or a public toilet. But that had been tough-guy hyperbole. I'd never considered doing something as downright evil as ejecting a unique, feeling life-force into something so dead and repellent. However, it seemed Brad Larsen had no such reservations. Because here I was. A toilet.

As much as I hated to admit it, my current situation lent a great deal of credence to Fieldman's spaced-out dialogues. Here I was, a living entity, contained in an artificial environment. (At least it explained the poltergeist phenomena folks have been reporting for years.) The most I could hope for was that this apartment would go un-rented for a few months, during which time I could possibly find a way to kill myself. Maybe, eventually, some compassionate soul would clog me full of toilet paper and let me choke in peace.

* * *

Don't misunderstand. I wasn't feeling suicidal. But this was the first time in my entire life—from womb to death to soul absorption to current status—I'd felt completely and irrevocably lost. And then a thought occurred to me.

Was I completely powerless? Or did the abilities I'd been given transfer to my mind, and not the architecture of my physical reality? Could I still absorb—and transfer—a soul?

If Fieldman were to be believed, the powers lay within my physical brain. Which he called a computer of sorts. I refused to accept that model of my brain, of course. Anybody would. It reduced my core being to a machine.

But if *I* were to be believed, my powers still remained within me. Which would mean I could still shuttle souls—including my own—back and forth between objects as easily as a four-year-old arranges alphabet blocks. My mind possessed those powers—not my physical brain.

The only problem: I only knew one way to transfer a soul, and that way required direct eye contact. Absolutely nothing in my bathroom had eyes: not my toothbrush, razor, washrag, bar of Ivory soap . . . nor the toilet.

I had to transfer into something alive. And having bumped into some of the sad-sack residents of this apartment complex in the past couple of weeks, finding a living being was not going to be easy.

Then I remembered: Buddy.

Sweet, lovable, adorable, fur-ridden Buddy. Gift from Amy, Eater of Shoelaces, Ripper of Couches, Fearful of Own Shadow, Savior from Heaven. But how could I call him? I couldn't very well do that *pss-wss-wss-wss* thing as a toilet. No lips. No access to Cat Chow to tempt him, either. I had to use a distracting noise, something to stir the bugger's innate curiosity. Then, lure him close enough to look inside the bowl itself, the watery core of my being . . .

I realized what I *could* do. I started to shake my arm—now, the toilet handle.

C'mon, Buddy. Come out and be a cat.

I jiggled the handle again. *C'mon.*

Jiggled it again. And again.

Finally, I could sense tiny pawsteps skittering across the bathroom tiles. Right on! I felt padded, furry feet against my bowl. I saw the feline head peek over the water, up at the handle. Good boy, good boy! I wanted to shout.

Then I heard a key fumble in the apartment door. Buddy turned his head, interested in the new sound. I was curious, too, but no matter now. I jiggled the handle more furiously. Buddy looked at it, then spun his head around again.

I jiggled the handle that was my hand with all of my porcelain might. *Look at it, you stupid fur-brained . . .* The apartment door opened, full of ear-splitting, rusty squeaks and wood groans . . . *Look! Look!*

And then the handle came loose, dropped onto the rim, and flipped over into the bowl. Buddy followed it with his green feline eyes. Through rings of concentric, watery circles, I looked into them.

* * *

"Del? You home?"

Well, sort of. It was a terribly strange adjustment. And I thought the toilet was bad. At least it had been a porcelain constant; the brain of a cat was something wholly different. I locked on to its primitive brain structure easily, and established myself as the commander-in-chief, but I still had to surrender myself to cat logic.

Cat logic: whatever seemed to be the most reasonable course of action at any given moment, do the opposite.

Whenever you absolutely, positively have to accomplish a task, run off and find something else to occupy your attention.

I wanted to see Amy, but Buddy yanked the reins out of my hands and leapt into the bathtub. *No, Buddy,* I commanded. But he regarded the master's voice inside his tiny cat brain as he did the master's voice in real life: he completely ignored it. Buddy started scratching at the drain, apparently trying to kill tiny droplets of condensation.

"Del?" Amy called from the room.

Come on, Buddy. Go see Amy. Go see Amy.

Did he know who Amy was? Did my thoughts translate into cat language inside his skull? Didn't really matter, it seemed. Buddy was still fascinated with the drain. I swore I'd keep the bugger out of the bathroom from now on, as punishment.

Fortunately, Amy popped her head into the bathroom. "Hey, Buddy!" she squealed, and then started going *pss-wss-wss-wsss*.

You should have heard the sirens go off in the cat's Lilliputian brain. Suddenly, there was nothing more important in the entire world than to seek out and identify that alluring sound. I felt our furry, muscular body tense, spin around and hurtle out of the bathtub. It made my stomach—or at least, my own internal concept of "stomach"—flip. We bounded ahead until we encountered our target: the Woman's Shins. Then he thrust our body forward, rubbing our entire length against the Woman.

If I ever say I want to absorb the soul of a cat, talk me out of it. Fast. The only thing more uncontrollable than a cat is the weather.

Amy picked us up and started stroking our head absent-mindedly. "Where's your daddy?" she cooed, but not looking at us. She still scanned the apartment, as if I would be hidden under my desk or something.

I'm here! I tried to yell, but it came out as a purr.

She put us down, and Buddy tried to skitter away. But this time I was ready for him. I flexed every last bit of mental energy and clamped down on the scruff of his neck. Buddy jolted forward, then froze. He started to growl, but I cut it off. Then, slowly, I forced his head up to look at Amy.

She was reading something on a piece of notepaper, twiddling an apartment key in her free hand. Then I realized: *Hey. That's probably my apartment key. What's going on? What day is this, anyway?* Amy sighed, folded the note, put it in her jeans pocket, and started for the door.

If I was going to get any answers, I needed to jump into Amy's body. Quick.

Okay, fur lips. Let's move it.

I jerked one front leg forward, then the next. One back leg, the next. Buddy was fighting me the entire way. You know cats can make themselves heavier when they don't want you to pick them up? Well, believe me, they can do the same thing mentally. I'm sure if Amy was paying any attention to Buddy, she'd have immediately called a combination vet/exorcist.

Amy was at the door.

Leg, leg, leg, leg . . .

Amy was unlocking and opening the door.

We were a foot away. Time to go for broke. I summoned every ounce of mental control I thought I had over this cat and sent it to his back legs. It sprung up in the air like a jackrabbit who's had a carrot rammed up his ass.

We crashed into Amy's moving legs and did an ungraceful flop to the floor. Apparently, my presence negated Buddy's ability to land on all four feet.

Amy let out a startled, "Oh!" then looked down at us. Pathetic. Which, apparently, worked wonders. Amy squealed with pity and snatched us up into her arms, stroked our head and ran her knuckles beneath our mouth. Tremors shot throughout our body; our tail flicked wildly, joyously. *Oh, don't stop, don't stop.* Then I remembered what I had been going for.

I lifted our head so it bumped Amy's jaw. "Buddy, slow down," she said.

I bumped her again, rubbed our head across her cheek, and bumped her again.

"Buddy!"

Amy nudged our head up with a finger. "What's wrong with you, kit—"

We looked into her eyes.

22

ELECTRIC AMY

Whammo. The world did a backflip.

By this point, I was feeling like a world traveler. From the Country of Porcelain to the strange, exotic turf of Feline, right into the uncharted territory known as the Female Mind. Oddly, Amy's mind felt closer to the toilet than the cat.

This is not meant as an insult—honest. The foundations of her psyche were unlike anything I'd ever encountered, and I'd encountered many a psyche.

I/Amy blinked, dimly aware that Buddy had wriggled free, leapt back down to the floor and scrambled away, probably looking for a place to hole up and bathe himself for a couple of hours.

Where am I? I heard Amy ask.

There was no Brain Hotel in here, to be sure. Just an ordinary human mind. Or was it?

No matter the environment, I had to create a suitable meeting place for our two minds. Right now, no doubt, Amy's consciousness was tumbling around in the void of her own brain, wondering how she'd lost her grip on reality so quickly.

I started to slap up a large room with wood-paneled walls, a comfortable rug, a desk, a couch, a few paintings. Then I realized a strange room like that would probably disorient her even more. I needed something familiar. So, I recreated my own apartment the best I could. That way, when I summoned her soul here, she would think she'd momentarily passed out. I could explain it away, without fear of her losing her mind.

When I'd finished, I called out to her. "Amy! Amy, wake up."

AMY IS AWAKE.

The voice didn't come from any single location. The voice, for lack of a better description, came from *all* locations. I was in the voice, right here in the recreation of my own apartment. I felt like a mere puff of breath within the voice.

"Amy where are you?"

AMY IS WITH YOU.

"Can I see Amy?"

AMY IS ALL AROUND YOU.

This line of questioning was getting me nowhere. Where was her soul? According to the rules (at least, as I'd come to understand them), it had to be around here somewhere. I checked the kitchen area—in the fridge, in the stove, in the limited cupboard space. Nowhere. I checked the bathroom. Not there, either. The only place left was my closet. But there was a sign tacked to the front of it:

WARNING! DO NOT ENTER.

Now that hadn't been in my real apartment. And I sure as heck didn't invent it for this reproduction. What was going on? The damned thing was sealed shut, too—some kind of gray caulk pasting up the crack between the door and its frame, and a dozen metal hinges locking it in place.

Not that this was a problem. Hell, if I could recreate an entire apartment, I sure as hell could whip up something as simple as a Brain chainsaw.

So, I did, and the crazy thing came alive in my hands, its sudden weight straining my arms. I thrust it into the closet door, and the chips started to fly. And as I did, the words on the door sign changed right before my eyes:

STOP! DO NOT CONTINUE.

"Oh yeah?" I shouted over the din of the saw. "Or what?" And I pushed the speeding blade deeper into the wood, cutting across toward the frame. Sparks popped as I hit a metal staple.

The sign changed again:

Interesting. "Well then," I shouted, "tell the Devil to pull out his best china, 'cause he's gonna have a guest!" I sawed back through the groove I'd already cut and finished the job on the opposite side of the door. The last staple sparked, and the door immediately folded up into itself and was sucked back into the darkness.

And that was what I found within my pseudo-apartment closet: utter and perfect darkness. *Miner's lamp*, I thought, and one appeared on my head. *Double-barrel shotgun*, I thought, too—just to be sure. Who knows what kind of heat Satan was packing?

This had to be a trip for the record books. From the bowl of a Philadelphia toilet to the bowels of Hell. Yee-haw.

I stepped into the closet. The air got thick fast. To take a step meant pushing my way through air as heavy as beach sand. I found that if I pushed hard enough to one side, the space would part easier for me, but only for a second or two before the pressure came crashing back.

After what seemed like hours, I came up against a barrier. I reached out and touched it—smooth, like wood. I knocked on it. Sounded like wood. Was this a coffin I'd wormed myself into? That would teach me a *Twilight Zone*-esque lesson, I supposed. *Dead Guy steps into a doorway to Hell and ends up in a coffin, finally, where he belongs. Justice is served. Cue Rod Serling's Monday morning wrap-up.*

But it wasn't a coffin lid. It was a door. I found what felt like a long brass handle and turned it.

Outside the door was a beautifully furnished bedroom.

Welcome to Hell, here are your robe and slippers, make yourself at home?

* * *

I had no idea where I was supposed to be. This certainly wasn't a bedroom I'd encountered before. It must be one of Amy Langtree's memories. I wondered if her consciousness extended this far. "Amy?" I called out. "Are you there?"

Amy popped her head through the door. "What? Did you call me?"

She'd startled me. I breathed heavily, then said: "Oh, God. There you are."

She came into the room, wearing nothing but a sheer white bra and low-cut panties. "Did you say, Amy?"

"Uh . . . yes?"

Amy frowned. "Brad, we've been married for almost a year now, and you still can't remember my name?"

Brad? I stole a glimpse of myself in a dresser mirror. Yep, I still had Brad Larsen's face plastered to my skull, even in the weird Brain world inside Amy's head. But how did Amy Langtree know Brad Larsen?

Then it hit me like a softball bat upside the head. Of course. "I'm sorry, Alison."

She walked up to me and put her arms around my chest, then gave me a squeeze. "You'd better remember, mister. So who's this Amy tramp? Some ex-girlfriend? A secretary at work?"

I faked a laugh and squeezed her in return. "Nothing like that. It was a fumble of the tongue." I kissed her on top of her head. Her hair was damp and smelled like peach shampoo.

Amy/Alison looked up at me. "You need help with your tongue?" She moved her mouth over mine and flicked her tongue across my teeth.

Not what I needed right now. Forget traveling from a toilet to the bowels of Hell—this was far weirder. Making out with a woman's repressed memory inside her own head? I politely and quickly kissed her back, then broke the embrace. "Wait, wait. I wanted to ask you something." I was lying, of course. "Do you know where my day planner is?"

Amy/Alison wrinkled her forehead. "You don't have a day planner. We write everything on the calendar on the desk."

"Right," I said. "That's what I meant. The desk calendar."

"Then why did you ask me where it was? It's been on the desk all year long."

"Of course," I said, and kissed her again, strongly tempted to linger. But I couldn't. There was too much to sort out. Already, the pieces were connecting in my mind. And those few connections were scaring the hell out of me. I needed time to think.

I headed for the bedroom door. "Be back in a second," I said, then walked through it. The layout of the house was completely unfamiliar. I wandered down a plush-carpeted hallway and opened the door, which turned out to be the bathroom. (I gave the toilet a nod, out of professional courtesy.) I doubled back and checked out a few more doors, but they were closets. Finally, I went downstairs and poked around the living room— hardwood floors, curio cabinets, real art on the walls—and then I saw the sign.

DO NOT ENTER UNDER PENALTY OF DEATH!

It was attached to a door. Another gateway to another Hell? If this house was Hell, I could only assume the door led to the Taj Mahal or something. I opened the door and stepped through. Suddenly, I was outside. And this outside was familiar. Dishearteningly familiar.

It was the Witness Protection house in Woody Creek—the one that was supposed to have been razed to the ground, as per Special Agent Nevins' orders. And no doubt, it had been. Only this one was the one from Amy/Alison's memories, locked away where she couldn't (or wouldn't dare) find them.

Alison Larsen's life was stowed away in the back compartments of Amy Langtree's mind. But where did that leave the real Amy? As a cover identity for the real soul, Alison, or a separate and distinct entity herself? And what was housing Amy/Alison—a Brain that could support a collection of souls, like my own Brain? (A Brain that, I remembered, had been hijacked a few hours ago by Brad Larsen.) Or was it an artificial repository?

My God—was Amy even real?

For once, I wished I had annoying Fieldman here to explain things to me. But, of course, he was probably the one who helped build all of this. He and Brad Larsen, in secret alliance to find the killers themselves, letting me poke around in the dark on my own. Brad Larsen was central to his mission; not me. I had been declared obsolete. All this time I assumed myself to be special, gifted, and it turned out I was just another schlump spinning his wheels day after day, thinking he was making a difference, but not doing a damn thing worthwhile to anyone. Utterly disposable. A man you could flush down a toilet without an ounce of pity. A nothing man. A dead man.

With nothing better to do, I looked around at the scenery. It was nice here. The grass, the trees, the sloping gravel walk up to the house. Maybe this is where I should stay—hole myself up in a literal ghost house forever. Let the real men handle the tough work. Sit and read and listen to the Beatles albums I remembered, and relax.

I went to the front door and walked inside. The interior was how I remembered it—minus the blood and cops milling about, mind you. Nice, respectable piece of property. There was a portable radio on a small card table. "The Air That I Breathe" was playing.

There was a knock at the door behind me.

I spun my head to look at it and, when I turned back to the room, I saw Brad Larsen, sitting at a desk, reading something out of a thick textbook. I was about to call out to him, but I turned my attention to the door and opened it, not thinking. Halfway open, it occurred to me this was probably a bad idea.

And it was. Ray Loogan's eyebrows lifted, and then there was an explosion that blew out my eardrums, and the next thing I knew, my throat had exploded. I inhaled. It was like drinking flaming oil. My mouth and lungs burned. I couldn't catch my breath. I heard a man screaming, furniture breaking. I could feel the ground shake beneath my head with every stomp and kick.

I heard glasses rattling, grunting noises.

After a while, I couldn't hear anything.

Then a gunshot.

Then nothing.

* * *

Of course, I knew what was happening to me. I was reliving Alison Larsen's death, which had been locked away deep within her mind. But why? If Brad was trying to bring back his dead wife through Amy, why keep the painful memories at all? And why was this taking so long?

I knew the answer to that one, too. The human soul doesn't always depart its body right away. If it has a reason to, it can hang around for a day, maybe even longer. And Alison had plenty of reason to hang around.

Thus, I hung around in Alison Larsen's rapidly cooling corpse. I watched a woman step over my body, but I couldn't make out a face. Then I watched the same woman drag the man who'd shot me out of the house. They were both careful to avoid my body. I listened to the radio for longer than I cared to, though I couldn't distinguish any of the songs, or the announcements, or advertisements. Every song, in fact, sounded like the Hollies' "The Air That I Breathe." The rest was meaningless garbage. I sensed the sun setting and darkness filling the corners of the house. Somewhere deep in my mind there was a sense of urgency, a need to escape this situation and return to my own life . . . whoever I was . . . and back on the case. Whatever that was. The dark hours rolled by. My soul hung on to the corpse, like a piece of wet tissue paper on a shoe.

Then, light again. A new morning, and warmth—slight warmth, not nearly the degree I was used to. Then, a child's face. At first, he looked shocked; then amused, the corners of his mouth curling up, eyes alive with mischief. He ran away. About a half-hour later, he returned with a few of his buddies. The Secret Dead Woman Club. They started by unbuttoning my blouse, already dried and sticky with blood. They stared at my breasts and touched my nipples with short, grubby fingers.

I don't wish to recount the details of their petty experiments and probings. This record is not meant to degrade the memory of Alison Larsen. Suffice to say, they left no taboo untried. I wish I could have protected Alison . . .

The thought reminded me: I was not Alison Larsen. I was trapped in her memories. I was . . . *who was I?* No names would come. I didn't remember who I was, or much of my purpose here. All I knew was that I was Not Alison.

Eventually, the tortures stopped—the children chased away by a postal worker. Presumably, he called the proper authorities, for not twenty minutes later my dead body was visited by Sheriff Daniel Alford. But even now, I felt myself slipping further away from my body, as if it had gone through its required mourning and was now ready to travel to the afterlife, wherever that may be. I saw more police arrive, dimly, and men in suits, and photographers and eventually a white sheet. I saw nothing, and patiently awaited whatever lay ahead. At least it would be an educational experience. Then something whipped the sheet away from my face.

And everything stopped.

Not that I was in Heaven or Hell—I mean the scene froze, with my body on a gurney being ferried by two EMTs, who looked like department-store mannequins. No tree branches moved, not a blade of grass. No wind. But no, *something* was moving. A man. He stepped through the static lawn toward me, smiling. I knew I recognized his face, but I couldn't place him immediately.

"I'm sorry I couldn't be here sooner," he said, "but there are rules about these kinds of things."

"Who are you?" I heard myself say. But I hadn't said anything.

"I'm a friend of your husband, Ms. Larsen. I'm here to take you away from all of this."

"Is he with you?!" I gasped, involuntarily.

"Yes, he is. And he'll be with you soon. But you need to speed someplace and rest for a while. You won't feel any pain anymore. No loss. Nothing but happiness and comfort. I promise."

"Take me to Brad," I said.

The man walked over to me and touched my cold forehead. Then he placed a weird-looking machine that looked like a crucifix over me, and I heard an electric snap and everything dissolved like Alka-Seltzer in a tumbler of water and—

* * *

"I am not going to live inside *that*," I said.

It was an indeterminate amount of time later. The man had guided me through entire worlds of darkness and blue lightning—kind of a speeded-up version of some of the freakier scenes in *2001: A Space Odyssey*—to a room that looked like a college laboratory. On the table rested a machine that vaguely resembled a human. If humans had long, wiry tentacles popping out of every available orifice.

The man shook his head. "You must. Otherwise, your soul is unprotected."

"Not that . . . *thing*."

"The simulacrum is not complete, Alison. Not without you inside it. Then it comes to life and becomes fully human. And I mean that. Human. Without a soul, a body is only meat. Without you, this machine is nothing but engineered tissue."

I started to cry, without meaning to.

The man placed his hand on the area of space that would have been my back. "It's the only way," he said, soothingly. "This is the way to your husband."

I sniffled, then agreed to it all.

* * *

The past was erased. I had a new life now. My name was Amy Langtree, and I was an art student who lived in a studio at 1530 Spruce Street and everything was great. I met a cute guy who lived a couple of floors below me, and I hoped he'd ask me out.

Wait—no I'm not. I'm Not Alison. I mean, I'm me. Del Farmer Me. Del Farmer, Soul Collector.

And with that realization, I found myself in my own apartment again. At least, in the Brain simulation of my apartment.

Goddamn, how long was I buried in that gruesome memory? A couple of days, at least. It all came flooding back to me at once—JP Bafoures, the murder investigation, the Susannah/Lana thing, the Brad/Fieldman/toilet thing . . .

Finally, the story was becoming clear. The being who had rescued Alison's soul and put her in the robot was Fieldman. I recognized him now. How did he pull it off? Beat me. I wasn't quite sure how he managed to rip my own consciousness from its body and throw it into a toilet, either. Fieldman always said he "existed out of linear time," and I suppose that loosely translates into: "I'm always going to be two steps ahead of you."

Alison's soul—her memories, her emotions, her quirks— were stored inside this body. This "simulacrum," as Fieldman had described it. She had always looked—and felt—so damn *real*. Weren't robots supposed to be made of cold metal and beeping or something? But she wasn't. Not as far as I could tell.

"You're home?" I heard a voice ask. Amy was standing behind me. Or at least, the visual representation of *her* soul was standing behind me. Actually, we were two souls, standing inside a mental replication of my apartment.

"Yes, I am. I have a favor to ask."

She walked over to the couch, looking for the cat. "Psss-wsss . . . Here, kitty." She turned her head back to me. "Sure. What is it?"

"Just hang out here, and wait for me to call. I have something to take care of."

"No problem. Where's the furball?"

Uh-oh. The furball's soul wasn't currently absorbed in this simulation.

"I'm sure he's just hiding," I said.

"Not many places to hide," Amy said.

"Be right back." I hoped she didn't start digging around too much. I walked out the door of the apartment. It worked just like the front doors in the Brain Hotel lobby.

It brought me back to Reality.

* * *

I opened our eyes. I had to move if I was ever going to get my physical body back. I felt inside her pocket for my apartment key and instead found a piece of paper. A note. From Del Farmer.

Amy—

I'm sorry about what happened. I want to make this work. I know we can. Please stop down later. I'll be home around 9:00. I've left this key for you to let yourself in. Make yourself at home. I left a present for you on my writing desk.

All my love,
Del

P.S. After you see the present, turn this page over.

"All my love?" Christ, I would never write something like that. I always signed correspondence with a "sincerely," or perhaps "best," if I knew the recipient well. Even with the infrequent love interests I'd had I would sign "yours." And that was pushing it.

I checked Amy's watch. 6:40 p.m. My God, it must be Friday already, I thought. I must have been a toilet for over . . . twenty hours? If so, this meant the infamous party—the Best of Philly, where Susannah would be all alone, needing Paul's protection—started in twenty minutes. And if my hunch was correct, it wouldn't be Paul showing up to take care of her. It would be Brad Larsen, showing up to really take care of her. And I had to stop him before he scotched my entire investigation.

I flipped the note over. On the back was nothing but an address:

473 Winding Way, Merion PA.

I didn't recognize the address—I wasn't even sure if it was close to the city. Merion? Could be a small hamlet outside of Pittsburgh. What was Amy/Alison supposed to do with it?

The answer was sitting across the room, on my desk, in the form of a present.

* * *

I walked over to the record player on my desk. It had a silver bow and a yellow note attached to it: *Play Me*. There was a forty-five record on the platter. The label had been ripped off. I lifted the arm and dropped the needle into the groove. A familiar guitar note wailed, and rhythm guitars kicked in.

I could feel the tears forming in my/Alison's eyes, and our body starting to tremble. She was remembering. Triggered by the Hollies' "The Air That I Breathe." The song she died to. The song that would blast open all the doors in her psyche. In a split second, I relived every torment. And so did Amy/Alison. After all, songs pinned down times and places like nothing else.

Bodily control was jerked away from me, and I was back in the Brain simulation of my apartment. (It was kind of like the two different viewpoints you get when you shut one eye, then the other. Subtle, but a shift nonetheless.) I felt us moving toward a mirror. Amy/Alison glared into it, hair in her face, cheeks wet. "Who am I?"

I formed a mental mike and spoke to her. *It's me, Del. I'm here to help you Am— Alison.*

"I remember," she said.

I know you do.

"I remember everything."

Yes, I understand.

"I want my husband back."

Okay, Alison. Let's go get him.

23

THE SPIRITS OF '76

Finding the party wasn't tough. The Philadelphia Museum of Art was one of the most obvious landmarks in the world. Somebody had decided to put it right at the end of a parkway that cut a diagonal across the ordinarily precise grid that was Center City. (Just to shake things up, one presumes.) And that night, in case you were confused, helpful folks in tuxedos were only too glad to point you in the right direction. A year later, a movie about a scrappy boxer from the slums would seal the museum's fate, and countless tourists would be compelled to run up this marble torture mountain.

The hardest part was walking in two-inch heels. It was the dressiest thing Amy/Alison had in her closet, and they made those damned museum steps an absolute horror. It was the goddamned Mount Everest of Culture. Do people love art this much? At the top of the forty-two million steps, another kid in a tux told us the entrance for the party was around back. I asked Alison if she was okay with taking over her body for a while—after all, she had more experience with these things. She agreed.

We walked around the huge piece of land, and up a sloped driveway to the back, which was littered with Cadillacs dropping people off. At the door, a pimply kid in a ruffled tux shirt three sizes too big asked us for our ticket. Alison started to stammer, so I offered to take over again. We were a spiritual tag team.

"We're on the list," I said.

"We?" he repeated.

Whoops.

"I mean, I'm on the list. With my guest."

The kid nodded and checked his list—a tattered mimeograph. Then he frowned and looked back at us. "Uh, what's your name?"

"Guest of Richard Gard."

It took him a full five minutes to find the Gs. "Right. Gard. He's already inside. With a guest."

"I'm his mistress," I said, and pushed my way past him.

"Wait!" he called after me. "You forgot your sticker!"

"Stick'er up your ass," I shouted back, which earned me strange looks from some well-dressed bystanders. I smiled coquettishly and kept walking. It was fun being a woman.

I walked down a hallway and into the main hall, the heart of the party. This wasn't your usual swanky affair. The room looked more like a carnival, with booths and tables set along the perimeter of the hall, stocked with beef and booze and desserts and whatever else the editors of the city magazine had deemed "the best." Smelled like a scam to me. Taste was a highly subjective thing. Frankly, this seemed like a lame excuse to stock a room full of advertisers and have them cater the thing for free. Including, no doubt, the mini Big Band wailing a jazzed-up version of "Turn the Beat Around" over in the corner of the museum.

I nabbed a cup of beer and a cracker full of some kind of seafood and started the search for my body.

* * *

Before long, I found it. Brad and our client were standing near a booth sponsored by Wyborowa Vodka, which was giving away free samples in tiny cups. It looked as if Brad had told a joke, because Susannah was laughing and brushing her brown hair back over her ears. Clearly, he hadn't told her yet. I doubt her reaction to "By the way, you're the bitch who knifed me" would be laughter. What was he waiting for?

I passed a silver punch bowl and caught my reflection, which answered my own question. Of course. He's waiting for me. The Alison me.

No, Brad wasn't expecting his bride-in-a-robot to show up here, now. He'd intended her to show up much later in the evening, around 9:30, say, at 473 Winding Way in Merion. For whatever reason.

It was time to liven this party up.

"Hi there, Pauly boy," I said. Because in this context, it was his name. Paul After. Protector of Innocents. Killer of Men. "Long time, no see. Who's the tramp?"

I watched Susannah's eyebrows lift in confusion, then suddenly plummet in contempt. "Paul . . .?" she asked.

The color drained from Brad/Paul's face. I could practically smell the smoke burning in his fevered brain. Was he trying to figure out how his dead wife showed up here, ahead of schedule? Or was he trying to calculate a way out of this without ruining his master plan?

Either way, it didn't matter. I used the opportunity to launch myself out of Amy/Alison's body, right into his eyes, and back into my own body.

* * *

To be honest, I wasn't sure I could do something like that. It'd always been the opposite: sucking somebody else in—absorption, not active possession. The thing seemed to work both ways, however. I saw the world in front of me enlarge, as if I were moving my head closer and closer to a photograph. Brad/Paul's eyes grew as immense as national monuments, and I dove right in.

It's hard to describe what happened next in physical terms. Kind of like tackling somebody to the ground, only using your head. In other words, it hurt like the dickens.

Next thing I knew, Brad/Paul and I were rolling around on the Brain Hotel lobby floor. I was back. Yes, praise the Lord, I was home. I lifted myself up to my knees. It was time to reassume command of this vessel, damn it.

Brad/Paul threw a fist into my gut.

Or, to be technical about it, he threw a fist into the part of my soul that equated with the human stomach. I buckled over for a moment, then tossed a fist back into the part of him equated with the human nose.

It snapped and spurted out the soul equivalent of blood.

I jumped to my feet. Brad/Paul was snarling like an angry dog. "Bastard! You don't know when you're finished, do you?"

"Nope," I said, then dove through the lobby doors.

I woke up in the real world.

* * *

Unfortunately, in the real world I was lying on a collapsed table, soaked in Stoli vodka. Susannah and Amy/Alison were both holding one of my hands, rubbing and tapping as if to snap me out of it.

A couple of confused-looking men in black tie—presumably, representatives of the Stoli company—stood behind them, no doubt checking the damage to their booth.

"I'm sorry," I said, struggling to my feet. Both women helped me up. "Very, very sorry. Susannah, will you pardon me for a moment?"

"What's happening, Paul?" she asked, touching my shoulder. "Are you okay?"

"Fine, fine. Just need a second to myself." I stumbled forward and took Amy/Alison's arm. "Follow me," I whispered. I felt like I was in some absurd sitcom double-date scenario. Torn between two lovers.

We walked to the back of the hall—the only clear space I could find. On the way, however, I took care of some urgent business. For the first time, I ejected a human soul out into an inanimate object in the real world.

I sent Brad Larsen's soul into the spinning corpse of a roasted pig mounted on a metal spit. I'm not sure what company had sponsored that.

* * *

"Alison, there are many things I need to tell you." I was trying like hell to sound like Brad. I figured this was no time to tell Alison her husband's soul was stuck inside a roasted pig.

"Brad, I'm confused. All I hear are voices . . ."

"Shhh. I know." I grabbed her and held her close to me.

"You gotta hang on for me. I have to go and do something, then I'll be right back to take you away from here."

"What do you have to do?"

I wasn't about to tell her the truth: I had to take my ex-client outside, kill her, then absorb her soul for later interrogation. Instead I told her, "Nothing important."

Alison looked like a cat trapped in a corner. "I don't know any of these people. What am I supposed to do?"

"Here." I reached around to the table behind her and snatched up a tiny portion of a cheesesteak, skewered on a plastic toothpick. "Have something to eat. There's plenty of free food here." I wondered: did robots eat? Then I remembered her attacking her burritos with gusto on our date at Casa Tequila. God, how long ago that seemed.

"Okay," she said, taking the sandwich and sinking her teeth into it. I was disturbed how different she seemed now—like a compliant child. I promised myself I would sort everything out for her when this was over. I owed her that.

* * *

I needed a moment to think about the best way to kill Susannah. This party was not the ideal place, but enough was enough. I had to do it *now*. Absorb her soul, get whatever info I could out of her, then head west. If I could pick up a beat on the ever-elusive Ray Loogan, great. I'd kill him, too. Either way, I was certainly going to force Brad Larsen to spill whatever beans he had left. The gig was over.

The best way to think straight, if you're a guy, is to take a piss. Following a few taped paper signs with black arrows, I stumbled into an ornate men's room with too many stalls to count. I walked along a long mirror above the row of sinks. I told myself the key was to keep it simple, basic. Maybe invite her outside for a breath of fresh air, then slit her throat? No, no, too much mess. Strangulation? Always an iffy proposition. Although I was steeped up to my eyeballs in death, I had amazingly little experience with murder. This, technically, would be my first.

I chose a urinal near the end. I stared into my own eyes reflected in the shiny steel piping. This wasn't murder, though. Susannah Winston—or Lana Lewalski, or Lulu Lakawana, or whatever the hell her real name was—would live on in the Brain Hotel. I could give her a better life than any adulterous lawyer could. Hell, if I could find Paul's soul, the two of them would make a happy couple.

My self-justifications were interrupted when the stall door opened behind me. Before I could stop the stream of piss, a hunk of metal was pressed to the back of my head.

"Hello, Paul."

"Uh, hello," I said. "Leah, isn't it?"

"Very funny. You and the slut are going to die tonight."

"I see."

"You had to fuck with your only lifeline, didn't you? With me, you had a chance. Ray wanted to kill you both from the word go."

"Oddly enough, Leah, I wish you'd listened to Ray."

That did it. Leah threw up an arm and smashed it into my face, pinning my head against the clammy tile wall. The pistol pressed into the back of my neck.

"Stop fucking around with me," she hissed.

I closed my eyes and sighed.

Big mistake.

* * *

Without warning, I found myself standing in the Brain Hotel lobby. Fieldman was standing there, holding his metal gizmo. "It is imperative you leave this situation to me, Collective."

"Sorry," I said. "No assholes allowed." I stormed off toward the lobby doors and walked through them. I walked smack into a brick wall. My brick wall.

"Do keep trying," Fieldman said. "Try until you crack your spectral head."

"What's going on?"

"You've lost control," Fieldman said. He was suddenly standing right behind me. "Stop fighting it."

To accent the "it," Fieldman shoved the gizmo deep into my spectral body. I felt a white heat wash over me. My Brain limbs turned to jelly, and I fell to the carpet, at which point the gizmo tunneled through my chest and locked into the carpet. I tried to sit up, but it hurt so bad I didn't try again. I could barely breathe—or at least, perform the soul equivalent of breathing—without spasms of pain.

Fieldman smiled at me, waved, then faded back into Reality. As usual, without going through the lobby doors.

But this time Fieldman did something new.

I watched, impaled to the lobby floor, as Fieldman resumed control of my body. Leah was looking down at my body on the bathroom floor, directly in front of the urinals. I must have collapsed when Fieldman yanked me back inside.

"Get up," she commanded, nudging Fieldman's/our chest with her gun. "C'mon, I didn't hit you that hard."

"My pleasure," Fieldman said. "Could you give me a hand?"

To my surprise, she did. She kept the gun trained on him the entire time, though.

Fieldman brushed the wrinkles out of his/our suit and adjusted the tie. "I understand you and Mr. Loogan wish to kill us? Excellent. In fact, I'll even supply you with the address where we'll be staying this evening. The only thing I ask is that you wait a couple of hours, which will give me time to call my insurance company and put a few things in order. Then I'm all yours. Please do stop over. Shoot me in the head. Shoot Ms. Winston in the head. Shoot everyone in the head, if you please."

"You," Leah said, "are still fucking with me?"

"No," Fieldman said, then whipped out his fist and smashed Leah in the jaw. She stumbled back. Fieldman punched her again, then smacked the gun out of her hand and used his forearm to bulldoze her back into the stall she'd originally popped out of. I watched as her head connected with porcelain. She was out.

"I gave that up long, long ago, Ms. Farrell."

Fieldman took a Magic Marker out of his/our suit pocket. He scratched out an address on a paper towel—the infamous 473 Winding Way—then balled it and gently tucked it down the front of Leah's dress.

He seemed to pause for a moment, then applied the marker to Leah's forehead. On it he wrote: BRING A DATE.

* * *

On the lobby screen, I watched Fieldman walk back out into the party, squeezing past hundreds of people shoveling food into their faces. No matter that they were all rich enough to sit at home and have a hundred Philly cheesesteaks delivered via limo without a second thought. The idea of hogging free food was too good to pass up.

Fieldman walked past the roasted pig, then paused. Nuts, I thought. He was collecting Brad again. True enough, within seconds, Brad appeared back in the lobby. He scowled at me, then started to laugh.

"You're lucky a large percentage of guests at the party don't eat swine."

"I should have dumped your soul in a keg of beer," I said.

"Don't go giving me any ideas, toilet-face." Brad walked over to the lobby doors, then paused to turn. "Let me send a friend of yours back to keep you company."

As Brad walked through the doors, Fieldman materialized next to my pinned spectral body. "That was exciting!"

He started to pace around me, looking at the gizmo lodged in my chest. "I had no idea of the machine's adaptability. Tell me—to what extent does your soul feel the paralysis?"

"I'll make you a deal. I'll tell you how much this goddamn thing hurts if you tell me what Brad is planning."

"This is quite amazing," Fieldman said, then touched the gizmo. "It was never intended to anchor a soul—only push it, like a cattle prod. Can you move your arms?"

I responded by flipping him the bird.

"That would be an affirmative." Fieldman stood up. He folded his arms and looked down at me with mock pity on his face. "You know, I could tell you more than what Brad is *planning* to do. I could tell you what Brad is *going* to do. I could tell you how you're going to die. I could tell you who will be elected president forty years from now. Which is really something, because there are still people who refuse to believe it."

"Because you exist out of linear time," I said.

"If our existence were a novel, I am able to flip ahead a few chapters."

"So," I said. "Did you see me dumping Brad's ass into the roast pig?"

Fieldman didn't have anything to say to that. *That would be in the negative*, I thought. "Okay, I give up. What is Brad *going* to do?"

"It doesn't matter, Collective. For you, this book is coming to a close."

"Then read me the last chapter."

"In less than twelve hours, you will undergo a profound and lasting change. You will question your immediate past and, by extension, your entire life. Everyone you know will be dead or speeding away from you. You'll be covered in blood. You'll be trapped in a dead body. Your investigation will be over."

"Couldn't you throw in a nuclear war or something, just for kicks?"

Fieldman laughed. "If you only knew."

I didn't like how this was going. The fact that I had a hunk of metal shoved where my astral perception of lungs should be didn't make me feel better, either. I decided to pick Fieldman's warped brain to see what angle he was working. After all, Buddha or not, he started out as an ordinary—well, almost ordinary—human being. There had to be something he *wanted*, enlightened or not.

"Where will *you* be in twelve hours?" I asked.

"Eating a luxurious breakfast with a breathtakingly beautiful woman, lounging over the morning paper. The meal will be soft-boiled eggs, with fresh croissants and six tiny jars of the freshest fruit preserves available. It will be the finest meal I've ever had. And then the new phase begins, and the woman and I will proceed to save the world. That's what this is all about, by the way."

Good Lord. Did I actually think I could reason with a person so obviously insane? There was nothing he wanted, except to take me to the nut-hatch with him. My only option was to pass the time listening to Fieldman ooze verbal diarrhea until Brad returned. What would I do then? No idea. But I figured my chances had to be better with Brad. He might be a homicidal maniac, hell-bent on avenging his dead wife, but he was still a reasonable human being.

Fieldman's attention had turned back to the reality on the lobby screen. "You might want to watch this, Collective," he said. "This is going to be wonderful."

The worst part: Fieldman was right.

* * *

Brad, in our body, had finally spied Susannah and walked over to her. She smiled and made a tiny wave. What was Brad planning to do? Cut her open right here in the middle of the party?

"I was wondering where you went," Susannah said. "What am I paying you for, anyway?" But Brad didn't say a word. He reached out and clamped his hands down on her hips.

"What are you doing?" she demanded.

Brad cleared his throat. "I want to dance with you."

"Right now? There's nobody else dancing."

"There will be. There'll be plenty of dancing."

As if on cue—and come to think of it, it probably was—the freebie Big Band started to play the opening bars of "The Air That I Breathe." Oh no, I thought. I searched the screen for a sign of Amy/Alison, but she was nowhere in sight. What the hell was Brad doing? Trying to drive his own wife nuts?

"This next one's a request," said the band leader through a crackling, tinny mike. "With love, to Ray and Lana, from Brad and Alison."

Oh boy.

Brad grabbed Susannah and pulled her into a bear hug. Her face practically bounced off the screen in the hotel lobby. She looked confused. Maybe she was trying to figure out why someone had spoken the names Ray and Lana out loud. Maybe she was wondering why her bodyguard was suddenly pawing at her.

"What are you doing, Paul?"

Brad didn't say a word. He forced her to rock back and forth in an awful parody of a slow dance.

"Paul, say something."

"I'm remembering this beautiful song."

"Yeah," she said, nervously. "It's nice. But it doesn't explain why you're touching me like this."

"Do you remember the last time you heard this?"

251

"Not really."

"I do, Susannah." Brad's hands slid up and locked onto her forearms. "Lana. Susannah. Whatever your fucking name is."

Susannah's eyes went wide.

"The last time I heard this song," Brad continued, "I was in Woody Creek, Illinois. It had started playing on the radio, and I turned around to watch my wife blown away with a shotgun."

"*Ohjesusgod,*" Susannah whispered, stark terror blossoming in her eyes.

"The last time I heard this song, I was beating the shit out of the guy who killed my wife, and I'd almost killed him when somebody stabbed me from behind."

Susannah's head started to shake.

"The last time I heard this inane fucking song, you took a stiletto and stabbed me in the back, and then stabbed me again in the chest, and in the arm, and in my ribs . . ." Brad shook her arms with every body part mentioned.

"No," she said. "No, no, no . . ."

"And now I'm going to repay the favor, Lana."

Brad released her arms. Susannah was no dummy. She spun and ran away, pushing through the crowd toward the front of the museum. Nearly everyone was staring at Brad, probably wondering what he'd done to drive that pretty young girl away. I'm glad I didn't have to explain it to them.

* * *

"Absolute genius," Fieldman said. "Better than he'd described it."

"What do you mean?" I asked. "She got away."

"Try to keep up, Collective. Brad can't kill the woman here. He never intended to. You arriving with his wife in tow may have confused things for a moment, but we've recovered splendidly. Things are back on schedule. We've been planning this for too long to have it go awry."

"How long, exactly?"

"Oh," Fieldman said. "A little over eight months."

"That isn't possible. You only died a month ago. Remember? Nevada? Flaming Datsun? Pan-Fried Fieldman?"

Fieldman sighed as if he were speaking to someone with severe mental impairment. And you know what? Maybe he was.

"Collective, once I returned to be with you, it was as if I had been with you all along."

The gods must have taken pity upon my poor soul and showered enlightenment down upon me, because in an instant I understood what Fieldman was talking about. Memories in my own head now seemed elastic, gelatin, pliable. What had gone on for those eight months? I had no idea. They were no longer my own months. They were my Fieldman months. They were supple as a dream and painful as reality.

"You and Brad were plotting this sicko revenge thing the whole time," I mumbled. "Right under my nose."

"Sometimes even using your nose. Along with the rest of your physical body. Remember the stomach flu you had back in February? Knocked you out? I did that. Gave us use of your body for weeks. You still believe it was a matter of coincidence the Brown Agency assigned you this case?"

"But . . . *why*?"

Fieldman saw that I was still confused. "Oh, Collective! To lay the trap! And it's working. She's walking right into it. No chance she'll go back to her hotel apartment—not after her bodyguard—who not only has the address but a set of keys—

just threatened to kill her. Nor does she have anyplace else to go
... except 473 Winding Way."

Something clicked. "Wait. That's ..."

"That, dear Collective, is the same address I scribbled on a
paper towel and stuffed between the breasts of Ms. Farrell. Do I
have to explain everything to you?"

"I think so."

Fieldman laughed. "Of course I have to explain it to you,
because you haven't been there yet, but you will be. 473
Winding Way is Susannah Winston's hideaway. Richard gave
her the keys in case of an emergency. That's where she'll run."

And that's where Amy/Alison was going to run. And now,
Leah Farrell. And undoubtedly, Ray Loogan. A Woody Creek
reunion. I was forced to agree with Fieldman. I had to admit it
was brilliant, from a vengeance-is-mine point of view.

"And this will save the world *how*, exactly?" I asked.

"It won't," Fieldman replied. "But it will save Alison. And
she's extremely important to our future."

* * *

Up on the screen Brad was trying to make his way through the
crowd. Along a few of the more popular tables, nobody was
budging. Standing in line for twenty minutes for a free Dixie
Cup full of booze had the Philadelphia socialites returning to
their baser instincts. They weren't letting anybody through.
Finally, after making his way around the long way, Brad found
Amy/Alison. She had been standing in a corner, eating Jell-O
from a cup with a plastic spoon. "Alison."

She looked up at him and smiled. "I want to go to bed,
Brad."

"I know, sweetie. There's something we've got to do first. Then we can leave."

"Back to our house? Back to California?"

"Right back home, sweetie."

I'd been in their home—or at least a memory of their home—not too many hours ago. A comfortable place. I'm sure Alison was desperate to go back there, maybe burn some incense, roll herself up in a thick quilt, and fall asleep for about ten years in a climate-controlled room. She'd never wanted to leave it in the first place, but Brad had insisted on the trip to Woody Creek, Illinois, to the "vacation cottage" by the river so he could finish his dissertation on John Donne. She'd gone along, not expecting to have someone knock at their door and her life to change in five abrupt seconds. Funny, the things you could intuit about someone after you've lived through their death.

Brad led Amy/Alison by the hand and headed back through the feeding frenzy. Along the way, he grabbed a couple of crackers and hunks of mozzarella cheese—Amy/Alison was still hungry. They made their way toward the museum's main entrance, which was closed to the public for tonight's party, but served as a shortcut to the Ben Franklin Parkway, where they could easily find a cab to take them to 473 Winding Way.

It was an ornate set-up; three marble staircases, one leading down to the front glass doors, and two twins leading to a second floor. Brad paused to take it all in. I supposed there was no hurry now—why not soak up a bit of culture with the wife? All the pieces were falling into place; Brad Larsen simply needed to catch a cab out to the suburbs, stash Amy/Alison somewhere safe, then watch the fun ensue.

"Hello, Paul," said a voice.

Much to our collective surprise, Susannah was standing on the staircase to the left. And aiming a pistol at us.

"No," Fieldman muttered.

Brad thought fast. "I was looking for you. I wanted to see if you were all right."

Amy/Alison touched his arm and shot him a look—you know, one of those *wife* looks.

"Stop it," Susannah said. "Just stop it. No more insults, no more games. One call to Richard and your life is over."

"This is none of Richard Gard's business."

Susannah paused, as if she were turning something over in her head. "I suppose you're right. This is between you and me, isn't it?"

"Right," Brad repeated. "You and me."

"And her." Susannah lifted the pistol slightly and pulled the trigger. The bullet caught Amy/Alison high in the chest—not quite her throat, though not exactly at her heart. The impact knocked her down to the marble floor.

Blind fury ripped through Brad. I could feel the Brain Hotel quake.

"This is not going to be good," Fieldman told me. Those were the first words to pass his lips that I ever completely believed.

Susannah lowered the pistol to her hip and laughed—a hollow, high-octave chirp. "It's better this way, Paul. I don't think she could have withstood the shock of hearing about how I sucked your dick the other night."

Brad launched forward, ready to rip the woman's flesh from her bones.

Susannah took careful aim and shot Brad in the head. As awful as it must have been, I'm sure this was nowhere near as painful—I would assume—as seeing your wife killed. Again.

The view on the lobby screen flipped back and around. With a start, I realized that I wasn't a detached observer. Shit—*I was shot in the head, too!*

* * *

"Take this thing out of my chest and let me up," I said in the most commanding voice I could muster.

"I can't do that, Collective," Fieldman said.

"If you don't let me up, we're all dead."

"We're *already* dead."

Up on the lobby screen, Susannah Winston's face came into fuzzy view. Amazingly, our eyes were still transmitting, but our ears weren't. She was saying something I couldn't make out. Probably something nasty. Not to have sympathy for the Devil, or anything, but I couldn't help but wonder what Susannah made of all of this. The poor woman was probably never going to trust another man for as long as she lived.

"You'll feel the fire, wench," Fieldman said to the lobby screen with an unusual intensity.

Susannah walked off-screen.

24

H-BOMB IN VEGAS

Within minutes the Brain Hotel lobby was reduced to chattering chaos. Souls started flooding into the room, throwing a million questions at me. Tucked away in their own apartments, absorbed in their own pursuits, I guess they all had felt the shot to our collective head. I tried to explain things to everyone, even with the metal gizmo still lodged in my chest, which nobody seemed to notice. "Listen, everybody," I said. "If we're all going to live, we're going to have to seize the body back from Brad."

"Not-gonna-happen," Fieldman said in a sing-songy voice.

"Where's Paul?" Doug asked. "He takes care of this sort of thing."

"Paul is dead," I explained.

"That was a goddamned hoax," a voice from the back cried out. "You've been listening to that Walrus song too much."

"Shut up, Tom," somebody else said.

"Tell me one thing, buddy-boy." It was Special Agent Kevin Kennedy. I hadn't spoken to him for eight months. He'd been lounging in his own retirement resort ever since I'd gotten him—or at least, his memory—in serious trouble with the Feds. Maybe his keen, analytical mind had noticed something important, something I'd overlooked.

"What's that?" I asked.

"How long before we all die and get out of this weird mental hell?"

I decided to go back to ignoring him.

Fieldman looked over the crowd of worried souls and lifted his arms like a priest giving a blessing. "Calm yourselves! Your struggle is almost over!"

"Shut up, asshole"—or a similar sentiment—was the collective reply. Making this Collective proud.

I checked the lobby screen. A crowd of magazine staffers and drunken lawyers and floozies from steno pools across Center City—basically, anybody with an excuse to be here—started pouring down the stairs. Among them was Leah, who took one look at our bleeding body, then kept walking, a tiny smile on her face.

It was a surreal moment. A crowd of souls in an artificially constructed hotel lobby within a single human brain, watching a crowd of the living—completely unaware they themselves were being watched—mediated by the body of a man with a massive head wound. I would have spent time pondering it, had my body not been fading away so fast.

Some of the *Philadelphia* magazine staffers—you could tell by the colored name stickers—started a debate on how to help the poor man who seemed to have been shot in the head. One in particular started to poke around authoritatively. "All right—move back, people. I know what I'm doing. Somebody call 911? Somebody call NOW, please!"

"Don't bother, pal," said Kennedy. "We're toast. We've bitten the bag and squirted wet shit."

The magazine guy started foraging around in our jacket, and finally managed to fish out a wallet. He started flipping through my forged IDs, and finally settled on one—my fake driver's license. "Let's see here. Okay. Who are ya?" the man said to himself. "Hmm. Del Winter. Says you're a power company employee."

A woman piped up: "God, Tim, shouldn't we move him or something?"

"You can't," said Tim. "You're likely to paralyze him. Now, we've got to keep the body still until the paramedics arrive. Speaking of, has somebody called 911 yet? I mean, for Pete's sake, our friend . . ." He looked at my ID again. ". . . our friend Del here is losing quarts by the second."

A bloody hand reached up and wrapped around the license. Tim's eyes widened. Brad was still alive, for the time being.

But perhaps he wasn't reaching for the license after all. I saw another face peek from behind the crowd of magazine staffers. It was Amy/Alison.

"She was shot," I said, mostly thinking out loud more than anything else. "How can she stand there like that?"

"You seem to forget: she's been reborn into a cyborg body," said Fieldman.

"A what?"

"Android, robot—whatever word you care to use. Surely, you know this. You arrived at the party inside her."

Indeed, I did know. Amy/Alison's lips trembled as she tried to move closer. Tim's bushy black hair obscured part of her face, but Amy/Alison's eyes remained transfixed. Her bright, blue eyes.

Oh God. Now I knew why Fieldman was acting smug.

"Brad, don't!" I shouted, even though I was nowhere near the lobby mike. "Don't do it!" Maybe my anguish would transmit through the pulpy brain and shattered skull into his consciousness. Either way, it wouldn't matter. Because Brad did it.

He jumped into Amy/Alison's body. He even looked right back down at us, and winked, with Amy/Alison's face.

I felt the conscious presence leave immediately. The house lights dimmed, as if there were a sudden power shortage somewhere else in the world, and electricity was being sucked away to be shared elsewhere. The lobby screen went blank.

"I'll be with you always," Fieldman said apropos of nothing, and vanished from our sight.

Leaving the rest of us inside our dying body.

* * *

Remember how I was complaining about being trapped in a toilet? A fate worse than death, right?

I was wrong. There is something worse.

* * *

The moment Fieldman vanished, the metal gizmo that had affixed me to the floor vanished, too. I was a free man. Wowee. A free man, trapped in a soon-to-be corpse.

Kevin Kennedy slapped me on my soul-shoulder. "I guess this brings the case to a close, doesn't it, buddy? I always knew somebody would get the better of you. Hell, this is the happiest day of my life. Or should I say death?"

"Nobody's dying," I said. "I mean, not permanently."

I couldn't have picked a worse time to say those words, for the Brain Hotel chose that moment to start to collapse. It started in the uppermost floors, where a few of the more solitary souls resided: a loud, thunderous rumbling, like God bowling in an empty dancehall. Then it became louder and louder, as if each floor were collapsing and falling down on the next, and so on. For all I knew, they were.

"Come, Father Death, come!" Kennedy was shouting.

But it wasn't Kennedy who got it first. A large chunk of ceiling exploded right above a group of souls gathered by the doorway—including Doug and Old Tom. Then, to rub salt into the wound, the floor beneath them erupted upward a second later. I could only assume that everything—plaster, bricks, souls—met halfway, violently. Hopefully, the stoner bastard never knew what hit him.

I bolted for the stairway. The booming from above pounded closer and closer. I quickly decided the stairs were not an ideal escape route. I spun, and the wall I was now facing shattered into a million pieces, flying debris cutting Kevin Kennedy into an equal number of individual pieces. I tucked myself into a ball on the lobby carpet, waiting for something to rip me apart, too. The only mystery was the direction.

I heard plenty of explosions, but nothing so much as a flying brick touched me.

After a minute or so, I dared to stand up and look. I was still standing on a patch of the lobby carpet, but the carpet was positioned in the middle of a vast field of green, reaching into the distance. No debris, no bodies. Then again, souls didn't have bodies, I supposed. Just astral perceptions of bodies. Every last astral perception, it seemed, had been blown to smithereens.

The Brain Hotel was gone. But what was this surrounding me? I'd never built any kind of landscape around the hotel. I was never a big fan of mowing lawns, Brain-conjured or not.

There was more, too—another hotel complex a mile away, across a green field—a superhotel, the Las Vegas variety. Behind it, the fields rolled outward into a blue infinity, occasionally interrupted by patches of gold lines and other, hotel-like structures. The more I stared, the more I could make out another piece of land, across the blue infinity. An island. Where the hell was I?

"I was wondering when you'd arrive," a voice said. I snapped my head around. It was Paul After.

"Brad told me you were dead," I said.

"I've been dead as long as you've known me."

Even *I* was getting tired of the dead cracks. "Do you know where we are?"

Paul puffed up his chest, and started to look around, as if he were a tour guide. "The best I can figure is that this is the place between death and whatever lies beyond it. I'm not even sure how long I've been here. Do you know?"

"Not too long. I think it's been about a day since Brad told me he offed you."

"Oh. Right." Paul's eyebrows furrowed. "Brad was pretty pissed. Of course, he had every reason to be."

"So, you *knew* you were one and the same?"

"No, no," Paul insisted. "I never lied to you. I didn't realize who I was until I was sent to this place. It gave me a sense of clarity I've never felt before. That's when I realized I was—*am*—nothing more than an invented personality. I was John Paul Bafoures, criminal mastermind, and Brad was the normal, upright, tax-paying citizen. It was brilliant. Most killers invent a cover, some ordinary boring life, to avoid detection; Brad Larsen actually lived it. I was the aberration."

"He made you up?"

"Yep," Paul said. "And I finally remembered what I did to piss him off."

"Spit in his Cheerios one morning?"

"Last July, Brad decided to turn himself into the Witness Protection Program—to protect Alison and start over, with a clean slate, I presume. Or maybe start up business someplace else. He decided to erase me, pretend I didn't exist. Naturally, this didn't make me happy. So I sent an order to have *him* killed."

"You what? But you *were* Brad."

"No, I was part of Brad. A distinct personality within his own. I wanted revenge. Don't forget—I was a ruthless, bloodthirsty killer. Brad made me that way."

"How did you pull it off?"

"One night, when Brad was sleeping, I took over his body, and made a quick phone call to Las Vegas. Asked an associate of ours to arrange a quick assassination. I suppose he picked this Ray Loogan guy—an absolute nobody."

"Then why was the paycheck half a million?" I asked.

"It was the price I'd set. After all, JP Bafoures was good for it. I wanted to wipe the slate as clean as possible."

When I thought about it, I realized how right Paul was. Nine months ago, I didn't know who this "JP Bafoures" was, either. I assumed it was a cover name for some higher-up in

The Association who'd decided to screw his buddies over. The tip I heard was simple gossip: Bafoures was having some guy in Illinois killed. I inferred that this Larsen must be damned important if The Association was going to send a killer across a couple of states and give him half a mil to boot. I happened to absorb a local Fed named Kevin Kennedy around the same time and the rest is recent history.

Only there was no Association. There was no JP Bafoures. There was no Paul After.

There was no point.

* * *

"So, what brought *you* to this lovely place?" Paul asked.

I took a deep breath. This was going to be the best story Paul After would ever hear in this life. And quite possibly the next one. "Right after your . . . uh, experience with our client, Brad and Fieldman confronted me in the hotel lobby. Said they didn't need me anymore. Told me they'd killed you and they were taking over the operation—and, zappo, the next thing I know, my soul is in a toilet. I hitch a ride on our cat, when suddenly Amy from upstairs shows up. I jump into her, only she's not her, she's a robot, and what's more, she contains the soul of Alison Larsen."

Paul whistled. If I were him, I would have whistled, too.

"Yeah. And then I live through her grisly death, bullet to the throat and post-mortem torture by eight-year-olds, then wake up and put on a goddamned cocktail dress and hightail it over to the art museum before Brad starts killing everybody. A body swap here, a body swap there, Brad takes over and the next thing I know, I'm lying on a cold slab of museum marble with my brains hanging out of my skull. The hotel flips out, the whole place goes up in nuclear hellfire, and I find myself here, talking to you."

"Wait a minute," Paul said. "You mean our physical body is dying?"

"If not already dead."

"Uh-oh."

"What? What do you mean by uh-oh?"

"It's only a theory," Paul said, "but I was beginning to surmise the only thing keeping me here, in this place between Death and the Next, was that your physical body was still alive."

"And what's Next?"

"I think we're about to find out."

* * *

As if on cue, the first mushroom cloud appeared over a tiny island in the deep, hazy distance. It looked unreal, like a cheap animation.

And then another. Closer this time, less cartoon-like. A hotel out in the distance exploded upon impact. Then another—each one more like an angry geyser of steam than an H-bomb, but burning everything nonetheless.

"Maybe they'll miss us."

"I don't think so," Paul said.

Another nuclear blast, even closer. I felt the air sizzle around us. This was how I'd always imagined a nuclear attack to be, way back when I was a grade-schooler and forced to tuck myself under my desk during an air-raid siren.

Naturally, I instinctually understood that all this carnage and destruction was merely my brain's representation of itself dying, shutting down. The same creative powers I'd harnessed to build the Brain Hotel were now turned against me, showing me my own personal apocalypse with the very things that had always terrified me the most. This knowledge did not help me from being scared out of my mind.

Paul said, "In case I don't see you again, it was nice working with you."

"Me, too," I said.

Finally, as I'd feared, the hotel complex directly across the way imploded and funneled up high into the sky, like white foam from a faucet shooting in the wrong direction. *That was too close*, I thought. And the air became alive with electricity and burning, and everything burned out like a photographic negative . . .

* * *

That was what it was like for me to die from a bullet to the head.

25

SOUL GUN

I woke up sometime later. The sun hadn't come up yet, but I could feel myself in bed. I had the blankets pulled up all the way over my head. I was freezing. Who cranked the air-conditioning in this room? And the bed felt like a sheet of cold steel.

Which, of course, it was.

I was lying on a slab in the morgue.

All I had witnessed countless times in the past had, at last, come to pass for me: I was dead. And my discorporated soul was hanging around the flesh, as if it had nothing better to do. I tried calling out to Paul, but I heard no response. Was he in the Next Place already? I hoped so. Even cold-blooded killers needed a rest.

So, this was death. Visited many times, never wanted to live there. When I'd died the first time, and Robert had absorbed my soul, I had only been hanging around my body for an hour or so. My flesh was still relatively warm, and rigor mortis was a long ways down the road. Now, however, I could feel my physical body turn traitor. It longed to crawl in some cool earth and break down, chemically, into nutrients to feed future plant life. I wanted to carry on thinking and being and knowing and learning. We were at cross purposes. But I wasn't going to give up without a fight.

I just prayed I would still be able to do a resurrection.

Granted, I'd never tried it on myself. Performing one took a lot out of me when I was alive—God only knows what it would do now I was dead. Truly, completely, utterly dead, I mean.

* * *

Many souls have asked me what it's like to perform a resurrection. I don't know if they're curious about the process or if they're trying to glom some information for their own purposes.

Nevertheless, my answer is always the same: I honestly don't know. Bringing a soul back from the dead is an art that was passed down to me from Robert, and I suppose he'd learned it from the man who'd done the same for him. Maybe it went back centuries—dare I say back to the time of Christ, when he worked his mojo on poor old Lazarus? Was someone around then to learn the trick? And were they able to describe it?

If pressed to explain it, I guess I would say it's like struggling to remember something. You don't quite know what you're doing when you're "racking your brain," but clearly, some kind of mechanical process is in effect. Then, all of sudden, the memory pops back. Or it doesn't.

That's the same deal with resurrection.

I lay there and tried to remember how to raise somebody— namely, myself—from the dead. I ran through every possible train of thought: my own death and rebirth; the first time I brought somebody else back, seeing Brad Larsen dead in the muddy waters of Woody Creek . . .

And then, it worked. I immediately forgot exactly how it worked, but it did.

I started to come back to life.

* * *

After a while, I sat up, and the sheet dropped from my face. Boy, did I feel like a lump of shit. This was a hundred times worse than the worst hangover or flu I'd ever known, easy. My physical body was not happy with me one bit. My physical body wanted to check in at Hotel Deep Six as soon as possible.

I threw one leg over the table, then the other, then slid my ass off, landed on my feet, and managed to stay there for a second. Then my entire naked form collapsed and smacked into the cold tile floor. Fortunately, my body was too involved in its own internal suffering to acknowledge the blow.

Eventually, I got to my feet and surveyed my surroundings. Definitely a morgue. I needed to find the ME's office, and hope he kept a spare pair of pants around, or at the very least, hospital scrubs. Maybe they even had my own clothes around here somewhere, sealed up in a plastic baggie. I opened up a couple of drawers but didn't find a thing. Just a lot of doctor toys—cotton balls, bottles of rubbing alcohol, tongue depressors, scalpels.

The ME's office was down the hall. Predictably, the door was locked.

Across the room was a fire extinguisher and a fireman's axe, sealed in a box with a glass door. I thought about smashing it with my fist, but then I'd have yet another cut to heal, and I wasn't sure my newly resurrected form could keep up with me. I grabbed a sheet from a nearby stiff, wrapped it around my elbow, then shattered the sucker with a quick jab. I took the axe back to the ME's office and chopped at the handle.

"What the hell are you doing?"

I turned around. A young woman in blue scrubs was staring at me. I had to think fast. A reasonable explanation for a naked, supposedly dead man trying to break into an office? Yeah, sure. Then it came to me.

I lifted up the axe and started to lurch toward her, zombie-style.

My gambit paid off. The woman, who surely must have seen George Romero's *Night of the Living Dead* at some drive-in, took off screaming down the hall. It gave me enough time to finish my work on the door handle and force my way in. Bingo. Found my bloodied suit wrapped up in plastic with DEL WINTER, 6/76—ah, my brilliant alias—written in marker on the front.

I got dressed, washed up as best I could, then set off to look for an elevator.

* * *

This was a nice hospital, which was a relief. I wasn't stuck in a city morgue—apparently, somebody had tried to fight to save my life. I felt a bit of gratitude. Had I the time, I would have hunted down that surgeon and bought him a drink to thank him for the effort. Maybe even to tell him, "Hey—it worked!"

Finally, I located a set of stairs, which led up a level to an elevator. I was apparently still a floor or two underground. I pressed the button with the up arrow and waited. After a few short moments, the doors opened. There were four other people in the elevator. I stepped into the car, and everyone collectively gasped and inched themselves backward. Of course they would—after all, I was a walking corpse in a bloody tuxedo, carrying an axe. I felt the need to explain things.

"Head wounds," I said. "They bleed like anything. One tiny cut on the top of your head? Boom—all of a sudden, it starts gushing like the geyser at Yellowstone Park."

Nobody said a word. They stared at everything else in the car—the lit numbers, the walls, the reflective security mirror, the translucent buttons—everything but me.

"Nobody worry—I'm going to be fine," I said. I put the axe down and rested it against the wall, a sign of good faith.

One woman broke the holding pattern. She stared at me, looking as if she were going to burst.

"What?" I asked her.

"But your head, sir . . . your head . . ."

"It looks bad, I know. But I'm fine, honest."

The woman swallowed. "Sir . . . *your head is still bleeding.*"

Now that I looked at my own shadow on the elevator wall, I could see she was right. Tiny jets of liquid were still shooting out from the top of my head. Must be an aftershock of the resurrection, I thought. Or the simple fact that I was ambulatory again, moving limbs, breathing air, pumping blood once more.

I eyed the woman up and down, then reached out and ripped her blue scarf right from around her neck. "Thanks," I told her, wrapping it around my head.

Then I pushed the **CLOSE DOOR** button.

The woman fainted dead away. I felt bad about that.

* * *

I left the hospital and got my bearings. The sign out front read **JEFFERSON UNIVERSITY HOSPITAL**, and the sign plate on the corner of a nearby building read CHESTNUT STREET. Thankfully, I knew where I was. I'd passed here a couple of days ago—rather, Paul had passed here a couple of days ago, with Susannah, on a shopping excursion.

But unless I could find a mode of transportation, I had a long walk to 473 Winding Way ahead of me. And I doubted this body was going to make it that far. I'd be lucky if I could drag this slightly warmed-over corpse back to the art museum.

I started down Chestnut Street, in a direction I thought would take me closer to City Hall. I walked close to the parked cars, scanning for unlocked doors. No luck. I crossed Tenth Street and the same—zilch. This was ridiculous. I could hail a cab, but I didn't know what I'd pay the driver with. Under ordinary circumstances, I could have walked back to my apartment from here to pick up some cash, but this would assume I had cash to be picked up, which I of course didn't. (Damn Gard, that check-bouncing prick!) All I had to my name was a bloody tuxedo and a fire axe.

It would have to do.

I picked an older model car, thinking they'd be easier to work with. A 1968 Chevrolet something or other. I removed my jacket, wrapped it around the handle, and hammered the thing into the passenger window. It merely bumped the glass and slid off. I almost lost my balance and got dizzy. A couple of my leg muscles were starting to freeze up. Rigor mortis? Quite possibly.

I tried again, with more force. Same thing. Now people on the street were starting to notice and point at me. To hell with it. I grabbed the axe with both hands and swung the business end into the window. It hurt my back like hell, but the window shattered spectacularly.

I lifted the lock, brushed glass off the seat, and slid in behind the wheel. Of course, I had no idea what I was going to do next. I'd always counted on Doug to perform these petty criminal acts. And, right now, Doug's soul was probably busy haunting the entrance to the Philadelphia Museum of Art. I doubt he'd help now even if he could. I'd let them all down.

My bout of self-pity was cut short by a tapping on the glass.

It was a cop with a flashlight, his cruiser (and partner) right behind. He twirled his finger around. "Open up."

I looked up at him and smiled. I'd been down this road before.

He returned the smile.

And then I jumped into his body.

* * *

The cop was a tough bastard—he fought the possession every step of the way. But I was thrilled to discover I still had the magic, damnit. Resurrections, soul jumps, you name it. The kid was back.

I put the fuzz in his place and assumed control. When I opened my eyes, I found myself looking at my old body slumped over in the seat. I opened the door and turned my own face around with a gloved finger. I wasn't looking too good. It was probably for the best that I'd changed bodies.

Still, I wasn't anxious to leave it. Sure, the face had changed a couple of times, and I was starting to grow a spare tire, but until tonight it had been a perfectly useful body. "What is it?" a voice said.

Ah. My new partner.

I turned around to face him and said, "It's nothing now. The guy's dead."

"You're kidding," he said, opening the door. His name tag read SLATKOWSKI.

"See for yourself."

Slatkowski did. He shuddered. "God. This guy is ripe. You sure you saw him moving in here?"

"Yeah," I said. "I think."

"Man. Probably some hop-head, trying to make one last boost."

In a bloodied tux? With an axe? And with those boyish good looks? Yeah, that sure fitted the drug-addict profile. But I let it pass as an easy way out to 473 Winding Way came to mind.

"Hey," I said, snapping my fingers. "I recognize this guy. He was the one involved in the art museum shooting tonight."

Slatkowski frowned. "How the hell do you know that? You've been with me all night, and I sure as shit don't—"

I interrupted him before he got carried away with the logic. "There's no time," I said. "We've got to get over there right away." I ran around to the driver's seat and hopped in, then hammered the gas pedal before my new partner had a chance to join me. I heard him scream for a full five seconds, then I turned a corner.

I must have set a land-speed record on the drive back to the art museum. I tried to estimate how much time I had before Slatkowski called for backup. Not much—probably the amount of time it would take for him to find a public phone. Most cops kept a taped roll of dimes handy in case of emergency. I had a couple of minutes. Maybe. That's why I felt it necessary to drive the police cruiser over the sidewalk and up the fourteen million steps to the front door. My front fender even snapped one of those POLICE LINE—DO NOT CROSS banners clean in half. Gratuitous? Maybe to somebody else. I refused to walk up those goddamn steps twice in one night.

There were still a few forensics boys on the scene. They looked panicked. In all fairness, I would, too, if I saw a blue-and-white fly up a forty-five-degree marble-stepped incline and screech to a halt.

I gave them all a nod and walked right past. One of them made a wisecrack about free parking, but one of his buddies gave him an elbow and a "Shhh!" Good.

"Watch my wheels," I said.

* * *

I swept around the entirety of the grand entrance, and one by one re-collected every one of my Brain Hotel residents. The forensics team must have thought I'd gone daft, but who did I have to impress? Hell, I wasn't even in my own body anymore.

I found Doug hiding in a thick medieval rug. I could feel him when I stepped on it and he yelled. Imagine an eternity of grubby tourists stepping on your soul? A touch to a Grecian urn revealed my good friend Kevin Kennedy. *Sorry*, I told him.

No death today. Old Tom was lounged out in a wall tapestry. Just like Old Tom to be hangin' around. Genevieve. Harlan. Fredric. Lynda, George, Mort. They were all happy to see me.

The only soul I couldn't find was Paul Bafoures/After. I suppose he had moved into whatever dimension lay beyond this one. The one Robert escaped to five years ago. I envied Paul. For one, he was enjoying a retirement I longed for someday. Secondly, he wouldn't have to be here on Earth, headed to Merion, to deal with the shit I was going to have to deal with.

"All right, boys," I announced over the Brain Hotel courtesy telephone. I didn't have time to reconstruct the entire Brain Hotel, but I did slap a decent replica of the lobby, and this time included an open bar. Old Tom manned the taps.

"We're going on a field trip."

26

GALLANTLY SCREAMING

Twenty-five minutes later, we finally arrived at 473 Winding Way, in Lower Merion Township. It wasn't easy. As it turned out, not a single one of my souls knew Philadelphia and its suburbs well enough to give directions. Someone—I think it was Kevin Kennedy—briefly mentioned the idea of killing and absorbing a cab driver, but that seemed gratuitous.

Then it struck me: I was currently housing a soul who was intimately familiar with the area. The cop.

His name was Bill Madia, and he was a tough nut to crack. I tried reasoning with him, explaining the situation. Nothing. I promised him favors, offered to buy him a dozen Boston Crèmes at Dunkin' Donuts. No go. In fact, he wouldn't say a single word until I demonstrated the horrors of having your soul trapped in an inanimate object. (In his case, the steering wheel.) And even then, it was just to spit out the words, "Screw you, punk."

Finally, Old Tom came to my rescue. He seemed to recall something about Lynda, the Brain hooker who had given me the Ray Loogan info in the first place. She had grown up in the Philly suburbs before running away and into a life of ill repute.

Lynda stepped forward in the lobby, looking all bashful. "Yeah, I know the way to Merion."

"God bless you," I told her.

"Can I drive?"

About three or four of the souls shouted "No!!!" simultaneously. I guess they'd already seen her drive, in a manner of speaking.

So, it was up to me. Of course, I'd wrecked the suspension on the police cruiser when I assaulted Mount Art Museum, but no matter. I didn't plan to take that car anyway—too easy for Slatkowski to find. I made one of the forensic geeks offer up his car keys. "Keep my spot open," I'd told him.

I drove while Lynda directed.

* * *

The house on Winding Way was meant to be unlike every other house on the block, but that was the problem: they were all different in the same exact way. All colonial-looking mini-mansions. Palatial, but oh-so tasteful. It didn't seem like Susannah Winston's style. Or Lana Lewalski's, for that matter.

I approached the front yard of 473. The mailbox read J. GARD in metal-embossed letters. A relative of Richard's—most

279

likely his parents. I opened the box and saw it was stuffed with letters and bills: Philadelphia Gas and Electric. American Express. Something thick from the Republicans for Ford/Dole '76. It was all addressed to Mr. and Mrs. Jasper Gard. Yep, parents for sure.

A scenario painted itself in my mind: middle of June, parents away at a summer cottage, most likely the South Jersey Shore. They give trustworthy lawyer son keys to the pad to check up on it every once in a while. Lawyer son gives a copy of the keys to his mistress, for out-of-town rendezvous. Mistress treats it as her retreat from reality.

But how did Brad and Fieldman know all this? Hey, I never claimed to be the world's greatest detective. I suppose it had something to do with Fieldman being "out of linear time." The enlightenment I had enjoyed earlier, while speaking to Fieldman, had long faded away. Maybe that's because I'd died again. Did Christ rise on the third day feeling dumber than ever? I'd almost bet on it.

I crept up to the front door, which I saw was ajar. I could hear voices from deep within the house. "Do it. Come on, do it." I couldn't place the voice, though. I withdrew Officer Madia's pistol from his holster and stepped inside.

* * *

Not surprisingly, the first thing I found was a dead body. It was Leah Farrell, chest soaked with blood. Her own, I assumed. The words BRING A DATE were still on her forehead, but faded a bit, as if she'd tried to scrub them away. I crept down to feel what was left of her neck for a pulse, but found none. Instead, I found a close-range bullet wound to the throat. Just like Alison Larsen's. So far, quite an amazing reproduction, I had to admit.

I walked down a narrow hallway, next to a staircase, which led back to what I took to be the living room. Living was a strange word to be associated with what I saw going on in there.

A man was affixed to an antique sofa with what looked like barbecue skewers and coarse rope—the ever-mysterious Ray Loogan. He wasn't a terribly tough-looking guy, to be honest. I guess I'd built him up in my mind to be so much more that seeing him now disappointed me. Then again, *anybody* tied to a couch and poked with sharp pieces of metal will look kind of pathetic. Next to him was Susannah, who was bound in a similar manner, only without the skewers. In front of them stood Amy Langtree/Alison Larsen, holding a pistol. She heard me and spun around. I could still see the bullet hole through the top of her evening dress.

"Hi, Alison," I said. "I see you have a few guests over for the evening."

"Thank God!" Susannah cried, giving me her most alluring-yet-pitying look.

"Shut up," I said. "I'm not here to save you. In fact, I've got half a mind to finish the job myself." I turned my attention back to Amy/Alison. "Care to step outside?"

The corners of Amy/Alison's robot mouth curled up. But it wasn't her soul talking. "It's *you*, isn't it?" she asked. "God, you're a resilient bastard when you want to be."

"One of my more charming qualities."

"Agent Fieldman, do you want to take care of this?" she asked.

"Officer, please!" Susannah cried. "Help us?"

Amy/Alison was still talking to herself. "Oh . . . Of course. You're right."

My vision went black.

* * *

When I could see again, the first thing my eyes focused on was a balled fist. It collided with my face.

My head snapped to the right. I regained focus for a second, and realized I was back in the rebuilt Brain Hotel lobby inside my own head. I saw a bunch of the souls, gawking at me. Goddamnit, how did Brad keep doing this to me? When I looked back up, I found my answer. Brad had Fieldman's soul-gizmo.

Being no dummy, I went for it. But Brad was no dummy, either. He swiped it away at the last second, then used his free hand to sock me in the face again. All I saw was a yellow flash. By the time I tuned my eyes back in, Brad was gone.

Doug came to my side. "You okay, chief? Brad wailed on your face pretty hard."

"I'm fine," I said, standing. "Just fine. And thanks, all of you." I was raising my voice. "Thanks a whole friggin' lot."

Everybody in the room, of course, started hemming and hawing.

"It was too damn fast, boss."

"He had that soul-zapper thing."

"Hey, I'm only here for the drinks."

Abruptly, somebody changed his tune. "Wait! Look!"

We all looked at the lobby screen. Brad was in control, and had our body looking in a mirror, which was situated in the hallway next to the stairs. It was Officer Bill Madia's face, of course, looking back. "That's me," said a voice from the back of the room. "What in hell am I doing up there?"

Up on the screen, Brad/Officer Madia turned his head. Amy/Alison was standing in the hallway with him.

"So how do I do this?" Brad/Officer Madia asked.

"The transducer modifiers need an image to work from," said Amy/Alison. "Close your eyes, and picture yourself in your mind to the closest detail possible. Then click the OK icon in your peripheral vision and the muscles will start to work on themselves."

That didn't sound like Alison at all. Jesus—that sounded just like Buddha Fieldman. After a couple of weeks in electronics school.

On screen, Brad/Officer Madia turned back to the mirror. Then, blackness. Slowly, a dim image of Brad's real face started to appear, like a photographic negative burning itself into vivid color. Skin stretched and settled into new forms; the skull itself seemed to grow and shrink in different places.

Of course, he was pulling the old change-your-face trick. A trick I was intimately familiar with. But Brad didn't seem to have as much trouble with the process as I did. He didn't even flinch.

Brad closed his eyes, and our viewing screen in the Brain Hotel lobby went blank. When he opened his eyes again, Brad was looking at his own, real face in the mirror. "At last," he said, beaming, "they'll see the face of vengeance!"

"And the wife of vengeance," said Amy/Alison/Fieldman's robot body, off-screen.

There was a despairing cry from the back of the lobby: "Holy shit! What happened to my face?!" Officer Bill Madia. Poor guy. This was a lot to see in one night.

"Hope you had a picture somewhere," I told him.

Brad started down the hallway, taking Amy/Alison/Fieldman by the hand. After a few steps, she stopped. "Wait—

we should do something about our mental luggage," she said. "We don't want any further interference at this stage, do we?"

Brad looked around the house, then spied Leah's dead body. "In there, for now?"

"Capital idea."

Amy/Alison/Fieldman took Brad by the shoulders and stared straight into his eyes, as if she could see right through the screen, down into the Brain Hotel lobby.

"Sorry to do this to you again, Collective."

Before I had a chance to hurl a retort at the screen, we were all gone.

* * *

By now, this kind of thing was becoming familiar to me: the cold, the rigor mortis, fighting the strong tides of the decomposition process. But the rest of the souls were scared to death. All they saw was their new haven start to rot before their eyes. Amazing how closely linked physicality is with human creativity. With all this mind power in the room, we should have had no problem maintaining a clean, safe environment in which to live for any period of time. After all, I was living (sort of) proof that a human soul can exist in whatever physical form it inhabits. In other words, if a guy can survive in a toilet, he can certainly survive in a dead woman's body. Maybe not as dead as I'd thought.

Standing before me was a confused Leah Farrell. I hadn't had to absorb her soul; she was still here, in her own mind. Which meant there must be some brain activity left in her body. "Don't tell me this is the afterlife," Leah said, frowning. "A bunch of hungry-eyed chumps, sitting around a fleabag hotel?"

"Leah," I said. "Relax. I can explain. But I need you to help me first."

"Who are you? Do I know you?"

"We've had a few drinks together," I said. "Don't you remember?"

"Look, buddy. I have a lot of drinks with a lot of guys. You can stop the happy talk and tell me how to get the hell out of this place."

I touched her shoulder. "First, tell me how you got here."

She slapped my hand away. "Don't fucking touch me."

"Tell me the last thing you remember."

It took quite a bit of coaxing (and even more sarcastic banter), but Leah finally told me enough to help me piece together what had happened before I arrived at the house. Right after Susannah had flipped and shot us at the art museum, Leah hauled ass to retrieve Ray. (They'd both rented a cheap room in Fairmount oddly enough, not one mile from where Susannah had set up camp. Philly can be a small city that way.) She showed Ray the address Paul had stuffed down her shirt and they decided to check it out. They hopped in a cab and high-tailed it over to Merion, then split up: Ray took the back entrance, Leah the front. Leah picked wrong. She opened the door and got a bullet in her throat for her trouble. The last thing she heard was glass shattering somewhere in the house. Then she ended up here.

"Your turn," she said. "Start explaining."

"I'm going to borrow your body for a moment."

"What?"

"I'll be right back." I created a pair of doors with my mind and walked through them. My eyes—actually, Leah's eyes—fluttered open back in Reality.

All I can say is, thank the sweet Lord the bullet had severed Leah's vocal cords, because I would have screamed to Heaven and awoken all the angels. This body *hurt*. I could barely suck down air, let alone stand up. But I was determined to go back to the living room. I threw out a hand, experimentally, and let it drop onto the rug. My newly borrowed fingers gathered up every fiber I could, then used it to turn the body over.

Then I started to crawl, hand over hand, down the length of the hallway. The rug created an almost insurmountable degree of friction; it was slow going. I could only imagine the electric shock I was building up. One touch from this body oughta kill the entire room. Halfway there I paused to cough. I was surprised to see blood jet from my mouth. No time to pause for lost fluids. I kept crawling toward the living room.

* * *

Finally, I reached an acceptable vantage point. I guess I'd missed a lot of pre-revenge chit-chat, because not much had changed in the living room. Ray was still skewered and tied to the couch. Susannah was still next to him, but now untied. Brad held a gun to her head. Amy/Alison was standing with her back to me. I wondered if the real Alison was in control again, or if Fieldman was still running the robot?

She removed a wrapped present from her purse, then tossed it to Susannah. "I believe this belongs to you, Ms. Winston."

Well *that* answered my question.

Susannah, to her credit, caught it mid-air. Most people aren't terribly agile with guns to their heads. She hesitated, then ripped the paper off. A stiletto.

I'm guessing it was the same one she'd used on Brad—although I can't fathom how they could have fished it out of the creek without me knowing. Maybe it was just the same make and model? I couldn't help but be impressed. Brad had this planned down to the last sticking detail.

"Now use it," Brad said.

"What?" Susannah asked.

Brad raised his pistol and pulled back the hammer. "You heard me. Use the knife on your boyfriend. I'm thinking fourteen or fifteen stabs ought to do the trick. That is, if you pick non-vital parts first."

"You're insane," she said.

"C'mon, Lana—I fished it out of the creek for you and everything!"

Ray Loogan, for his part, didn't look like he was enjoying this part of the discussion. He started to panic and tried to crawl up the back of the couch, even if it meant pulling skewers through his skin. I almost felt bad for him. I couldn't help it. All this time I'd thought of him as this suave, genius killer who managed to elude me for the better part of a year. But now, all I saw was a kid who'd been overly trusting of the women in his life, and now he was scared out of his mind. He was going to *die*.

"Do it," Brad said. He thrust the gun in her face.

"Sorry, Ray."

Ray started to cry. Susannah lifted the stiletto into the air and paused, as if trying to delay the inevitable. Then she struck down—hard. The blade slid into one of Ray's thighs. He howled. Susannah jerked it out, aimed, and plunged it again, inches higher. And again. Each stroke was more frenzied than the last. I couldn't see everything because Amy/Alison partially blocked my view. But it was enough. And I could hear everything—every grunt, cry, and thud.

Soon enough, Ray stopped crying. Susannah was covered in droplets of her ex-boyfriend's blood. She had the strangest expression on her face—part rage, part fear, part confusion.

"Good show, Susannah," Brad said. "Wouldn't you say, sweetheart?"

Amy/Alison didn't say anything. She took a step back. Her heel dug into my outstretched hand. I shrieked, but it came out as a series of gurgles.

By way of pure reflex, Brad spun around and shot me in the shoulder.

"Owww shit," I said, and rolled over. To be perfectly honest, my hand hurt a lot more than the bullet wound. I managed to spit out the words, "*It's Del.*" As if it would matter to Brad.

"Christ," he said. "Don't you know when to play dead?"

I would have shot a pithy remark back at him, but I was too busy trying to line my eyes up with Ray Loogan's. He was a dead man, of course. But luckily for me, he'd chosen to expire with his eyelids rolled up in his head.

"Looks like I'll have to teach you." Brad took careful aim at my head and squeezed the trigger.

Or should I say, took careful aim at my ex-head. Because as the bullet was flying through the air, my soul was flinging across the space of the room, right into Ray's body. I was getting better and better at this. I jerked up my head in time to see Leah Farrell's head do a JFK.

And I'll be damned if Ray's body didn't hurt a hundred times worse than Leah's abused corpse. I didn't know where to register pain first. I turned my new head to the left, experimentally and saw Susannah staring at me in mute horror.

"Hi, sweetie," I said.

That broke her stunned silence. She screamed and slid down to the floor, and started to crawl backward until she bumped into Amy/Alison. Brad, once again, spun around to face me. "You . . . !"

I realized I had to do some fast talking. I was running out of bodies. And at the rate at which Brad was blowing their heads off . . .

"Hold it, tough guy," I said. "I have something important to say. To Agent Fieldman."

"I doubt it," Fieldman said, from within Amy/Alison's robot body.

"This exercise in revenge isn't going to solve anything. You're treating the symptom, not the disease. This is an entirely wasted effort." It must have seemed too funny to watch a dead guy wax philosophical about the uses of revenge.

"Ah," Fieldman said. "This is where I'm supposed to have an epiphany about violence begetting violence? Spare me the philosophy, Collective. This store isn't buying. The 'exercise' you see before you *is* going to solve everything. I've been trying to explain this to your tiny mind, but will you listen? No. This is much, much bigger than you or I, or anybody in this world."

"Okay, Buddha. Maybe everything you're saying is true. If it is, fine. You want some kind of higher justice served? Bully for you. But it still doesn't address my earlier point: what are we going to do about the killer?"

"We have the killer. Killers, to be precise."

"No, not this pathetic errand boy, or the dizzy wench. I mean the real killer." I looked at Brad. The face of the killer, accusing the victim.

"What?" he asked.

"You don't see it, do you Brad? You killed your wife, and yourself!"

"Shut up," he said.

"It was you. You hired these two pathetic people to do it."

"I did not!"

"Perhaps not the personality known as Brad Larsen," I said. "But the name on the dotted line was John Paul Bafoures. And you were, in fact, John Paul Bafoures."

I could see a dim bulb lighting in Brad's mind. "No . . ." he said weakly, but he was finally getting it.

Amy/Alison's face wrinkled up in confusion. "What are you saying . . . *he* hired them?"

"Sorry, Fieldman. I suppose you would have had no way of knowing, looking at our boring linear timeline from the outside. But Paul and I had a nice chat inside a dying brain, and it turns out, Brad wanted out of his professional rackets and decided to bury the murderous side of him. Only problem, the murderous side resented it. So, he decided to cash in everybody's chips, all at once."

"You . . ." Fieldman said. It sure looked weird coming out of Amy/Alison's mouth. "All this . . . for nothing!"

I saw the fire die in Amy/Alison's eyes, and something invisible pound in Brad's body, flinging him back against the wall. Amy/Alison took two wobbly steps backward, found her back against the wall, then slid down. She started to cry. At last, the real Alison Larsen, the woman I knew as Amy Langtree, finally regained control of her artificial body. Had she been watching the whole time? I had no way of knowing. She simply lowered her head into her folded arms and sobbed.

Brad, on the other hand, was on the floor convulsing. Clearly, Fieldman had jumped in there, and there was some kind of battle royale going on in that skull. I probably shouldn't have waited this long to play my trump card, but hell, hindsight is twenty/twenty. And, to be honest, I had no idea Fieldman would be this upset. To think that would have meant believing his crazy stories and schemes. And now—after seeing how this damned thing was turning out—maybe I was. Maybe this case was bigger than all of us.

Finally, a victor emerged. Brad stopped shaking. He rolled over on his side, then scrambled to his feet. He paused to straighten out his police uniform and looked at me. "I owe you an apology, Collective," he said. "And the soul of Brad Larsen will have to answer for his crimes."

I was about to accept Fieldman's apology when I saw Susannah pick up the cop's revolver from the floor and shove it in his face.

"Cool your tool, fool," she said.

As if on cue, a siren screamed outside.

"Talk about timing," I said.

Fieldman nodded. "Yes. Brad had arranged for that. He figured the FBI was here at the beginning, might as well call them in at the end. I can't believe how clouded my judgment has been."

"Hello!" Susannah yelled. "Can't you see I have a fucking gun to your head?"

"Sorry," Fieldman said.

I was growing tired of the interruptions. Part of me wished I had shown up after Brad had deep-sixed both of them. "Lady, listen to me," I said from Ray's bleeding body. "Do you still think you can control this situation? After all you've seen tonight?"

Susannah didn't bother to give me a rational answer. Instead, she whipped the pistol around and fired, screaming, "AND YOU!"

The shot was amazing. It planted directly beneath my right eye, dug a few inches into my skull, then exploded back and out. All in all, a much more professional shot than the one she'd delivered to my other head mere hours ago. Talk about a learning curve.

When my vision dimmed and my head flopped to the left, I started to worry. This was beyond my bag of resurrection tricks. If someone were to poke out Ray Loogan's remaining eye, I'd be screwed, blued, and tattooed. And as much as I've complained before about all the miserable places my soul had been shuttled to, this was by far the King Daddy shit-pick of the year.

I could still see, though, out of my remaining eye. Susannah had the gun back on Fieldman. Why didn't he use the distraction to disarm her?

"The law is coming for you," Fieldman said.

"Don't worry," she said. "I'll explain everything to them. How you killed all of these nasty people. How you tried to kill me."

"They won't believe you, Ms. Lewalski."

"No, but they *will* believe Susannah Winston. She has powerful friends. She has a powerful father. She can explain her way out of anything."

Feds kicked in the front door; footsteps thundered up the hallway. My old buddy—Special Agent in Charge Dean

Nevins—whipped out his pistol, doing the best Dirty Harry impression he could muster. "Drop your weapon!"

"Oh, can she?" Fieldman whispered, looking directly into her eyes. "*Explain this.*"

Susannah's trigger finger twitched, enough to fire the gun. At first, I thought she'd flinched, but then it became clear what had happened. God, that clever, stupid bastard. His face—which looked like Brad's, but used to belong to a Philadelphia police officer—exploded in a blur of wet crimson, and his body flipped back to the ground. I wonder what kind of gizmo he'd used to do *that*. The look on Susannah's face was priceless. Absolute and complete horror.

One might say what happened next spoke volumes about the self-control of Dean Nevins—after all, any other agent would have immediately started pumping lead into the psycho bitch. But Nevins didn't do that. He calmly and sternly repeated himself. "*Drop your weapon now, woman!*"

Susannah turned to face him, gun still in her hand. Ooh, bad form, girl.

"Drop it!" Nevins squawked. His entire body seemed to tense.

"God, NO! *He* did this—"

"I said DROP IT!"

"Yes, yes, of course . . ." Susannah bent down to put the gun on the floor.

"That's it."

Susannah complied, even offering a weak, vulnerable smile.

"Now just step away from the body . . ."

I couldn't believe it. Despite Fieldman's last-minute efforts to the contrary, it looked as if Susannah Winston was going to explain her way out of this one, too. Her whole life had been lying her way into bigger and better social circles—shit desert town to gun moll, gun moll to high-society mistress, high-society mistress to . . . what? Directrix of the FBI?

Thankfully, it wasn't to be. A thirst for justice runs in the Larsen family.

From behind, Amy/Alison slid her hand across Nevins' beefy forearm. For a brief second, he looked confused: why was this attractive woman touching his arm? A sudden manifestation of gratitude for saving her life?

Of course, a second was all that Alison Larsen—robot, simulacrum, android, whatever—needed. She found Nevins' trigger finger and managed to squeeze off three shots before he could stop her. Susannah's chest and face exploded in near tandem. She choked and flung her hands to her throat, then stumbled and collapsed back to the floor.

Nevins wrestled the gun away and threw Amy/Alison to the ground. He stared at the bodies on the floor, then at Amy/Alison. He lowered his gun and closed his eyes tightly.

I let a sigh escape my dead lips, and then I involuntarily passed out.

* * *

I heard movement, then decided it was okay to open my one working eye again.

Amy/Alison had scrambled up from the floor and run to Brad's side. She was ignoring Susannah, who was lying nearby and choking on her own blood. Amy/Alison grabbed her husband's hand, crying. "Brad, please . . . please don't go now . . . *not now.*" She took his face in her hands, rubbed his forehead, passed her thumbs over his eyes.

And then the crying stopped. Amy/Alison sniffled, then cleared her throat.

"Sorry it has to end this way, Larsen," she whispered. But it wasn't Alison talking anymore.

Brad's corpse didn't make a sound, but something inside must have.

"No," Amy/Alison/Fieldman said. "You've done enough for now. It's time for you to rest." Another pause. "Shhh. See you on the flip side."

Amy/Alison walked over to me and forced open my eyelids. "Your investigation's officially over."

I didn't reply. I knew it was Fieldman talking, and I knew it would be useless to resist. For the first time, I was ready to accept that my investigation *was* over.

She was the last thing I saw before my own, borrowed, dead eye fluttered shut.

27

FOUR AND A HALF DEAD BODIES

The next time they opened I was staring at Special Agent Dean Nevins. My long-lost friend in the bureau. After spending a month with Fieldman, I was almost happy to see him. Nevins forced my eyelid up with a fat thumb.

"Hello, dead guy," he said, deadpan. "And what happened to you?"

I decided it was time to work the magic just one more time.

"The usual," I said. I watched his face turn white and his eyes bulge—very, very wide—and then I jumped into his body.

* * *

Practice must make perfect, I guess. Nevins' knees didn't even buckle. I stood up and started barking orders, just like Nevins would have done himself. *Get these bodies tagged and ID'd. Where are the print guys? Come on, fellas—are we running an investigation, or a three-ring circus here?* At that moment, the phone rang. One of the other agents answered it. He seemed to listen for a long time, then turned to me.

"Boss? It's a Mr. Gard. He's asking for Susannah Winston or Paul After?"

"I'll take the call," I said. "Hello, Gard? Hi. Special Agent Nevins of the Federal Bureau of Investigation. How are you doing tonight?"

"What's going on there?"

"Well, there are a bunch of dead bodies scattered all over the living room floor of your parents' house. Including your mistress, Susannah Winston, nee Lana Lewalski, a hooker from Las Vegas wanted for murder. Pinned to your parents' couch is her ex-boyfriend, cheap hood Ray Loogan, also wanted for murder. Then across the room is Leah Farrell, yet another piece of Vegas scum. She had her throat blasted open. Lastly, there's a guy whose face has been blasted beyond all recognition. Frankly, we don't know who he is. Quite possibly, he's a rogue FBI agent we've been looking for."

"Who?" Gard asked. "What . . . what are you talking about? I . . . *I don't know these people!*"

"Yeah, well that's the funny thing, Gard," I said. "Right after I got here, I ran into the PI you hired. He wanted me to pass on a message to you."

"Wh-Wh-What?"

"He said if you ever bounce a check on him again, he'll feed you your own spleen. Have a nice day." I hung up.

Next order of business: rescuing the souls I'd left behind in Leah's body. I figured they were probably flung out into the space of the room when Leah's head went up like a melon with a Roman candle inside. I checked pieces of furniture, the shag rugs, nature paintings, dopey white plastic World Class Father and Mother statuettes, lamps, but nothing. Not a glimmer of life.

Fieldman must have taken them with him in the Cyborg Alison body. Or perhaps they'd all made it to the Great Beyond. For all of their sakes—even that pain-in-the-ass Harlan, even cranky Kevin Kennedy—I hoped that was the case.

There was a final piece of business to take care of, though. I approached a young-looking agent holding a clipboard. Most likely, Fieldman's replacement on Nevins' team. "Call the cleaners in here. I want this house razed to the ground."

"But, sir," Agent Boy said, "this is a private residence. It belongs to . . ." he glanced down at a clipboard, "a Mr. and Mrs. Jasper Gard."

"You want everyone to know the Witness Protection Program can't be trusted? That the very fabric of our judicial system is consistently being ripped out like some Tijuana whore's panties?"

Agent Boy got the idea.

* * *

I sat across the street in Nevins' car, sipping a Styrofoam cup full of coffee. Still lukewarm and milky, but I didn't mind. This was the first fully functional body I'd been in all night, and it felt like a dream. I didn't even mind that Nevins had polluted his liver and treated his lungs like smokestacks. This was the healthiest I'd felt in years.

What was my next move? That was the best question I'd asked myself in a long time. I realized how much time and effort I'd wasted by only reacting to life. I'd been reacting for five years. Now, there was nothing left to react to. My long-awaited, Association-smashing information was non-existent. Hell, there wasn't even an Association to smash.

Was this how it felt to want to quit a job? I wasn't sure. I'd always loved the only job I'd ever had—newspaper reporting. That particular career had been ended for me, and this new one thrust into my hands. Being the consummate professional, I expended the same, tireless amount of energy on it. But was my heart in it? Was it ever?

I sat in Agent Nevins' body, and his car, for a long, long time. When dawn broke over Merion, I turned on the ignition and started to drive back to Philadelphia. After all, the Bicentennial was only a few days away.

It was something to look forward to.

AUTHOR'S NOTE

This novel is largely set in the year 1976, which was an interesting year for me. On the Bicentennial, when I was four years old, I got lost. Right in the middle of festivities, in the heart of downtown Philadelphia.

My father was working that day—playing in a band hired to perform outside of Winston's Restaurant in Old City Philadelphia. The name of the band was the Shuttlebums, and since my dad was also a carpenter, he came up with the idea of making business cards for the band on tiny slats of wood. Someday, when the bombs drop and cockroaches start throwing their own Bicentennial celebrations, those business cards will be around.

Since my father had a gig, and my mother was the Shuttlebums' de facto manager, I was brought along too, as well as my year-old baby brother. I don't remember much of the gig, except that it was in front of Winston's Restaurant, near Second and Chestnut Street, three blocks from where the Declaration of Independence was signed. I also remember what was going through my young brain: Big Boat. Very Cool Big Boat.

You see, my father's full-time carpentry gig was on this restaurant ship called the Moshulu, which, in 1976 (and again, about twenty years later), was docked at Penn's Landing, three blocks east of Winston's. I somehow put the geography together, and I knew if I walked over the Very Big Bridge (in actuality, a pedestrian footbridge over I-95), I could see the Very Cool Big Boat. So, in the middle of the largest crowd ever gathered in Old City Philadelphia, I ran away.

But not alone. I took an accomplice along with me: my Aunt Diane. Relieved? Don't be. She was only nine months older than me at the time. (My grandmother became pregnant with her late in life—the last in a series of five girls, spanning twenty-two years or so. God bless my grandpop Lou.) Why Diane followed me, I'll never know. I've never been the persuasive type. And you'd figure a five-year-old would know better. But, oh well.

I don't remember the walk over there. It was probably scary as hell, and I've blocked it from my memory. But I do remember walking into the restaurant portion of the boat, and Diane and I sliding into two seats at a table. A frazzled waitress with a nameplate emblazoned VICKY came over and dropped two menus and a large wicker bowl of popcorn on the table. She must have assumed we were brother and sister, and our parents were nearby. Of course, this was not the case. We were alone and lost.

For about five minutes.

A man in a big suit appeared next to our table, looking down at us with a strange expression on his face. I remember worrying we were about to get yelled at, but he didn't. "You two aren't supposed to be here, are you?" he asked, smiling.

Neither Diane nor I made a peep.

The man pulled out a chair and sat down with us. "Well, that's okay. I'm not supposed to be here, either." I watched him pull a cigarette out of a steel case in his pocket, and saw a big thick belt under his arm, with a Big Gun inside of it. Wow. That was even cooler than being on a Big Boat. But the man quickly covered it up, lit the cigarette, and stared at us both. Then I saw him look up, behind us.

I felt the thin, scratchy breeze of fabric across the back of my neck and caught a whiff of perfume. A woman sat down at the table. I recall her being incredibly beautiful—almost as beautiful as Lori, my babysitter.

"Who are these two?" she asked.

"I've been busy in the past couple of weeks," the man said.

"Very funny," the woman said. "Are they lost?"

"Yeah. The waitress clued me in to them. I'm just doing my job."

The woman smiled. "Funny to hear you say that, after all this time."

"Well, I was kind of forced out of my old one," he said.

"Now, now, Collective. Don't be bitter. You know this was for the best. You're not supposed to complete every task. Some have to be finished by others."

"I know. If I didn't, I'd plant a bullet in you right now."

The woman was quiet for a moment. I got bored and started

to eyeball the popcorn basket. I loved popcorn. But Diane beat me to the punch: she already had her hand in the basket, almost tipping it over.

"I have a question for you," the man said. "How much of that stuff you'd always tell me—you know, about what I am . . ."

"Yes?"

"Well. How much of it was true?"

The woman smiled. "Excellent question. I'd say you could place my factual accuracy at about fifty percent. Some things were outright lies, meant to keep you confused, or bitter, or a little of both. But everything else was the truth. More than you know, actually. More than you'll ever want to know."

"What *are* you going to do now?" the man asked, righting the basket before we lost all of the popcorn.

"Well, first I have a small matter concerning a certain hotel here in Center City Philadelphia. There's going to be a plague this holiday, and I have to make sure it doesn't spread to end life on Earth."

"Oh," the man said. "I guess that's important."

"You might say that."

The man nodded, then turned to look at us kids. I always got uncomfortable when grown-ups stared at me, so I started to fidget with the tablecloth. Eventually—thankfully—the man turned away.

"And what about you?" the woman asked. "Any plans for the immediate future?"

"I'm going to make sure these kids get back to their parents. Nothing beyond that. Nothing I can think of, at least."

"You need anything? Money?"

"Only the air that I breathe."

"Catchy," the woman said, smiling. "It would make a good song."

The man sat there, staring at the basket of popcorn on the table. Which, of course, prompted me to grab a handful and stuff it in my mouth. I looked at the man to see if he was going to stop me, but he didn't. He looked like he was going to cry. I'd never seen that in an adult man before. It was weird.

"I know what you're thinking," the woman said. "Rest assured, I'll take care of her. She's happy here."

"Can I say something to her? Just for a second?"

"Sure. But remember: I've wiped her memories away. The bad ones, I mean." The woman swallowed and closed her eyes.

Again, I reached out with my tiny fingers and grabbed as much popcorn as I could hold, then tried to shove it all into my mouth. Most of it missed.

"Hi," the woman said.

"Hello," the man said. "It's been a while."

"I'm sorry, but I don't remember you."

"Of course you don't. I look different now. I wanted to wish you luck in the future. You deserve it. In fact, you deserve the world. I wish I were the one who'd be able to give it to you."

"Oh, okay," the woman said. "Uh, thanks." The woman blinked, and then sighed. Then she stood up from the table, patted us both on the heads, and said, "Be good."

The man sat with us for a while longer, not saying anything. Diane and I made short work of the popcorn basket, and the waitress brought over a full one when the man stopped her, smiled, and then took us both by the hand and led us off the ship, back across the bridge, back to the corner of Second and Chestnut, back to my parents. I don't remember their reaction;

I can only assume they were overwhelmed with the urge to hug us and choke the living shit out of us, simultaneously.

My last memory of being a four-year-old was this: the man in the suit walking away.

I never saw him again.

ACKNOWLEDGEMENTS

Special thanks to Theresa Dougherty and Marianne McQueen (for the spelling), James Roache (for "The Most Dangerous Game"), Michael DeMeo (for the Stephen King), Albin Dixon (for the detective stories), Robert Dunbar (for *The Pines*), Gabe Fagan (for *The Waste Lands*), Bill Wine (for the sick puppy), Loren Feldman (for the career), Art Bourgeau (for the hardboiled talks), David Hale Smith (for the faith), Allan Guthrie (for the sunshine), and Rufus Purdy (for the extra brain).

Honorary guests of the Brain Hotel include Farhad Amid, Charles Ardai, Ray Banks, Lou Boxer, Ken Bruen, Katharine Carroll, Bill Crider, Katherine Fausset, McKenna Jordan, Peter Katz, Bahar Kutluk, Paul Leyden, Natasha MacKenzie,

Myatt Murphy, Louise Pearce, Jason Rekulak, Rich Rys, George Sandison, Robert Sheckley, Kevin Burton Smith, Dutch Southern, David Thompson, Jim Warren, and Lou Wojciechowski.

Meredith, Parker, and Evie enjoy luxury suites in the heart of the Brain Hotel.

ABOUT THE AUTHOR

Duane Swierczynski is the two-time Edgar-nominated author of fifteen novels, including *Revolver*, *Canary*, *The Wheelman*, *The Blonde*, and *Severance Package*. His very first novel, *Secret Dead Men*—extensively re-edited for this twentieth-anniversary Titan Books edition—was originally published by PointBlank in 2004.

Duane's short story "Lush" was included in *The Best American Mystery Stories 2019*, and is currently being adapted into a feature by director Chad Stahelski (*John Wick*) for Lionsgate. He has also written various bestselling comics for Marvel, DC, Dark Horse, Archie, and Valiant, including *Cable*, *Deadpool*, *The Immortal Iron Fist*, *Punisher MAX*, *Birds of Prey*,

Star Wars: Rogue One, Godzilla, Bloodshot as well as his creator-owned *Breakneck* and *John Carpenter's Tales of Science Fiction Presents: Redhead*.

Duane has also collaborated with bestselling novelist James Patterson on three Audible Original radio dramas. The first, *The Guilty*, starred John Lithgow, Bryce Dallas Howard, and Aldis Hodge. He also co-wrote a series of bestselling "digi-novels" with *CSI* creator Anthony E. Zuiker.

Duane is also the author of six non-fiction books about vice and crime, including *The Perfect Drink for Every Occasion*, *The Big Book of Beer*, and *This Here's A Stick-Up: The Big Bad Book of American Bank Robbery*. Earlier in his career, Duane worked as an editor at *Details*, *Men's Health*, and *Philadelphia* magazines, and served as the editor-in-chief of the *Philadelphia City Paper*.

A native Philadelphian, Duane now lives in Southern California with his family.

Find Duane at gleefulmayhem.com or on Twitter/X and Instagram at @swierczy

MIDNIGHT STREETS

Phil Lecomber

George Harley is a cockney private detective in late 1920s London. While investigating a series of grisly murders, he uncovers a trail of hidden clues that link the crimes to an infamous figure from the past. Convinced the police have the wrong man, Harley must use all his skills to negotiate the dark underbelly of the city and track down the real killer. The investigation leads to a clash with an occult mastermind, an encounter which will have dire consequences for the rest of his life.

Set during the Golden Age of Crime Fiction, Harley's world is a far cry from the English country house of an Agatha Christie whodunnit. Its working-class hero does his "sherlocking" in the frowsy alleyways and sleazy nightclubs of Soho—the city's underbelly, peopled with lowlife ponces, jaded streetwalkers and East End mobsters. It's a world of grubby bedsits, all-night cafés, egg and chips, and Gold Flake cigarettes. Unlike the American noir of Chandler and Hammett, this is a strictly British affair, where the villains are more likely to be wielding cutthroat razors than Tommy guns, and the wise-cracking Lauren Bacalls are louche bohemians with belladonna eyes and ladders in their stockings.

The midnight streets are black as pitch and Harley finds himself embroiled in the macabre mysteries of a city in which truth is as murky as the mustard-yellow smog and the sins are as dark and bitter as stout porter beer.

Midnight Streets is the first novel in the Piccadilly Noir series.

THE BUTCHER'S DAUGHTER
THE HITHERTO UNTOLD STORY OF MRS. LOVETT

Corinne Leigh Clark & David Demchuk

Famed for being the baker who stuffed her pies with the flesh of Sweeney Todd's victims, the notorious Mrs. Lovett has long been in the diabolical shadow of Fleet Street's murderous barber. But what could lead a woman who began life as a hard-working butcher's daughter to such distasteful crimes?

When young Margaret Evans's skill with the knife and saw brings her to the attention of a well-to-do doctor in early Victorian London, she is whisked from the offal-streaked streets of Whitechapel and installed in his Highgate home as a maid and sometime medical assistant. And thus begins a hellish journey straight out of the penny dreadfuls of the day—one in which Margaret must employ all her wit and resourcefulness to avoid the clutches of crazed anatomists, sinister child-snatchers, and the seemingly all-seeing gentlemen freemasons who seek to take away her liberty.

Nobody can keep an East End butcher's daughter down though. When, by nefarious means, she takes ownership of a little Fleet Street pie shop, and discovers the sinister barber who plies his trade upstairs takes the name of his cutthroat razor a little too literally, Margaret finds a way to turn the situation to her advantage. But with so many of the gentlemen who've come to Todd's parlour in search of a shave disappearing without trace, how long can she keep herself from suffering the same deadly fate?

THE REFORMATORY

Tananarive Due

"You're in for a treat. *The Reformatory* is one of those books you
can't put down. Tananarive Due hit it out of the park."
Stephen King

"*The Reformatory* is a masterpiece—a new American classic of the uncanny.
I was gripped from the first lines to the catch-your-breath desperation of the
final pages. Even in the tale's grimmest moments, Tananarive Due insists on the
almost supernatural power of simple kindness. You have to read this book."
Joe Hill, *New York Times* bestselling author of *The Fireman* and *Heart-Shaped Box*

Jim Crow Florida, 1950.

Twelve-year-old Robert Stephens Jr., who for a trivial scuffle with a white boy
is sent to The Gracetown School for Boys. But the segregated reformatory is
a chamber of horrors, haunted by the boys that have died there.

Robbie has a talent for seeing ghosts, or haints. But what was once a comfort
to him after the loss of his mother has become a window to the truth of what
happens at the reformatory. Boys forced to work to remediate their so-called
crimes have gone missing, but the haints Robbie sees hint at worse things.

In order to survive the school governor and his Funhouse, Robert must
enlist the help of the school's ghosts—only they have their own motivations...